Ki
Shadow

A novel set in the wilds of Borneo before
and during the Second World War

Steve Morris

Visit us online at www.authorsonline.co.uk

A Bright Pen Book

ISBN 978 07552 1198 2

Authors OnLine Ltd
19 The Cinques
Gamlingay, Sandy
Bedfordshire SG19 3NU
England

This book is dedicated to the many
brave people worldwide who selflessly
fight the darkness of oppression
so that others may live in the sun.

SOUTHEAST ASIA

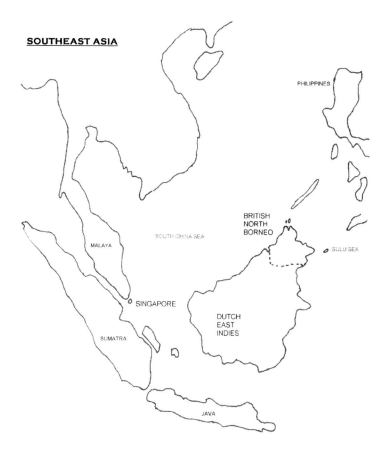

PHILIPPINES

BRITISH
NORTH
BORNEO

SULU SEA

SOUTH CHINA SEA

MALAYA

SINGAPORE

SUMATRA

DUTCH
EAST
INDIES

JAVA

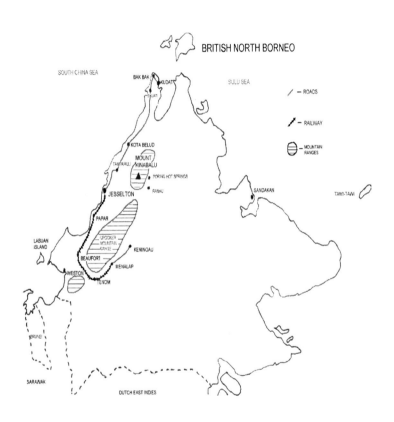

BRITISH NORTH BORNEO

SOUTH CHINA SEA

SULU SEA

BAK BAK · ·KUDAT

·KOTA BELUD

TAMPARULI · MOUNT KINABALU

·PORING HOT SPRINGS

·RANAU

JESSELTON

SANDAKAN

TAWI-TAWI

PAPAR

CROCKER MOUNTAIN RANGE

LABUAN ISLAND

·KENINGAU

BEAUFORT

MENALAP

·WESTON ·TENOM

BRUNEI

SARAWAK

DUTCH EAST INDIES

/ — ROADS

/ — RAILWAY

⊖ — MOUNTAIN RANGES

Prologue

He felt his hair being tugged from behind, not hard, but sufficient to cause his head to tilt back slightly. There was a strange dragging sensation across his throat without pain and then, clearly and dispassionately, as if watching a film, he saw a red jet of liquid spurt across the low wooden table in front of him engulfing the remnants of the feast. He looked across and noticed with detached amusement that the fellow officer sitting opposite him had somehow affected a beaming red smile that appeared to have slipped down off his face. Suddenly, fearfully, and with great clarity, he realised what was happening. That was his final thought.

Minutes earlier he had sat back contentedly on his heels, musing on the excellent meal they had just finished and considering how it had completed a most satisfying day. He was Kiyo Konno, the senior officer in command of the occupying force. His position gave him great power that he enjoyed more than any other pleasures life held for him. He was very proud to have risen so high in the Imperial Army and knew his family back home in Kyoto were equally pleased with his exalted position. He looked forward to marching in full dress uniform down the dusty road to his modest house, looking straight ahead and apparently unconcerned but secretly revelling in the admiring and envious glances of his neighbours.

The food at the feast had proved to be the best he had eaten in a long time, certainly far superior to the boring Japanese army rations of rice and a few stringy vegetables. So much red meat! He had consumed at least five bowls of succulent roast deer and buffalo with two large helpings of steamed rice and many glasses of the local *tapai* or rice wine. He hoped his digestive system would be able to cope with such a rare rush of protein and alcohol. The day had been such a triumph and one he never expected to have experienced as relationships with the native people had been strained since he had been part of the

1

invasion of North Borneo in December 1941. He considered it must definitely be because of his personal charisma and undoubted charm that the local headman had invited him and his fellow officers to the longhouse for the meal. After all, his wife back home had constantly told him that it was his friendly persona that had attracted her to him. The dancing on the sprung longhouse floor while they ate had also proved to be a most entertaining diversion. The rhythmic beat of the drums and gongs had been as hypnotic as the sinuous movements of the young nubile female dancers. He had not really taken a great deal of notice of Murut girls before as they had seemed rather dark-skinned and coarse featured to him but the repetitive dance steps and the erotic swaying had aroused him and he thought that a perfect end to a perfect day would be a few hours with one of the girls in a very private dance. It had been a long time since he had fucked a willing female. The comfort girls from Korea in the military brothels were unresponsive and clearly showed their hate and contempt for the soldiers in their eyes if not in their movements. There was little pleasure to be had from such encounters and there was always the nagging thought at the back of his mind that he might be receiving more than just physical relief. It made the whole experience a trial that he only indulged in to prevent his fellow officers talking behind his back implying he might be less of a man than them. He looked around to see which girl he favoured most but they all seemed to have departed. Never mind, he mused, they will no doubt soon be back and then I will be able to honour one of them with my personal attention. Possibly the slightly taller shy one who had been at the end of the dance line and had, he felt sure, looked at him with coy admiration. It was a good thought and he leaned back to fantasise about what he would do to her and what she would do to him. This was when he felt the hand tug his hair and the knife slit his throat.

The same fate befell his fellow officers at exactly the same moment. Each of them had been waited upon personally by a male member of the longhouse and at a given signal the waiters each dispatched the Japanese soldier they had previously been serving with much fawning and obsequious gestures. The guards the Japanese had left outside the longhouse had already been similarly dealt with by the cooks who had taken them their food to eat at their posts. Not one invited guest or guard was alive to relate what had occurred and be able to help identify the perpetrators. The native warriors knew there could be vicious reprisals but considered the exercise to be worthwhile if it helped to rid the island of the hated invaders who had taken all their food and possessions.

Within an hour all the bodies had been buried minus their heads. These were taken as trophies to be kept and treasured in the head house at the end of their longhouse. But not this particular longhouse. This longhouse vanished into the jungle by the evening and all the evidence of the afternoon's work had gone. The notched pole that served as the ladder to enter the house had been broken up; the *atap* roof strewn in the undergrowth; the bamboo walls and floors smashed and the wooden frame demolished and disposed of over a wide area. This longhouse had been specially constructed, rather like a film set, solely for the day and, being made of jungle materials, was easily concealed in the dense vegetation that grew in smothering profusion thanks to the tropical heat and rain. They knew that the jungle would soon reclaim the whole scene of slaughter and leave no evidence of their handiwork. By nightfall, before any alarm was raised at the failure of the soldiers and their officers to return to their barracks in the town, the men and the girls set off with their cooking pots, utensils, *tapai* jars and musical instruments on a twenty mile trek deeper into the jungle in the shadow of the towering and brooding bulk of Mount Kinabalu, the highest mountain in south-east Asia.

By daybreak they arrived at their destination, a genuine longhouse in a small clearing, and climbed the ladder at the end of the house to the general living area on the left of the row of small sleeping rooms that housed the twenty or more families who made it their home. It was rather like a village street with

3

the road and the pavement outside the cottages being used for work, play and general socialising. On normal days the women did all the domestic work and the men sat around smoking foul-smelling tobacco wrapped in thin dried leaves as they gossiped or retold ancient tales of bravery and cunning. These tales embraced both of the main areas of their lives; hunting game and hunting people. Before the arrival of the white men and the imposition of the Indian Penal Law Code they had been constantly at war with neighbouring tribes and were very adept jungle fighters. They took the heads of their enemies in the belief that they would take the bravery and courage of their victims for themselves. They were not cannibals and showed great respect to their adversaries. The heads were kept in the head house together with large jars containing the remains of their own ancestors whose bodies had been dried by being hung up over a fire and the desiccated remains stuffed into the jars to be brought out on auspicious occasions and informed of all the latest events; both triumphs and disasters.

As the group moved down the longhouse a figure emerged from one of the rooms. By his height, he was well over six foot, he was obviously not one of their tribe but his skin was a similar dark shade of brown. The main difference, however, was the crop of dirty blond hair that sprouted in wild profusion over his head. He sat down with them and looked at the baskets full of their souvenirs of the night's work.

'Did you take all of them?' he enquired mildly as if they had just brought him his weekly shopping.

'Yes *tuan*,' replied the headman, 'all the officers and their guards are here and are ready for our women to work on them and make them look pretty.'

'Well done,' he answered, 'but remember that when the war is over you must stop taking heads to add to your collection.'

'Agreed *tuan*, but these do not really count as the men were not real warriors – their hands were too soft and they are not fighters. They are not used to the jungle and must have been clerks or shopkeepers before becoming soldiers. We will not

4

gain much power from their heads.'

It was true that the Japanese soldiers and their Korean conscripts were no match for the skilled jungle hunters who moved stealthily through the forests and killed their prey equally silently with blowpipes and poisoned darts.

The women took away the heads and left them at the edge of the jungle for the ants and other insects to remove the flesh from the bones. A couple of children stayed with the heads to ward off any larger mammals that might have fancied running off with a free meal. Later the heads were boiled to clean them and then hung up with the much older trophies. The men carefully cleaned and polished their razor-sharp knives smiling contentedly and dreaming of when they would next use them.

Chapter 1

Mary Field leaned on the heat-blistered wooden rail of the SS Vyner Brooke as it slid slowly towards the small wharf thrusting out into the South China Sea from the neat little town of Kudat at the northerly tip of British North Borneo, one of the Empire's smaller colonies. She could see the wooden godowns near the wharf and, from her elevated position on the top deck, the single main street lined with shophouses and deep storm drains. A sweet and sickly smell suddenly assailed her nose and invaded her mouth and throat; so thick it seemed solid and almost chewable. She turned to her husband of six weeks who was lounging in a rattan chair along the deck. Before she spoke she gazed at him and, as had happened many times, a feeling of complete disbelief nearly overwhelmed her. She observed, almost as a stranger, his strong torso and firm muscles seen in sketchy outline under his bush shirt. His tanned face, with the easy smile and the small dimple in his chin that had first caught her eye and her imagination during the last waltz at the 1937 Christmas company dance in Sydney. Again, as she had so often done, she wondered what he had seen in her, an insignificant twenty year old typist, when he could surely have had his pick of the girls in the city. Or even in the whole of Australia. Hopefully when they were settled on the estate these sporadic feelings of panic would subside and she would start to accept that he was for her alone. Her nose dragged her back again to the present.

'Tom,' she called, 'what is that dreadful smell?'

'Copra, the drying flesh of the coconut,' he replied, slowly unwinding from the chair and looking at her with his sea-green eyes. 'You'll soon accustom yourself to it and, after all, it's the coconut that pays our bills so it's really the smell of money.'

What, of course, she couldn't know was that he had been closely watching her through half-closed eyes. He had noted with intense pleasure the way her shoulder length dark blond hair wafted gently in the movement of air caused by the ship's progress. With the sun behind her the thin cotton dress she wore left little to the imagination and Tom felt a familiar stirring in his, luckily voluminous, tropical shorts. He reflected on his good fortune. Mary, he knew, would be the ideal companion and lover in this tropical paradise. She was everything, and more, than he had dared hope for. At the age of thirty-five and no longer living in Australia, he had thought himself too old and set in his ways for romance and had ruminated that the future would be one of lonely solitude on his estate. He had considered that there was nothing for him in Australia as both his parents had died of tuberculosis when he was young and he had been brought up by his father's parents who were now also dead. But this girl had bounced into his life and completely blown away all his preconceptions. If they hadn't met when they did then in time he might have taken a local girl as his mistress. Many of the European planters did this with the inevitable complications which resulted if they eventually married a girl from back home and brought them out to their plantation. It could be difficult to hide the small children running around the compound who were so obviously of mixed race. Luckily Tom had no such problems to hide away and his reputation in the area was one of a hard-working, fair and honest man. This was by both the indigenous people who worked with him and his fellow settlers.

Mary leaned back on the rail. The town looked pretty and, as they steamed nearer, quite busy with many workers hauling sacks to the wharf and others pushing long handled wooden carts with bicycle wheels. These were piled high, almost impossibly so, with boxes and tin drums. How they stayed on without falling was a mystery. Now she could see further inland and noticed a large expanse of green surrounded by painted wooden houses raised a few feet above the ground on piles. There was what looked like a very ornamental Chinese temple over to the left of the town on a road leading towards a small hill and a vista of gently swaying coconut trees stretching as far as she could see. To the left of the wharf was an untidy collection of rickety wooden shacks built on stilts over the sea. Like the loaded carts on the wharf they seemed to be in danger of toppling over at any time. There were children, many without a scrap of clothing, playing outside these houses on the bamboo walkways or even in the water. 'Why aren't they in school?' she asked Tom.

'Why aren't who in school?'

'The children playing over there by the houses over the water.'

'Oh, in Kampong Ayer you mean. Their families probably can't afford the fees. Anyway, they find them useful staying at home mending the fishing nets with their nimble fingers and the girls look after the younger children.'

They do seem happy, thought Mary, but without any education they must have a very limited future. 'I'm really looking forward to seeing our house and the coconut plantation. I know you've described them to me countless times but now we're so close to actually being there it suddenly seems unreal.'

'You do have the strangest ideas,' Tom laughed, 'and I thought you would just take it all in your stride like a true Aussie girl.'

By now the ship was almost at the wharf and the captain had the fore and aft lookouts guiding him slowly in. The Vyner Brooke gently nudged the wooden pier and thin ropes were thrown to waiting hands so that the heavier hawsers could then be pulled to the wharf and the ship securely berthed.

'Time to go,' Tom said. 'We'd better fetch our hand luggage from the cabin and keep an eye on the unloading of the trunks and boxes. We don't want anything left behind.'

The ship, one of the Straits Steamer Company fleet, had left Singapore almost a week earlier and Kudat was one of its many ports of call as it delivered goods and people along the northern coast of Borneo. It had already docked in Kuching,

Brunei, Labuan and Jesselton and, after Kudat, would steam on round the tip of Borneo to the town of Sandakan where it turned round and repeated the trip back to Singapore collecting its cargo of rubber, copra and other tropical produce to be taken for distribution round the world. The ship carried a small number of first class passengers who slept in small, cramped cabins with basic facilities. It was always hot despite the slight breeze as the temperature was constantly high and the humidity almost at saturation point. There was a bar and dining room where pleasant evenings could be spent with the Scottish captain and his senior officers knocking back Singapore slings and large gins with tonic or 'it' in them. The tonic, containing quinine, was supposed to guard against malaria and the gin was to take the edge off the medicine. Or so the colonialists liked to pretend. The food was adequate and uncompromisingly British with hearty stews and roasts followed by steamed puddings and custard. Not always ideal fare in a tropical climate. Other less fortunate passengers were lower down in the vessel with the third class or steerage passengers squashed on the open deck among the cargo. The classes never mixed. In fact, they even disembarked in class order with the steerage passengers having to wait until all the others, including their luggage, had cleared the quay.

Tom and Mary had joined the ship in Singapore after a tedious boat trip from Australia. It was May 1938 and a chilly winter was starting in Sydney when they left so they could hardly fail to notice the rapid rises in temperature and humidity as they neared the equator. They much preferred the smaller and somehow more cheerful Straits Steamer to the impersonal Australian liner and treated it rather like a belated honeymoon cruise. And now they would soon be heading for Tom's plantation a few miles along the coast from Kudat. Mary looked again at the town that was now directly under her nose and the busy scurry of workers. She looked for Tom, possibly for reassurance, but he had left the deck and she was alone with her thoughts. She knew she had no regrets about Tom but was still apprehensive about her new role in life. She wasn't sure an Australian upbringing would have adequately prepared her for life in this small country that was administered by the British North Borneo Company. Her father was the owner of a medium-sized engineering company in Sydney and, as a result, she had experienced a fairly privileged upbringing in the upmarket suburb of North Shore that had become a popular residential district since the opening of the Sydney Harbour Bridge in 1932. She had not, however, been spoilt as her two older brothers had made sure that she kept her feet firmly on the ground apart from when they were throwing her around the garden during their play fights. She certainly knew how to take a knock and gave as good as she took. It was a great childhood filled with many fond memories. Would she be able to cope away from the close family ties? Her mother Iris was a typical housewife who involved herself in the local community and maintained the detached house as a warm home for her husband and children. She loved and doted on them all. Mary remained unaware of how deeply her mother had felt the loss of her only daughter to a life so far away. Iris had always been convinced that Mary would marry a local boy and live within calling distance. And now she was thousands of miles away and couldn't even be contacted by 'phone. Iris thought she had kept her feelings to herself but her husband James knew that at night she often wept silently into her pillow. He was a bluff and hearty man who didn't know how to deal with such emotions so he just kept bright and cheerful and stressed to his wife how lucky their daughter was to be going on such an adventure and how they could all look forward to her return on leave in a few years time.

Tom and Mary disembarked and were met by an efficient looking Chinese man of about fifty years of age who greeted them warmly in good English and said that he had the truck waiting for them on the road at the end of the wharf. He then rushed off to organise a small group of labourers to carry their luggage to the truck.

'Who's that?' inquired Mary.

'He's my boy,' Tom replied.

'He's hardly a boy!' exclaimed Mary. 'He must be older than my father and obviously far too ancient to be called a boy.'

'I know that, but it is colonial tradition to call your main servant a boy. I hated it when I first came here ten years ago but I suppose I've got used to it and now it's become second nature. It isn't insulting and all the boys are extremely proud of their positions. They really are indispensable and run their households with ruthless efficiency. He's a cross between a British butler and a housekeeper.'

'I suppose he does the cleaning and cooking as well.'

'Oh no, we have a cook and a cleaner for those duties. Kim Bong would never be seen cleaning.'

'So he does have a name,' Mary said triumphantly. 'Then that's what I shall call him. He's not going to be my boy. And we definitely do not have servants. They are our employees.'

'I can see you're going to be trouble,' laughed Tom, 'but you'll soon find out that many people here are very wary of change and are comfortable with how things are. Try not to judge everyone and everything by Sydney's standards or you'll have many disappointments.'

They clambered up into the cab of the truck and Kim Bong gunned the engine. It grumbled into life and lurched noisily off through the town attracting the attention of the shopkeepers who sat or stood on their doorsteps watching out for likely customers. Once clear of the town they went up a small incline and turned right along a narrow track lined by coconut palms.

'Our plantation is at mile five,' explained Tom. 'That means that it's five miles from the town. Kudat used to be the capital of North Borneo and local distances are still measured from here. Now that Jesselton is the capital most distances in the south and the interior are measured from there.

At the mile five post they turned right again went up a gentle hill. At the top was a large bungalow with a veranda running down one side and round the back. A small group of people

11

stood on the steps as a welcoming committee. Looking over them from the rear of the group was a tall and rangy white man wearing an Australian bush hat. He came through the throng and down the steps waving his hand in greeting.

'Welcome back Tom. Is it really six months since we last had to look at your ugly mug? Who's that with you? I didn't know you had such a pretty sister.'

'This, Colin, as you well know, is not my sister but my lady wife. Her name is Mary and I found her waiting just for me in Sydney. How is the plantation? I trust it's not completely in disarray after half a year in your care.'

'Everything's running as if you were here. In fact probably smoother. I'll show you round after lunch. And a very warm welcome to the new Mrs Field.' Colin gave an elaborate sweeping bow in Mary's direction.

'Not so much of the new,' responded Mary with an equally ostentatious curtsey. 'You make it sound as if there's an old Mrs Field hiding somewhere that Tom has neglected to mention.'

The remaining group on the steps were then introduced to Mary. As she had surmised they were the other 'employees' and they all greeted her with little bobs and bows. They went indoors and Tom took Mary through to the back of the bungalow and on to the veranda. To her surprise Mary found herself looking far out over the palms to the deep blue sea from their high vantage point. She could see small fishing boats dotted about in the water. She grabbed Tom's arm and squeezed it. 'It's gorgeous,' she whispered breathlessly. 'Why didn't you tell me how beautiful it was?'

'I thought it would be a rather fine extra wedding present,' Tom slid his arm round her waist. 'It wouldn't have been right to tell you everything.'

'It's by far the best present I've had, thank you Tom for making my life perfect.'

'I'm pleased you like it. I'll take you down to the town later this afternoon so you can look in the shops and meet a few people and then we could call in at the club for a drink before dinner.'

'Time for lunch,' called Colin and they dutifully trailed back into the house and sat at the dining table.

Chapter 2

In Kota Belud, fifty miles to the south-east of Kudat, David Wong was also enjoying his lunch of boiled rice and vegetables wrapped in a banana palm leaf. It was peaceful in his small herbal medicine shop and one of his favourite times of day. He loved and enjoyed the company of his family but also revelled in the solitude he found among the dusty bunches of herbs and bottles of Chinese medicine that he dispensed to the grateful Chinese population. Kota Belud was a functional town of wooden shop-houses set around a square and alongside a large *padang,* the grassed recreation area. Like Kudat it was in an area of plantations but here the main crop was rubber and the orderly rows of trees stretched out from the town way into the distance. From Kota Belud it was only a thirty mile journey down the coast on a rough road to the capital Jesselton and a further track stretched south-west through the dense jungle and led to the foothills of Mount Kinabalu. Around the town lived the Bajaus, a local tribe who were fierce fighters and rode into town on their small ponies rather like cowboys let loose on a frontier town in America. They were also suspected to be involved in violent piracy and were thought to be responsible for raids on small settlements along the coast often leaving no one alive as witnesses. The Chinese shopkeepers maintained an uneasy truce with them but always ensured that their money and valuables were safely hidden away when the Bajaus came to town.

David was constantly worried about his growing family. They were growing both in size and number at a rather alarming rate and, with the older children now in their teens, he had considered a return to China as he thought they might have a better future there than in a tiny town in Borneo. The opportunities to further their education were limited in Borneo and the family were not rich enough to pay for expensive overseas education, even for the older boys. David had studied medicine in Shanghai and still yearned for the excitement of the big city. He had met his wife there and knew that she also missed being away from her family. An important factor against moving back was that China was at war with Japan and now in 1938 had been invaded with the Japanese army controlling most of the major ports. A return to China, even if possible, could mean his sons having to forgo their education and be enlisted to fight and possibly die. He couldn't bear the thought of that. After all, they had come to Borneo for the stability that the British brought to the colony and to leave now could be a disaster. On a more mundane level he also worried about his thinning hair that even his extensive and thorough training had given him no clue how to cure. He had tried a few of the more ordinary remedies and was now considering trying more outlandish recipes to see if he could at least halt the decline. At the back of his mind lingered the notion that if he found an effective treatment then he could market it and it would make him rich. That would solve all their problems.

All these thoughts were insidiously invading his consciousness so that he sometimes had to make a huge effort to ruminate on more pleasant possibilities such as the evening meal his wife Ah San would already be preparing for the family. He hoped that tonight it would be chicken as it was by far his favourite dish. He found too much soya bean curd boring even though he knew it was good for him.

His reflections were interrupted by the arrival in his dispensary of a tall distinguished Chinese gentleman of around forty years. David had not seen him in the town before but that was no real surprise as many travellers stopped off in Kota Belud en route to Kudat or to visit the weekly *tamu* and purchase bargains at the market stalls. There were even quite a few Europeans who stayed for a break in the town's rest house up the hill before continuing with their journeys to the interior or up the coast. But it was very unusual to see such a well dressed and obviously affluent Chinese business gentleman in the small settlement.

'You are Wong Kim Shui?' inquired the visitor.

'Yes, I am David Wong.'

'Then I have come to the correct place. I was informed of your expertise in medicine by friends in Jesselton and have come specially to consult you. I've been suffering with stomach trouble for many years and no western doctors have been able to give me relief from the pain. I hope you can help.' He looked with a fierce intensity at the slight man in front of him as if he were trying to read his mind and even enter his soul.

'I'll try my best. Please tell me the history of the ailment and about your general health and lifestyle.'

They sat down and David asked a lot of questions about the visitor's daily routine and medical history. Armed with this information he proceeded to a physical examination by palpating the man's stomach. After this he was able to recommend a course of treatment that would hopefully solve the problem. He set to mixing various ingredients and making the resulting powder into pills for his customer. As the visitor paid him he looked David straight in the eye again and said, 'Thank you for your time. My name is Lo Vun Lip and we may meet again. There are more ills to be cured in this world than just my insides and I think you might be of further assistance to me in the future. My work is indirectly with the Chinese Government and we are building up a network of loyal contacts outside the country to help stem the Japanese tide. May we keep in contact?'

David was astonished and rather scared at this suggestion. 'Why me?' he queried. 'I have no military background and certainly no political inclinations or even strong convictions. I much prefer a quiet life with my family and friends and never get involved in any sort of organisations.'

'That's not the point,' replied Vun Lip. 'You're much respected and we're looking for loyal Chinese patriots who have standing in their local communities to be coordinators if any action were felt to be needed. We're all aware of the ongoing threat from Japan and it's wise to be prepared. Obviously we hope that nothing will happen and you will be able to live peacefully with your family as you do now. I wish you well and will keep in contact if you are willing.'

'Alright,' David agreed reluctantly. 'I hope you're right and that nothing untoward happens but I am loyal and willing to uphold what we have worked for.'

The stranger left and David's mind was in even more turmoil than before. He was flattered and wondered if he should tell his wife and family of the encounter but decided that, for the moment, it was probably prudent to keep his own counsel. He would, however, mention it quietly to a few of his close friends who he knew also worried about the future. There was quite a strong community spirit in and around the town where many Chinese settlers had smallholdings and, on the nearby coast, fishing boats. David felt sure that many would be willing to rally against any possible threat to their families and livelihoods. And, after all, it would do no harm to be ready if things went wrong. The Chinese had little faith that the few British administrators could protect them. They were not military men and were often young ex-public school boys fresh from completing a degree and a short training course in Cambridge. North Borneo had no army presence at all and only a small armed police force to keep the peace. The British felt that they were invincible and looked to the great naval base at Singapore to ensure their safety.

David shut up the shop a little early and made his way to the large *atap* roofed house on stilts where his family lived. As he drew closer he could hear the laughter of his younger children and his sombre mood lifted a little as he fixed a smile on his face to greet them. They heard him open the metal gate to the compound and ran to him with the little ones clutching his trousers and dragging him to his usual chair in the shade of the large mango tree.

'What's for dinner?' he called to his wife.

'A nice piece of salt fish.'

David was mildly disappointed but made no comment.

He knew his wife was very careful with her housekeeping allowance and often put money aside for little treats at Chinese New Year and also Christmas, which they had learned to celebrate since their arrival. This was because the children attended the mission school and part of their education included compulsory religious education in Christianity. David and his wife didn't mind this as it seemed a fair swap for the English education they received. He made sure was they also attended a separate Saturday school to learn how to read and write in Chinese. It was good, he thought, that they were getting such a varied diet of learning but the mission school only taught up to the secondary school certificate level and there were no universities or colleges in the country for further education.

Ah San brought out the dinner and the family sat round the large table in the space underneath the house. She was only slightly shorter than David but definitely larger in girth with her hair pulled back in a bun held in place by a tortoiseshell comb. Her ready smile, that had attracted David to her in the first place, spread upwards over her face and lit up her eyes. She took great pleasure in putting a good meal on the table and derived even more enjoyment from watching it disappear. The fish was accompanied by a large pot of boiled rice and some vegetable soup into which a whisked egg had been dropped making a sort of lacy pattern in the hot liquid. There was also a large plate of soya curd and a small dish of chilli sauce to dip the fish in. The meal was soon devoured and they sat back to drink tea and discuss the day's events. The children were asked about school and, in common with children worldwide, gave noncommittal replies. David mentioned his visitor but not in any great detail and Ah San complained about the rising prices in the market. It was all very low key and typical of family life everywhere.

Dinner over and a satisfied David went back to his favourite chair to smoke his third cigarette of the day. The fish had been better than expected and he enjoyed the comforting glow of satisfaction a good meal brought. He was still worried about the visitor but put his thoughts on hold so he could savour the sweet taste of the tobacco. There would, he thought, be sufficient time in the coming weeks to deal with any further complications to his life.

Chapter 3

'I'm on my way,' called Mary as she went down the veranda steps and turned towards the truck where Tom sat impatiently.

'Jump aboard; it's time you were introduced to the local dignitaries.'

'Are they that important?'

'Not really, but most of them think they are, especially the English who can be very stuffy and formal. When I first arrived I was thrown out of the club one evening because I was still wearing shorts and it was after six o'clock. Apparently it isn't the done thing for a gentleman to show his knees in public at such an hour.'

'I hope I don't do or say anything to offend them,' Mary answered with a frown.

'You'll be fine. Just watch them all fall in love with you!'

Tom started the engine and the truck rolled down the short drive to the track and soon they were approaching the town and the single main street of shop-houses. He parked outside one shop, got out and helped Mary down. They went into the gloomy interior and Mary had to close her eyes for a moment and then open them again to be able to see the vast array of goods spread out over the floor, up the walls and dangling from the ceiling. A stout Chinese man with a large mole on his chin from which sprouted a thick cluster of black hairs approached them from the back of the shop and bowed low.

'Welcome back Mr Tom,' he said, revealing a mouth full of gold bullion. 'I hope you had a pleasant trip. This must be your lady wife.'

'How on earth did he know that?' whispered Mary in Tom's ear.

'The local grapevine is very efficient,' he replied and then addressed the shopkeeper.

'Thank you Mr Tong, This is Mrs Mary and she will be

patronising your emporium regularly so please add her name to my account.'

Mary looked round and marvelled at the range of goods for sale. She had secretly thought that she would have to do without many luxuries and even some basic things but this shop seemed to stock just about everything from back home. She even spied a jar of what looked very like her favourite Vegemite but with Marmite on the label.

'We're not shopping now Mr Tong,' explained Tom. 'After a walk round the town we are calling in at the club for a quick drink. No doubt Mary will be back as soon as I've taught her to drive the truck.'

They left the shop and Mary caught Tom's arm. 'You never told me about driving,' she complained. 'Will I be able to handle such a large vehicle? And by the way, why do we address Mr Tong by his surname and he addresses us by our Christian names?'

'The answer to your first question is yes. And to the second it is because the Chinese write their names with the surname first followed by their given names. As we do it the other way round then it makes it is easier for everyone if we fall in with their custom.'

'Won't they think it odd that we have different names?'

'Not really, they think we're all odd anyway. Just wait until you meet some of the club members and you'll see why they're right to think like that!'

Arm in arm they walked slowly down the main street and many shopkeepers greeted them warmly and enquired about their health. It was obvious that they all wanted to see the new arrival and although they addressed Tom their eyes were fixed on Mary. She was making a very good impression if their gentle smiles were any indication. At the tailor's shop Tom stopped and pointed to a wizened old man hunched over an equally ancient treadle sewing machine. 'That's Mr Lee,' pointed out Tom. 'He's a fantastic tailor. Just bring in any of your dresses and he will make an exact copy in the material of your choice in a couple of days. When he knows your size he can also make you a dress from any picture you choose out of one of your fashion magazines.'

They strolled on until they came to a crossroads halfway down the street. To the right they could see a collection of single storey wooden buildings painted a brilliant white. 'Those are the District Offices,' Tom pointed out, 'and next to them is the Post Office where we can collect the mail from our box. On the other side of the Post Office is the Police Station. That's the brick building with the wire fence surrounding it.'

They walked on to the end of the street and stopped again. To their left was a two storey building with a first floor balcony facing the sea. 'The Club,' announced Tom grandly. 'But before we go in I should explain a little bit about it to save you any embarrassment. On the ground floor is the sports club and any local people are able to join and play badminton or snooker. On the first floor, up the outside staircase is The Club. This is for whites only and has a number of rules; you remember what I told you about the shorts?'

'Yes, just don't tell me there are rules for the ladies as well!' exclaimed Mary. 'I've always been hopeless at learning rules. I'll try my best to fit in but if I find a rule to be too ludicrous I shall say so. I'm no longer from a colony. Anyway, how many white people live in and around Kudat? There must be a lot of them to have their own club'

'Actually there are five white men including me and you'll make the third white lady.'

'Wow, It must be really crowded if everyone turns up at once. At least it's somewhere I can pop in for a lemonade after I've done the shopping.'

'Oh no you can't. First rule: membership of The Club is strictly white males only. You can only go in if I accompany you. You have to be my guest.'

'Hmm, I'm not sure I like the idea of this club. Let's see if anyone's around.'

They climbed the stairs and went into the large club room.

There was a scattering of tables with two or more chairs surrounding each one. At one of the tables sat two men who rose as one when Mary entered. The far end of the room housed a small bar behind which a round-faced Chinese barman idly polished some glasses. They made their way to the two standing men who, in looks, were the complete opposite of each other although they were of a similar age; around thirty-five. One was very well built and had a florid complexion with large beefy arms covered in thick black hair that in some strange way seemed to compensate for the lack of hair on his head. His left eye was missing. The other man was painfully thin and almost looked at death's door with his yellow skin and wasted muscles. Tom made the introductions and Mary learned that the larger one was the District Officer John Wilson and that the emaciated gentleman was a plantation manager named Cyril Fellowes. He was originally from England and his plantation was near their one but further down the Kudat peninsular towards the village of Sikuati. John, as District Officer was responsible for just about everything, including administering justice, in the Kudat district and far into the interior. He was supported by an Assistant District Officer named Philip Maltravers who had recently been promoted from being a Cadet in the Colonial Service and was, therefore, very new to the job and totally in fear and awe of his senior officer.

'Do join us,' growled John. 'I've been looking forward to Tom showing off his new bride. It looks as if he's made a fine choice.'

'Thank you sir,' Mary answered, 'but in actual fact I chose him. In Australia we always do things the other way round. It probably a result of living upside down on the other side of the world to you Brits.'

'That's told you John,' wheezed Cyril. 'I warned you these Australian girls were something to be reckoned with.'

Tom and Mary sat down and John ordered drinks from Apau the barman. When the drinks arrived he signed for them in a little book with his name on and the men settled back to discuss the finer points of golf. There was a six hole course that had recently been built around the *padang* complete with a sprinkling of bunkers. They sometimes played a round or two of an evening. After initially being the centre of attention Mary now felt left out so she rose and said that she would like to walk down to the shore on the other side of the field and look at the sea. After the usual courtesies she left and made her way across the rough grass to a small stand of trees on the water's edge and sat on a fallen log. She felt a little lonely and not for the first time she started to have doubts about being so far from home even though she knew Tom would do everything possible to make her happy and comfortable. She wondered if the rest of the small group of whites would be as formal and old-fashioned as the two she had just met. She hoped that at least one of the ladies would prove to be a friend and she would then have another woman to chat with about female things even though she wasn't altogether sure exactly what such things were. She suddenly became aware that someone was watching her and this was confirmed when a bout of shushing and giggling broke out from the foliage above her head. She looked up and saw two wide-eyed faces with even wider smiles peering through the leaves. Her responding smile seemed to act as a signal and the two swung down and stood, now solemn, in front of her. It was a boy and a girl and Mary guessed them to be about eight and ten with the girl being the older one. They were similarly dressed in shirts and shorts and were barefoot. The only other adornment was a dirty orange ribbon holding back the thick black hair of the girl. 'Hello,' smiled Mary. 'What are your names?' This triggered more giggling and it dawned on Mary that they couldn't understand her. In the best tradition of some of the American films she had seen she pointed to herself saying, 'me Mary.'

After more chuckling the girl pointed at Mary and said, 'me Mary.'

'No, just Mary.'

'Just Mary,' came the reply.

'What are your names?' asked Mary. No answer was forthcoming as the children didn't understand the amusing white woman who kept pointing at herself and them. Mary realised that even a basic conversation was obviously impossible. I need to start learning the local language as soon as possible she thought and this positive decision lifted her spirits enormously as she strode back to the club to persuade Tom to take her back to the plantation in good time for dinner.

Later, when showered and dressed for dinner Mary and Tom sat relaxing on the veranda each clutching a gin and tonic as an aperitif. 'The end of your first day in Kudat,' mused Tom. 'What's your impression of the place?'

'It's lovely. Both friendly and exotic. My only reservations about it are the overpowering smell of copra and the dinosaurs in the club.'

'You'll soon get used to both. I have but it took some time and I had to be careful not to become an old fossil myself. It's very easy to end up becoming a British bore when they are the only social contact you have.'

'But what about the local people? You must meet them all the time. Don't you ever socialise with them?'

'Not really. I meet a great many people through my work but it isn't really the done thing, as the English say, to be too friendly. It's like that in the town but up country is different and when I visit plantations in the interior I am able to mix much more with native tribes and enjoy their hospitality. One day I'll take you with me on a trip and you can experience it for yourself.'

'That would be wonderful,' Mary enthused. 'I was thinking earlier, while you were chatting in the club, about learning a local language. Which one would prove to be the most useful?'

'The only one that is widely spoken is *kadai* Malay. It is a simpler form of Malay and a *kadai* is a store so it means 'shop Malay' and is a basic way of communicating what you need. It's really only a vocabulary list as there are no plurals

25

or tenses to learn. You should pick up enough to make yourself understood in a matter of weeks. I could have the wife of one of my estate workers pop in and teach you the basics while I'm out working on the plantation. Would you like that?'

'Yes please, I want to start as soon as possible. When do you have to take over the reins from Colin?'

'Not for a day or so. Then he must return south to the plantation where he's an assistant. Looking after my plantation has been part of his company training. Before he goes I want to show you a little more of the area. We must have a day at Bak Bak beach very soon so you can swim with the tropical fish and then a trip to the Sunday *tamu* at Sikuati to see the real people of Borneo, admire their handicrafts and buy some locally grown produce. Actually we could do both in three days time on Sunday. If you like we could invite a few people and have a curry party on the beach after visiting the market. I promise it won't just be John and Cyril!'

'What a great idea. It will be the ideal opportunity to meet some more of your friends and acquaintances in less formal surroundings than The Club.'

'That's dandy. I'll send out the invitations tomorrow and tell the cook to prepare a large pot of curry and loads of rice. We can keep it hot in the hay box for when we eat. I must also buy some ice and lots of bottled beer and gin and tonic.'

With that settled they went inside for dinner.

Later that evening they were again seated on the veranda in the warm, still air with the incessant sounds of the night closing in around them and the perfume of the flowers seemed magnified by the darkness. Tom looked over to Mary and thought that he could never possibly feel so happy and contented ever again. He still couldn't believe his good fortune in meeting and then, to his total astonishment, marrying her. Rising from his rattan chair he went over and stood behind her. He rested his hands on her shoulders and gently stroked her dry, cool skin. She put her hands over his and moved them down to her firm breasts with the nipples already aroused. He nuzzled her neck and then in one swift movement released his hands from her grip and gathered her up in his arms. Still kissing her neck he manoeuvred her through to the bedroom and, pushing aside the mosquito net draped over the bed, managed to lay her down. Mary responded immediately by kissing him on the mouth and soon they were lying naked with Tom's fingers lightly brushing over Mary's body like delicate little butterflies. She thought she would scream with pleasure as the tips of his fingers moved away and then back to her smooth skin. His tongue started at her mouth and moved down gently licking and teasing her nipples and the further to her navel and the sensitive skin of her stomach. When Tom reached between her thighs and probed her most intimate parts she gasped and called out, 'Now, now.' He pulled her onto him and, with her legs crossed tightly behind his back; he penetrated her so deeply that her whole body felt near to exploding.

It didn't take long before both of them were lying back holding hands in the darkness. Mary hoped that time would stop so that they could stay just as they were for ever. She had never felt so fulfilled and it seemed to be so unfair that they had to do so many mundane things each day and not spend the whole time making love. They had made love many times in their six week marriage but this was the first time Mary had felt such intense passion. She smiled as she realised Tom was snoring softly and then she turned to hold him in her arms as she too fell into a contented sleep.

Sunday came and all the preparations for the picnic were in place. The small party of guests included the two from the club with Cyril's wife Rita. Philip Maltravers was invited together with Christina and Albert Bodin, a Dutch couple who were in charge of the small Basel Mission church and school at mile six. The plan was for Tom and Mary to go to the *tamu* at Sikuati in the morning and then they would all meet up at Bak Bak for a swim and a drink before lunch.

The couple set out for the short drive to Sikuati through the paddy fields and past some striking rocky outcrops before going over a wooden bridge and through a dark tunnel of trees to emerge in the blinding sunlight at the edge of a clearing. At the back of the clearing were a couple of shop-houses and a school building that had a roof but the walls finished at waist height. Inside, Mary could see some rough-hewn wooden desks and a blackboard. The market was in full swing. Scattered over the open ground were groups of people from the Kadazan tribe with some of the women dressed in traditional costume with copper bands wound round their legs from ankle to knee and on their forearms. Most of the clothes were black but often finely decorated with intricate patterns in gold and silver thread. The men were bare-chested with a loincloth or sarong tied at the waist and a loose open-topped turban. Their wares were spread on the ground on colourful cloths and ranged from various fruit and vegetables from their small market gardens to tobacco and hand-made tools, knives and farming implements. Mary and Tom wandered around the various traders and bought some fresh fruit for the picnic and Mary bought some bolts of cloth she thought could make interesting tablecloths as presents for her family in Australia. They each had a drink of sweet, refreshing cane sugar water squeezed fresh through an amazing contraption similar to a washing mangle that crushed the canes and the sweet liquid ran out down a tube into rather smeared glasses. A last look around and it was time to retrace part of their route and then go towards the coast to the small bay at Bak Bak.

They were the first to arrive so it gave them time to unload the food and drink and then the rugs for sitting on. Tom had brought a small table in the truck to keep the meal off the ground and, hopefully, out of reach of the ants. They had packed plates and cutlery as well as drinking glasses so all was set out ready before the others came. Tom opened a cold beer for himself and a bottle of lemonade for his wife and as they were toasting the success of the day when the harsh sound of a large motorcycle shattered the peaceful scene. It was the District Officer's assistant Philip and he swerved to a halt with a further revving of the engine and a squeal of brakes. 'Hello there,' he called as he wiped the dust from his face, 'you must be Mary. I'm Philip and very pleased to meet you at last. Tom told me about you in the Office and I must say he's an extremely fortunate man.'

'Thanks for the compliment,' replied Mary. 'I'm glad we've met as I thought I was to be the only young person round here.'

'Well that's not very flattering to me,' moaned Tom. 'I'm not totally over the hill yet.'

'I wasn't including you in my comment as I think of us as a couple and not individuals. So stop sulking and give Philip a drink.'

The rest of the lunch party arrived and they all sat on the rugs and surveyed the scenic view of the small tidy beach with a rocky headland at each end and the swaying palms giving them shade. It really was idyllic and Mary contemplated it with undisguised pleasure. The men then disappeared into the bushes at the back of the beach to change into their bathing costumes and after their return the three ladies did likewise. Tom had brought a couple of old inner tubes for those who were not very confident in water and so they were all able to splash about in the clear South China Sea. John, the district officer, cut a strange figure in a knitted woollen suit that hung down to his knees and made him look like an oversized baby in a rather full nappy. Mary, a strong swimmer thanks to her brothers' coaching, was able to go a further distance from the shore than the other ladies and dive down to explore the wonders of the coral reef. It was a magical world with pretty angel fish and belligerent clown fish in abundance. She saw sea cucumbers on the bottom together with spiny sea orchids. Tom had warned her not to put her feet on the sand in case she stood on something dangerous and to avoid contact with the pretty multi-coloured coral as a small cut or graze could easily turn sceptic. Taking these precautions did not prevent her enjoyment of the occasion and her day was complete when a shoal of electric blue fish darted around her in an underwater ballet.

The lunch was a huge success and everyone set to with gusto to demolish the large pan of curry with rice and chunks of newly baked bread. Having fresh fruit from the market rounded the meal off perfectly and the afternoon was spent in desultory conversation, napping and occasional half-hearted attempts at exercise. Mary soon chummed up with Christina Bodin from the Mission and they told each other respectively about their lives in Holland and Australia. They were amazed to find many similarities in their upbringing as they had both come from comfortable backgrounds. Christina, like Mary, had two older brothers and her parents were quite well to do. The main difference was that Christina had always wanted to travel and made all the advances to secure a husband and make the long voyage to Borneo.

Inevitably the men's conversation turned to the growing problems in China and the threat of a resurgent Germany in Europe.

'That Hitler fellow is really causing a lot of trouble. I think we would be wise to put him in his place as soon as possible. I doubt if the German people have the stomach for another war so soon after the last one,' opined John.

'Don't you believe it,' answered Albert Bodin who had recently returned from leave in Holland. 'They are all fired up and willing to follow Herr Hitler and his cronies in their lust for an all-conquering German Empire. They are already united against whole sections of their own population such as the Jews and those they consider different or who oppose their plans in any way. There are reports and rumours that many people have disappeared and might even have been killed. Hitler's ideal is for a pure German race that will rule all of Europe. They must be stopped at all cost.'

'It's probably more to do with economics,' observed Tom. 'Like the Japanese, the Germans are in need of raw materials and fuel for their manufacturing industries and, rather than buy it on the open market, prefer to take it by force. That way they consider that their supplies will be more secure as well as much cheaper. And they will have a captive market for the goods they produce.' Diplomatically he didn't add that the British had been doing exactly that for centuries.

Young Philip Maltravers looked at the others. 'I'll be the first to volunteer if it comes to a war,' he said with all the bravado and ignorance of youth. 'I'm sure we can easily defeat the Germans again.'

'I think our biggest threat out here is from the Japanese and their expansionist policy,' added Cyril Fellowes. 'They might not be satisfied with just China under their control and could move on to taking Malaya or even move south through the Dutch East Indies and possibly as far as Australia.'

John Wilson laughed at the suggestion. 'That's nonsense. They are too scared of the British Fleet in Singapore which is regularly patrolling the seas up to Hong Kong to try anything like that. Also, the garrison at Singapore is heavily armed and well-manned, ready to repel any attack from the sea. There will be no invasion of Malaya or any other British Colony in my lifetime.'

That ended the discussion but left Tom wondering if he had done the right thing in bringing his young bride to a country so far from the security of home. The picnic was now over and it was time to pack up and return to their respective homes to shower and dress for dinner. Again, they took turns to retreat to the bushes and change out of their bathing gear and then boarded their various transports and left Bak Bak to the wildlife whose peace had been so rudely disturbed for that day. Tom and Mary were the last to leave with the thanks of the others called to them as each vehicle departed. Mary was ready for a shower to wash off the salt, particularly from her hair that felt sticky and stiff. Tom also wanted a shower and wondered what Mary's reaction would be if he suggested they shared it. He mentioned it as casually as he could and was so surprised and pleased at her immediate acceptance that he drove almost recklessly to reach the bungalow as quickly as possible.

Chapter 4

In Kota Belud David Wong was also looking forward to his shower, albeit alone. His day had been quiet. Well, as quiet as most days were at home with six lively children aged three to sixteen. The older children, who had adopted western names like their father, had been studying in the afternoon following the compulsory attendance at church that enabled them to continue at the mission school. The eldest was Anthony who was very like his father in both looks and temperament and was keen to study medicine at university. At 16 he looked forward to going away from home and broadening his horizons. Lucy, aged 14, was next and a very pretty girl. She had aspirations to join the teaching profession and hoped that she would be able to qualify without travelling too far as she knew she would sorely miss her family. Peter, who was 12, had started in secondary school that year. He had no ideas for a future career and just wanted to enjoy life to the full. He was always up to some mischief but he was not malicious and most of the scrapes he found himself in were often more humorous than bad. Actually, he usually came off worst but he was not too analytical of his exploits and soon forgot any unfortunate consequences. All three of them had been successful in primary school and regularly passed the end of year tests which enabled them to move up to the next grade culminating in the very stiff and fiercely competitive examination in year six to gain entry to secondary education. David and his wife were quietly proud of them. Two of the younger children were still in primary school and were enjoying their lessons but had shown no real academic aptitude. David wasn't particularly worried and tried not to put too much pressure on them. He reasoned that they might blossom later and wanted them to have a love for education rather than be forced to learn by rote just to pass a test. He thought that there would be plenty of time for them to develop over the coming years.

Despite his earlier promise to himself he had shared with his wife the news of the mysterious visitor to his dispensary. She had been equally puzzled as to exact meaning and possible implications of the visit and had made him promise not to do anything that might upset or antagonise the British authorities as they were prone to repatriating any Chinese nationals they felt were acting or even thinking in a subversive way. He could also see the sense in that as he now had no doubts that a return to China with the Japanese occupying large swathes of the country would be a recipe for misery and possibly worse. His family came first over any other considerations and he would do anything to keep them safe and together. The love he felt for them was all-consuming and as much as he derived immense pleasure from their individual personalities he often also experienced occasional panic when the thought of the heavy burden he carried to keep them secure entered his head uninvited.

That evening, while the family rested after dinner, David wandered back down to the town coffee shop where he knew a few of his oldest friends would be chatting, playing chess or banging mah-jong tiles down on the marble-topped tables. He had decided to share with them the strange message from his visitor Lo Vun lip and canvas their ideas and opinions. Knowing that they were all in a similar position to himself with families to keep together he knew they wouldn't be rash and would carefully consider the outcomes of any decisions or actions. It was with confidence that he entered the shop and sat down at one of the tables and ordered a white coffee. It came in a glass with three distinct layers and a spoon held vertically in it. At the bottom was a thick layer of white sugar. On top of this some creamy condensed milk and the whole drink topped with black coffee. It was up to the customer to stir it or not, according to his taste. David opted, as he always did, to stir the mixture thoroughly so that it became a light brown and tasted so sickly sweet that any bitterness of the coffee was totally drowned out. It was just how he liked it.

After his first sip he looked around at the others and spoke. 'Friends, I have some rather interesting and surprising news for you.' He immediately had their full attention and even the mah-jong tiles stayed still and silent. They moved their chairs closer to him so they wouldn't miss a word of what he was to say. All held him in great esteem and knew that what he had to say must be important if it entailed addressing all of them at once. David outlined the stranger's visit and what had passed between them. They all listened intently and when David had finished speaking they sat without moving as they digested what he had told them.

At last one of them, the owner of a small general store spoke quietly and deliberately, 'What you have told us comes as no great surprise to me. The Japanese imperialist dream is well known and their occupation of our home country only serves to further underline that we must remain on our guard.'

Another man, a market gardener, added, 'Despite the protestations of the British that they can protect us I think we should start to make some concrete plans to encompass all eventualities. My suggestion is that we secretly start to build up a store of weapons such as rifles and handguns together with some explosives taken surreptitiously from the copper mines so that we can at least defend our families if we are attacked.'

Although some of the men nodded in agreement David felt he had to warn them that such action could be construed as rebellion against the British if they were discovered and the Japanese were still a thousand miles away. More discussion followed and after an hour or so they agreed that they would start to stockpile weapons but keep them separately so that there would be no obvious connection. They also decided to slowly build up stocks of tinned and dried food as they had heard tales of great hardship in China when the Japanese commandeered all the local food supplies for their troops. This settled, the men returned to their noisy games and David drifted off home.

As he walked along the road to his house with his hands thrust in his trouser pockets and his shoulders hunched he thought about what the future might hold. Deep inside he knew that his fears were real and that it was better to take some action rather than do nothing but a niggling idea kept cropping up and refused to go away. The thought was that it would be better to blend into the background and keep quiet so that nobody would bother him or his family. He wondered if this notion was really some form of cowardice and with a shake he straightened his back and walked a little taller to try to show that he preferred to stand out in a crowd rather than be just one of the herd. On reaching his house he had decided that he would never take the easy option and would happily fight for what was his and what was right. Ah San nodded to him as he took off his shoes and went to sit at the small table.

'When you went out you looked worried,' she observed, 'but now you've a much calmer countenance. Have you had some good news?'

'Not really. We just made some important decisions in the coffee shop. I won't bore you with all of them at this time but you must start to build up a stock of food in case of any emergency.'

Ah San smiled and nodded again. She was also well aware of what might happen if the Japanese invaded and was pleased that her husband was actively involved in determining their family's destiny. At the same time she worried for his safety and that of their precious children.

Chapter 5

'When did you last go horse riding?' Tom asked Mary as she tidied up the magazines on the coffee table.

'About two years ago. Why?'

'Because I have to go to one of our more remote plantations in the interior and I thought you might like to tag along. It's far from the coast and grows a rubber crop which makes it more labour intensive so you will see how different a manager's life is on such an estate. It's impossible to travel in the truck and to walk would take far too long so we'll have to go on horseback and carry everything we need. Two of our workers will accompany us and help with setting up camp each night and foraging for some of the food.'

'I'd like a few days to find my seat again,' Mary grimaced. 'Without some practice the going might be a little too painful.'

'That's fine; we don't need to go until next Wednesday so you've a full week to prepare your delicate regions.'

'But if travelling is so difficult how on earth do they manage to transport the rubber to the nearest port?'

'By river. Borneo has a great number of rivers leading to the coast. Unfortunately we can't go there by boat as the river used by this plantation does not end near here. It runs much further south near to the small market town of Kota Belud and there the cargo is transferred to trucks and taken by road to Jesselton for export.'

They had now been in Kudat for nearly three months and had settled in to a pleasant routine with Tom leaving for work each morning while Mary had her language lesson and then he returned for a quick lunch before working until around five o'clock. Each afternoon for Mary was different. Sometimes she went to town to do some shopping or she would visit Christina Bodin who had become a firm friend and confidante.

Occasionally she would read under the casuarina tree in the garden but more often than not this led to her finding focussing her eyes difficult and the book would slip from her grasp as she gently nodded off. Tom would often return to find her fast asleep in the wooden recliner with her book in her lap or fallen on the grass. He usually spent a few moments just gazing lovingly before rousing her from her reverie. A shower was then followed by dinner, a few drinks on the veranda and an early night. They were very contented and rarely socialised in the club. All they needed was each other. The prospect of a change in their lives left Mary with mixed feelings. She desperately wanted to see more of the country but at the same time wondered if the trip would somehow break the magical spell she felt governed their existence.

'I'll start riding again tomorrow if you can find me a suitably well-behaved pony. I'm not ready for a spirited horse so make sure it is either very old or extremely placid.'

'That's alright. You can have Sheba. She's sure footed and has an excellent temperament. I'll make a list of what we will need to take on our journey so you can start putting it all together and packing it in easy to manage bundles. We'll take a couple of pack horses with us so our nags won't be overloaded.' With that comment Tom went for his evening shower and Mary sat hugging her knees tightly, a slight frown on her brow.

After a week of regular riding Mary felt much better prepared and more confident. She had also packed all the items Tom had listed as well as a few extras of her own. He had not mentioned any toiletries or small home comforts and she was determined not to do without those. With all the baggage piled up in Tom's study it looked far too much and she considered trimming down the load by removing some of her luxury items such as her books and a large cushion. She then thought she would leave everything as it was and wait for Tom's reaction. Fortunately he didn't seem to notice the extra goods and they were soon loaded up on the horses and they were ready to depart. After a few final instructions to his staff Tom gave the signal and the small party set off towards Sikuati where they would leave the main track and head through the jungle towards the distant hills.

Their first night was spent by a small stream in some dense woodland. Mary had found the going reasonably easy and was still feeling fine when Tom stopped and announced that this would be their resting place until the morning when he intended to start off as soon as it was light. It was noticeably more humid in the jungle and Mary missed the refreshing sea breeze she had become accustomed to in Kudat. The lack of moving air made it seem much hotter and she was soaked through with sweat even though she hadn't really been exerting herself. There were also a lot of unfamiliar sounds and she found herself staring intently into the foliage. She was well aware of the dangers of snakes as these were a fact of life in Australia and she had heard of the white rhino and the rarely sighted elephant. Orang Utans, the so-called men of the jungle, she had seen as pets in some of the Chinese households and she hoped to observe some in their natural environment.

Her thoughts were broken by Tom calling her for dinner. It was an interesting concoction of rice, corned beef, eggs and dried salt fish. They ate it with spoons from small bowls whilst sitting on blankets and the whole experience reminded Mary of the Girl Guide camps she had attended when she was in her early teens. This was, she felt, a real adventure. Dinner over they washed their bowls in the stream and laid out their sleeping mats and bed rolls. These consisted of two blankets in a waterproof cover held together with little leather straps and buckles. A mosquito net was strung up from the overhanging branches and tucked under the mats to help them spend a more comfortable night. Darkness came suddenly as it does near to the equator. One of the men lit a couple of paraffin lamps but these only served to attract more insects so Mary and Tom retreated to the safe haven of their mosquito net and soon fell asleep. The two men stayed up longer and quietly talked until they too fell asleep under the jungle canopy wrapped in their sarongs with a small bundle of clothes serving as a pillow. They didn't have, or apparently need, the services of a net to protect them from bites.

The next day followed a similar pattern but towards late afternoon they came upon a river with a rather rickety looking rope bridge across it. Mary didn't like the look of it but said nothing. It was wide enough for the horses but they had to be led and were rather skittish as they didn't like the feeling of insecurity the wooden boards gave them. At last they all crossed safely and after a few more miles came upon a large clearing which only had a few small trees and bushes growing on it.

'Why is this part of the jungle so empty?' asked Mary.

'It's where a longhouse used to be,' Tom explained. 'The people must have moved on as there's no sign of a dwelling and the jungle is starting to grow back. They move their longhouses for various reasons. Sometimes it is because the headman has died and sometimes it is just because the land is no longer fertile enough to grow good crops. When they move they'll hack and burn another area to farm that they call a *ladang* and set up house again for another seven or so years. They never go very far so we'll probably meet them soon.'

Mary was not too sure she wanted to meet the inhabitants as she had heard the tales of their headhunting traditions. Tom assured her that they were friendly and that he almost certainly knew their headman from his previous visits to the area.

'I'm sure it'll be Asampit and his community. They're really very hospitable and will welcome us with great rejoicing. They'll offer us *tapai* to drink and be very offended if we refuse so just smile and wet your lips when the jar reaches you. It's only rice wine but is quite alcoholic and is a cloudy, greenish liquid with a sour taste. If we're lucky they might play their drums and gongs and make a bit of a party of the evening. At least you'll be able to sleep indoors on a well-sprung floor.'

About half a mile down the faint trail they came upon the new longhouse and were warmly greeted by a horde of naked children accompanied by a pack of light brown yelping dogs. The children surrounded Tom and Mary and grabbed their hands to pull them uncomplaining to the longhouse which stood proudly in the centre of the clearing. Down the notched log came an imposing figure. He wasn't particularly tall but was well-muscled and had his black hair in a long plait down his back. He wore a crimson loincloth and had colourful woven bands tied round his prominent biceps.

'That's Asampit,' whispered Tom in Mary's ear. 'He's the headmen or *orang tua*. I'm glad it's him as he's an old friend.'

Asampit approached them and the children drew back, not from fear but respect. He reached Tom and grabbed him firmly by the shoulders as he looked him straight in the eye. He spoke in Malay and Mary was very glad of the time she had spent on her lessons as she was able to understand quite a lot of what was said.

'Welcome to our village. It is good to see you again. I see you've brought a woman with you. Is she your wife? Do you have any fine sons or daughters?'

'One question at a time,' laughed Tom. 'Yes, this is Mary and she is my wife. We've only been together a short time so there are no children yet.'

'Welcome Mary. I'm sure you will give Tom many beautiful babies.'

Mary blushed but managed to put together a suitable reply. 'I'm sure we'll have a family before long and you'll be able to meet them on another visit.'

'Make it soon. I enjoy *tuan* Tom's company. Let's go inside and have a drink.'

Asampit almost ran up the steep log that led to the entrance. Tom ascended more gingerly as did Mary because the log was so old it was polished by constant use and very slippery. Inside the longhouse were some elderly women leaning against the walls of the various family rooms leading off the main thoroughfare. They gave the couple wide smiles showing their blackened teeth and bright red lips stained by the betel-nut they constantly chewed for its mild narcotic effect. There were plenty of men also sitting around chewing or smoking but no sign of any younger women.

'Where are all the girls and women?' asked Mary.

'They're working on the *ladang*,' explained Tom. 'A message will have been sent about our arrival so they should return soon to meet us.'

Tom and Asampit chatted for a few minutes about the harvest and how fertile the soil was and then Asampit told him that the next day was to be a special day for all of them as the whole village was teaming up with another one further up the small river they lived alongside for a fishing day. Tom knew these days were quite rare in the Murut calendar and looked forward to by everyone as it gave them some variety in their diet. He explained this to Mary and asked if she would mind staying an extra day so they could enjoy the spectacle. She readily agreed and they sat down to drink the *tapai*.

It came in a large jar with a bamboo straw protruding from the top. It was passed round and eventually it ended up in Mary's hands. She gazed into the murky liquid and with a fixed grin on her face raised it to her lips. She heeded Tom's warning and sipped cautiously but a little of the drink shot into her mouth before she could stop it. It tasted very yeasty but not really unpleasant so she swallowed it and sent the jar on its way to her neighbour. It was refilled and again made its rounds and this time Mary just touched the straw to her lips and didn't drink any. Eventually the women and girls returned as the party became a little louder and some of them went and fetched the brass gongs and wooden drums for the men to play. The girls of the village, for that is what a longhouse actually is, started a slow rhythmical dance with sinuous arm movements as they moved gracefully on the bamboo floor. Mary was mesmerised and much admired their lissom figures as they wove intricate patterns around each other and then moved seductively towards the seated men before turning away just out of reach. She thought it was far more sensual than the rather formal dancing she had experienced in Australia even though the longhouse dancers never actually made physical contact with each other.

When the dance ended Asampit clapped his hands and a seemingly endless procession of food appeared to be spread out before them on the floor. He took the first handful and this was the signal for a general free for all as the people jostled each other to take the tastiest morsels. Mary recognised chicken and pork but some of the other meat was a mystery to her. There were large tin bowls of rice and a large earthenware pot of some sort of vegetable soup which was poured over the rice using a wooden ladle. The whole feast was soon demolished and the men sat back with contented sighs and grunts of approval. They smoked their tobacco wrapped in the usual dried grass leaves. The women then cleared up and it was time for the storytelling to commence. The oral history of the village and their ancestors was related through stories handed down over countless generations. Most of the tales were of skirmishes with rival longhouses and the bravery of the warriors but some were humorous anecdotes of accidents and misunderstandings. It seemed that they had a gentle sense of the ridiculous and enjoyed nothing more than relating tales even if they themselves were the butt of the joke.

Eventually everyone retired to bed and Mary found that their bearers had set up their beds and mosquito net in an empty side room. Mary wanted to go to the lavatory but was frightened of going down the slippery pole and stumbling about in the dark. She confided her fears to Tom and he laughed and told her that there was no need to go outside as there were plenty of holes in the floor and any waste was soon scoffed by the pigs that lived underneath the house. Mary found this a tad distasteful but at least it saved her a frightening journey.

Early the next morning they were woken by the sounds of village life going on outside their flimsy split bamboo door. They went out and carefully descended to the ground so they could wash in the small river that provided the longhouse with water for all purposes. After a breakfast of fried bananas, rice cakes and weak tea they waited for the fishing expedition to commence. Mary asked Tom for some further details but he said that it was the first time he had been invited and had no idea what was to happen. He stressed that it was very important for all the villagers and would be an interesting day.

'They live a long way from the sea,' he explained, 'so fresh river fish is a highly prized food even though it's rather tasteless and full of tiny bones. It'll be fascinating to see how they set about catching the fish and why they need to band together with the other village.'

Mid-morning saw villagers of all ages clustered expectantly round Asampit who delegated the various tasks. Mary and Tom were to go in a canoe with his son Enduat who was a well-set young man of around twenty with thick black hair like his father's but done up in a bun held in place by a highly decorated bone pin. Other villagers had already been down to the river and built a dam from a lattice of tree trunks and bamboo poles at a narrow point. All were brandishing spears or carrying nets. Asampit explained to the couple exactly how the fish were caught. 'All last night our friends up the river have been preparing a surprise for the fish. They have been pounding a root called *tuba* so that it is now a pulp. It is put on wooden platforms over the river and then water is poured over it so that a white, milky liquid percolates down into the river below. It has a narcotic effect on the fish and they will rise to the surface unconscious to be gathered up in nets by the women and children. However, some of the cleverer fish race ahead of the drugged water and try to escape. They will reach us in a panic and when they encounter the dam they will attempt to leap over it. We will spear them as they try. That is why we will be in canoes and must be ready to act quickly as the fish arrive. At the end of the day we will get together with the others and share the catch out fairly.'

Tom and Mary glanced at each other and Tom took her hand. 'Keep close to me. This could be a bit chaotic.'

'Don't worry Tom. You know I'm a good swimmer.'

They paraded down to the river bank where the canoes were waiting. Each canoe was hewn from a solid section of a tree trunk and had a single wooden outrigger acting as a stabiliser lashed on one side. Despite looking heavy they were surprisingly manoeuvrable and the men propelled and steered them skilfully with wooden paddles. The women and children went off upstream to try and catch any comatose fish that floated past. Some of the men called out and pointed to the far bank where a bird hovered in the trees.

'That's a *nahagan*,' explained Enduat. 'It's a sign of good luck for the fishing. It means that the *tuba* will be strong and the fish plentiful.'

They clambered aboard the canoes. Asampit and two of his men were in the leading canoe closely followed by Enduat with Tom and Mary. Tom had been given a spear but felt that, as he had no experience, he might be more of a hindrance than a help and therefore decided to stay out of things as much as he could. Mary sat at the back of the canoe and waited with eager anticipation. The other canoes, four in all, came behind them and when they reached the dam they fanned out so that it would be difficult for any fish to escape their spears. Suddenly there came shouts and screams from upriver that slowly became louder. It was obvious that the fish were on their way and the men stood up and held their spears poised ready for action. In a moment all was in turmoil as the first fish tried to jump the obstacle barring their escape route. Enduat lifted his spear and caught one fish in mid-air. He dropped it on the floor of the canoe where it flapped and flopped about. Another fish that had leapt out of the water to escape managed to land in Mary's lap. Startled, she jumped up just as Enduat was poised for another thrust. The rocking caused him to lose his footing and in a flash he was overboard and in the river. Tom saw that he had hit his head on the bamboo dam as he fell and was slowly sinking under the murky water. Without a second thought Tom dived in and managed to get hold of his hair just before he sank from view. He held him up and trod water as Asampit came across in his canoe to help. Enduat was dragged into Asampit's canoe and Tom hauled himself up over the stern of his canoe behind Mary. She looked totally shocked and numb.

'It's alright,' spluttered Tom. 'All's well. Look, Enduat's

coming round so he can't be too badly injured.'

The fishing forgotten they made for the bank nearest the longhouse. Enduat was carried on to the grass and lay there looking dazed with his father Asampit supporting his head in the crook of his arm. The whole of the village stood in respectful silence as Enduat slowly recovered.

'What happened?' he enquired. 'One second I was about to spear a fish and the next I am lying on the ground with everyone staring at me.'

'You fell into the water and banged your head,' Asampit told him. 'Luckily *tuan* Tom saw you were in danger and rescued you.'

Seeing that his son was safe he gently put his head down and went over to where Tom was standing. As before, he put his hands on Tom's shoulders and gazed deep into his eyes. 'I owe my son's life to you,' he said with feeling. 'You are now also my son and I will never forget what you did. We are family. What is mine is yours.'

'You owe me nothing. I did what any man would do in the same circumstances. I am pleased to have been of some use and delighted that your son has recovered so quickly.'

It was now time for Tom and Mary to depart so they packed their bags, saddled the horses and set off with their bearers hoping to reach the rubber plantation before nightfall. As they neared the estate Mary suddenly became aware of a dark shape above the thinning trees. Its bulk towered over them and she could see that its topmost edge was jagged like a row of filed teeth. There were a few wispy clouds clinging to the almost vertical slab of rock that rose dramatically to its highest peaks. It was almost totally black and devoid of any softening vegetation. This was her first view of the mighty Mount Kinabalu. It was thought by the Chinese to be a slumbering dragon and by the native people as the resting place for their souls. Whatever their beliefs all who viewed it were united in being in awe and totally subdued by its mystical and overpowering malevolent presence.

'You're fortunate,' Tom said, invading her thoughts. 'At this time of day the mountain is usually completely shrouded in cloud. It is normally only at dawn that you can see it so clearly. Maybe one day you'll climb it as I did a few years ago. It isn't a difficult climb as there is a path leading up to the Paka Cave where you can rest before the final push to the summit in the early hours. There is no real rock climbing involved just a few scrambles over the large granite slabs and boulders. The view from the top is fantastic and you can look down into Low's Gully which is a near vertical drop of thousands of feet. We can complete the climb in two or three days.'

'First horse riding and now mountain climbing. I think I'll be an all action hero by the time you've finished with me. My name's Mary not Jane and you are certainly no Tarzan!'

The last film they had seen before leaving Sydney had been one of the Tarzan series featuring the legendary swimmer Johnny Weissmuller. It had helped to whet Mary's appetite for her rapidly approaching journey to the jungles of Borneo.

It only took a couple of days for Tom to finish his work at the plantation. There had been some problems with the workforce and he had used all his diplomatic skills to help iron them out. Having Mary with him had proved to be a bonus as the workers were fascinated by the first white woman they had encountered and her presence seemed to bestow on Tom even greater credibility. They decided to return to Kudat via Kota Belud as there was a convoy of boats heading that way down the river carrying the rubber and they could be accommodated on board with the two bearers and the horses. The river trip was uneventful and they found it quite relaxing just lying back and watching the swarms of insects over the water and the ever watchful birds swooping to snatch them up. They spent two nights camping on the river bank and this is when the insects took charge as they tormented the travellers until they retired beneath their mosquito nets.

Mary found Kota Belud a delightful little town. All the buildings were wooden and had a raised and covered walkway along the front so shoppers could wander along out of the rain. They had unfortunately missed the weekly *tamu* but were able to spend a few hours having a good meal in a Chinese cafe and a wander around the town and the shops. Most of the shops were similar to those in Kudat and the goods sold were no doubt identical but then Mary spotted the small Chinese medicine shop and gazed speculatively in the window at the intricate diagrams of the human body and the strange herbs and roots displayed on small dishes.

'I wonder how effective the medicine is?' she asked Tom. 'Most of the concoctions look quite disgusting and even deadly.'

Tom looked at her seriously. 'The Chinese have a long and proud history of medicine and they are able to cure many conditions using natural remedies. The most effective practitioners these days are very thoroughly trained and use a mix of Oriental and Western medicine to help people.'

David Wong heard these words from inside and came to the door to see who was responsible for uttering them. He was flattered by the praise and pleased to receive recognition from a white man. He looked at the striking couple who stood outside and greeted them with a short bow.

'I couldn't help but overhear your kind comments,' he said in excellent English. 'It is most gratifying that you consider my profession to be an honourable one. The majority of people from Europe regard me at best as some kind of witch doctor and at worst a complete charlatan.'

'That's because we're from Australia and not Europe,' laughed Tom. 'We have much more open minds.'

'Please feel free to avail yourself of my services if you are ever ill. I can see you are both in the best of health at present and the lady is positively blooming. It has been a pleasure meeting you and I hope we do so again'

They walked slowly away along the boardwalk outside the shops and Tom looked at Mary. To his surprise she appeared to be blushing and looked a little embarrassed.

'You weren't offended by his remarks were you?' he asked.

'He was only complimenting you on your good health.'

'Not at all. As you said he's obviously a good doctor and he saw something in me that I wasn't going to tell you about until we returned home. You see Tom, I'm three months pregnant.'

Tom stared at her then picked her up and whirled her round and round. He had a silly fixed grin that wouldn't fade. Eventually he put her down and holding both her hands said, 'How long have you known?'

'I wasn't certain until a few weeks ago.'

'Why didn't you tell me then? I would never have let you come on this trip if I'd known.'

'That's exactly why I didn't tell you. I desperately wanted to see more of the country and knew you would react like that. I'm not ill you know.'

'Three months?' mused Tom. 'That must mean that, er, well.'

'Yes, our first night in Kudat.'

David Wong watched them as they danced down the road and smiled a wry smile to himself. It must be their first, he thought, and the husband's just found out. They seem a well matched couple and I wish them every happiness. He thought about his own six children and the pleasure they had brought to him and his wife and wished the same good fortune on the disappearing pair.

Chapter 6

Their daughter was born in February 1939 and was named Sarah after Tom's grandmother who had died a few years earlier. Sarah was a real charmer and within six months had the whole household at her beck and call. Her parents doted on her and the servants vied for her affections. It was as if she had a real extended family and was surrounded by love and affection. Tom was only sorry that his grandparents had not lived to meet Sarah as he felt it would have made them extremely happy to know their great-granddaughter. At least he could take her to meet Mary's parents and her two uncles in Sydney. They would spoil her rotten.

Then the bad news from Europe reached Borneo. War had broken out and all its associated problems visited the small Kudat community of Europeans. Those with roots in England worried about their families back home and wondered whether they should return immediately. They waited for guidance from their employers and the British Government. The Bodins, being Dutch, were concerned about a possible German invasion of Holland and also considered returning as their parents were ageing and would possibly need them if there was any trouble. Tom and Mary were the least worried as their families were well away from the conflict and the threat from Japan had not yet materialised. Naturally they were concerned for the plight of their friends who had families so far away but there was little they could do to ease the uncertainty of not knowing what was actually going on. They decided to remain in Kudat for the time being and wait to see how the war panned out. As with all wars everyone hoped it would be over swiftly and that Germany would soon be defeated again. None of them really appreciated that warfare had moved on from the static trench conflict of the Great War and battles would now be fought at speed over the whole European continent and beyond.

The talk in the club was of little else and Tom found it more and more depressing so his visits, already infrequent, became even rarer. The English administrators still maintained that they would not be affected and that all they had to do was wait for the inevitable victory and nothing in their little world would change. Their routine would remain sacrosanct and Britain would continue to rule most of the world; benevolently and efficiently of course. Mary still regularly saw Christina Bodin but they deliberately steered clear of talking about the war and contented themselves with chats about the minutiae of their daily lives. A new dress, an interesting recipe, local gossip or the perpetual moans about the idiosyncrasies of their staff became the main topics of conversation. It suited them both and helped give a veneer of normality to their daily lives.

Tom's work continued and the copra crop was still shipped out regularly to Singapore. There it was processed and the oil and other products from the nut continued on their way by boat to Britain although now they had to go the long route round South Africa as the Suez Canal was no longer an option. If they missed the German U-boats patrolling the Atlantic then their precious cargo was very gratefully received by the now besieged Britons. The ordinariness of life in Kudat acted as a soporific to their more worrying thoughts and all the various groups of people gave little serious thought to the possibility of war ever reaching them.

Christmas 1939 was a muted affair with few messages or cards arriving from overseas to help cheer up the colonialists. It was the same throughout 1940 as the news that filtered through seemed to be all bad with little hope of an early end to hostilities in Europe and North Africa. By June Britain seemed to be more and more isolated in Europe as the German army had already reached the English Channel. Tom felt proud that the Australian government had put its support behind the British and that Australian troops were being deployed in many areas including Malaya and Singapore. These troops were enjoying a relatively quiet war and made the most of the swimming and sporting opportunities. To the south of British North Borneo and taking up the greater part of the large island of Borneo lay the Dutch East Indies and they had a reasonable Dutch army presence despite Holland now being under German occupation. There was even a small air force in bases scattered around their territory. There was talk that some of these bases were in secret locations in case of enemy attack. Mary asked the Bodins if they considered moving to the Dutch colony to be with their fellow countrymen but they felt their work was in Kudat and stayed put.

In April 1941 Mary realised joyfully that she was pregnant again and the birth would be in October. By now she desperately wanted to see her family again and thought that it would be wonderful if their second child could be born in Sydney with her mother in attendance. She discussed the matter with Tom and he agreed wholeheartedly but for slightly different reasons.

'It's a great idea,' he enthused. 'It's bound to be a boy this time and he should be born in Australia so he can play cricket, or even rugby, for his country when he grows up.'

'Well I suppose that's one reason for going back,' Mary chuckled. 'Do you think you'll be able to swing some leave?'

'No problem. We've been here for three years now and the company owe me home leave of around six months. I'll sort it out today. It takes a long time by boat so I'll see if I can persuade them to fly us home from Singapore by seaplane. We should be able to go back in August.'

Mary was overjoyed. She had never flown before and Tom's suggestion had her excited all over again at the prospect of another new adventure. She hoped that their little daughter Sarah would be able to cope with the gruelling journey now that she was two years old and bored easily.

It was duly arranged and once again they boarded the SS Vyner Brooke for the first leg of their trip home. Mary was delighted to be on this particular ship as she had always regarded it as their personal honeymoon boat. They flew out by sea plane from the harbour in Singapore and eventually reached Darwin on the northern tip of Australia. From here the plane lumbered on round the coast via Brisbane before landing in Sydney discharging its tired and dishevelled passengers. There were wild and emotional scenes of reunion when Tom, Mary and little Sarah eventually cleared the landing formalities and met the welcoming committee. Mary's brothers had made a huge banner saying, 'two leave – three return' which brought a smile to Mary's lips knowing it would soon be four. They were bundled into the waiting car and off to North Shore for a welcome home barbecue even though it was now winter and a little chilly outside.

Everyone admired and petted Sarah who soon forgot her tiredness and revelled in the attention. Eventually she succumbed to the rigours of the journey and was packed off to bed. After answering what seemed like a million questions Mary took out her photograph album to show her family exactly how they lived in Kudat. These prompted another barrage of questions until Tom had had enough and announced that they would be joining Sarah in the land of nod and all further queries would have to wait for the next day.

'What a reception,' Mary said as they prepared for bed. 'I'm glad we're home and somehow it makes the war seem even more distant.'

'Let's hope it stays that way.'

Chapter 7

The Japanese invasion of British North Borneo was fast, efficient and virtually unopposed. After the bombing of Pearl Harbour on December 7th 1941 there had been many telegraphic communications between the offices in Singapore and the administrators and planters in Jesselton and Kudat, resulting in a flurry of activity. Petrol stocks were destroyed and boats over ten feet in length hidden in the mangrove swamps. Kerosene and rice stocks were distributed to the native people and the railway line from Jesselton to Melalap in the interior, a distance of ninety-six miles, was commandeered as an escape route for the European women and children. The ruling powers and nearly all the colonialists did not believe that the Japanese would venture away from the coast and that by moving all supplies and people by rail they would remain safe. The British North Borneo Company hadn't given their employees in the local administration any directives telling them how to deal with an invasion. It was not included in their reams of rules and regulations so the District Officers and their assistants just carried on as if nothing was happening. None of them even considered the possibility of leaving their posts and moving inland to organise any resistance to an invading force.

The valuable oilfields at Miri and Kuching, the capital of Sarawak, were taken in mid-December. The island of Labuan by the end of the month and early in the New Year of 1942 the crack Japanese forces took Jesselton and Kudat. They suffered no casualties.

John Wilson, the District officer in Kudat, was at home shaving when the Japanese landed. They marched to his house and demanded he came out to surrender. He sent a message with his boy that he was not yet fully dressed and would see them at his office when he started work at eight o'clock. Predictably they stormed into the house and dragged him out at bayonet point. A large man, he towered over his captors and extremely angry and red of face was forcibly marched through the streets to the District Office. Chinese shopkeepers looked on in wonder at this amazing sight and then hastily moved indoors and set about concealing all their valuables and stocks of food. The victors soon rounded up the few other white residents, including Colin who was again looking after Tom's plantation, and incarcerated them in the police station. It all seemed surreal to the Europeans who had really not considered that this could actually happen to them. They seriously expected to see a British warship appear on the horizon at any moment and rescue them from their plight. It was not to be as both HMS Prince of Wales and HMS Repulse, sent to defend Singapore and the South China Sea, had both been sunk by the Japanese air force. Within a matter of days they were taken to a camp based in the barrack's stables in Jesselton. At this time they were not badly treated as they were all civilians and were not subjected to the scorn and derision the Japanese reserved for fighting men who surrendered. To them, surrender was the most shameful act a soldier could perform and made him totally unworthy of any respect or sympathy. They were taught to fight to the death whatever the odds against them and suicide was the only honourable action open if capture seemed inevitable.

Christina and Albert Bodin had been worried that they might be treated differently because they worked for a Christian mission and were not British. The Japanese, however, were not well versed in such niceties and simply treated them the same as the other internees. Cyril and Rita Fellowes, the English planters, were very optimistic about the whole experience. Nothing could ruffle their abiding belief that all would turn out right in the end and they would soon be back on their veranda each with a large pink gin in hand. Rita had packed a large trunk with her clothes and hats as if they were setting off on a cruise. Up to a point she was to be proved right but the trunk did not travel with her and was confiscated as soon as the Japanese saw it.

The Chinese population of North Borneo, despite their

mother country also being at war with Japan, were largely ignored and not considered to be much of a threat. This suited them admirably and they quietly went about their business as usual, keeping in the background and trying their best not to antagonise the invaders in any way. David Wong, in Kota Belud, also carried on as normally as he could and bowed low to any soldiers who passed his shop. This action always pleased the soldiers, especially the lower ranks, and brought nods and even occasional smiles from them. They enjoyed the feeling of superiority and revelled in the power they wielded. Food was in reasonable supply and, apart from a certain tension caused by uncertainty about the future, life carried on in the small market town. David hadn't heard from his earlier visitor Lo Vun Lip and there hadn't been any instructions telling him how to proceed. He reasoned that they were on their own now and would make their own decisions as the changing situation demanded.

At Asampit's longhouse there were also few signs of change. As with the Chinese they kept to themselves. A new invasion of their land wasn't something that unduly worried them as they felt they possessed nothing that the Japanese would want. The prospect of some fighting, however, excited them and they held long discussions about how they should react to any acts of aggression. The majority view was that they would stay calm until provoked and not take any action that might directly cause them to be attacked. If an attack came they knew they could deal with it and the younger warriors were anxious to prove themselves. It was up to the village elders led by Asampit to keep the lid on the ambitions of the young. They waited patiently for the drama to unfold without knowing the major part they were destined to play.

After eight boring weeks in the Jesselton camp the inmates were told that they were to be moved from the country by boat and to pack up their meagre belongings and prepare for departure. Rumours were rife. Some thought they might be going to Japan or to the Philippines; others were adamant it would be Singapore as that had been captured on February 15th and was now firmly under Japanese control. They were herded to the harbour and put aboard a small coastal vessel with an open deck and crew quarters aft. It was cramped and they hoped and prayed that it was going to be a short journey. When they set off it was clear they were going in the wrong direction for Japan or the Philippines but were heading for the island of Labuan which was only a short distance from Jesselton. When the boat sailed past Labuan and carried on down the coast they were perplexed but those who favoured the Singapore option felt vindicated. As it happened they remained in Borneo but in Sarawak and were put in two camps near Kuching with the men in one and the women and children in another. There was a camp for Australian and British prisoners of war nearby but they were kept strictly separate from this and conditions in the camps were very different. The civilian internees were held under a reasonably relaxed regime although the food was poor and the conditions extremely unsanitary. Some of their guards occasionally displayed small acts of kindness to them and the women were generally treated with respect and rarely molested. In contrast, the prisoners of war were very harshly treated with regular severe and gratuitous beatings and punishments. While they were able to be used as slave labour they were kept alive but when their usefulness ran out they were discarded and many starved to death or died of their illnesses. Rations were well below subsistence level and medical attention at its most basic. These conditions were replicated in all the Japanese POW camps with the conditions in the one in Sandakan on the east coast of North Borneo being even worse than in Kuching.

With North Borneo now devoid of all Europeans and Australians the Japanese could refocus on the Chinese and the indigenous people. They were very confident that it would be easy to control the small and well-scattered population. Also they knew they were safe from invasion by the allies as they had complete control of the air and the sea. The first project they decided to embark upon was the construction of four airstrips.

Three were on the coast at Jesselton, Sandakan, Kudat and the fourth inland at Keningau. All able-bodied men were rounded up and used as slave labour including clerks from offices and school teachers. The work was planned and supervised by the Japanese but of course they didn't join in with the labouring. They used some of the Japanese they had freed from the British internment camps as interpreters and eventually these were pressed into service in the Imperial Army. Most of these Japanese had been fishermen who lived on their boats and knew little of the ways of the native folk so the invasion force gleaned very little information of any use to them.

Eventually, as the situation stabilised, many of the experienced Japanese troops were moved out of Borneo and replaced by Korean conscripts who were often treated as badly by their officers as the local population. Overseeing the whole operation was the *Kempetai*, the Japanese secret police who were the equivalent in standing and cruelty to the German Gestapo. Their inventiveness when it came to punishment and torture knew no bounds and they delighted in devising new ways to humiliate and mutilate anyone who crossed them. They were based in the Sports Club in Jesselton and often meted out punishments for trivial or non-existent offences on the steps of the club for all the locals to see. One of their favourite punishments was to loosely tie up two prisoners and make them fight with the loser being severely beaten by the guards. This was to demonstrate the might of the Japanese people and was regarded as a sport to them and not a punishment. The most common offence was for a person not to bow low enough when passing a Japanese soldier. The usual punishment for this was a blow to the head with one fist followed by another from the other fist. If the miscreant fell at the first blow he would then be beaten unconscious. If he remained standing he was reprieved.

The Japanese army had no real supply lines. They depended on the land where they were to provide shelter and sustenance. Their demands for rice and other foodstuff became ever more insistent and this was the cause of many a beating as the local people resented their dwindling food stocks being raided. As they could no longer work on the land then the outlook was bleak and they realised that they stared starvation in the face. Even the Muruts in their longhouses did not escape from the demands until they realised that if they moved away from navigable rivers then they would be left alone. The Japanese did not like long jungle treks with all the associated hazards and mainly travelled the country by boat. They had no motorised transport to use on the few rough roads other than the trucks, cars and motorbikes they had taken from the Europeans. The people of North Borneo soon came to hate the invaders with a passion and there were many mutterings of discontent. In these early days there was no one individual willing to stand up and rally the people to the point of open rebellion. The country seethed, simmered and waited.

Chapter 8

'Tom,' called Mary. 'There's a soldier here to see you.'

She was standing in the doorway of the small house they had rented when they realised that return to Kudat was impossible. Much as she loved her family Mary felt that she wanted her own home again where she was in sole control and not having to compromise all the time over cooking and cleaning duties shared with her mother. Tom came to the door and eyed the broad shouldered upright officer with the small Clark Gable moustache. His air of authority made it plain he was of a fairly high rank and the pips on his shoulder reinforced that perception.

'Hello, I'm Colonel Barry Stephens. I hope this is a convenient time to visit you. I'd like a chat about your work in Borneo.'

Tom had not expected to be called up for the war as he was now nearly forty years of age and thought that soldiering would no longer be an option. He was working in his father-in-law's factory as assistant manager so that he had a regular income to keep Mary and his family that now consisted of two girls. The second child, Angela, had been born on time and although she was obviously not the cricketer or rugby player Tom would have liked she was very healthy and adored by her parents and older sister Sarah. Tom led Colonel Stephens to their compact sitting room and Mary went to make coffee. While it was being prepared Tom and the Colonel made everyday chitchat about sport and the weather; now that it was April and the cricket and summer were ending. Eventually they sat drinking coffee and eating homemade biscuits while Tom and Mary waited for the Colonel to start his interrogation and find out exactly what his intentions were.

'You see,' he began. 'I need to learn just about everything you know about North Borneo. It is a country with no up-to-date accurate maps available and we are gathering as much knowledge as we can for future military use. Is it true that you were a copra plantation manager for over ten years?'

'Yes sir, actually it's nearer fifteen now and my wife was there with me from 1938 until we returned here. In fact Sarah, our first child, was born in North Borneo.'

'Good, did you learn any of the languages and travel around the country at all?'

'Part of my job was visiting other estates, some of them growing rubber trees so I travelled fairy extensively along the coast and into the interior. I am reasonably fluent in the basic, local version of Malay and also know a few words of some of the tribal languages but not sufficient to hold a meaningful conversation.'

'Please tell me about the places you visited, how long the travelling took and the sort of terrain you encountered.'

Tom took out a large piece of paper from the writing bureau and placed it on the coffee table. He drew an outline of North Borneo and started by adding all the main towns and major rivers. As time went on he built up a fairly accurate map of the places he knew and, using one of Sarah's red crayons, traced on the map his usual routes and the time each section took to complete. The Colonel looked most impressed.

'That's already at least ten times better than any maps we have at headquarters and I'm sure you could even add more if you were given time.'

'Yes, but I don't want to descend into guesswork. If it's to be of any use then it must be as accurate as possible. Also, I've not shown the full extent of the Crocker Mountain Range and that's a very important feature of the area as it cuts that part of the country in half. It's south of the massive Mount Kinabalu that dominates the whole landscape. I could probably improve on the map by using your other, older maps as reference points or, better still, have you any aerial photos?'

The Colonel nodded. 'We do have some photographs together with the old maps at headquarters. Do you think you could call in one day and see if you can use them to make today's effort even better?'

'Of course,' Tom replied. 'But please tell me about your unit and where your headquarters is. So far we've only talked about me and I'd like to know more about your organisation.'

'Fair enough, we're a very new branch of the armed forces and not well known. In fact, we're hardly known at all and that's how we want it to remain. The outfit was formed in March and is similar to the British Special Overseas Executive that is responsible for clandestine missions behind enemy lines. We call ourselves the Service Reconnaissance Department or SRD for short and our aim is to gather information about the situation in Japanese held territories so that when the time comes for us to strike back we have as much useful knowledge as possible. Our base is in Melbourne.'

'I'm pleased to be able to help you. Does it mean that you want to recruit me as a member of the department or will my information be all you need?'

'At present all we want is your help with filling in the details about the country. If anything else develops and we think you can help then we'll contact you again.'

He gave Tom a card with the address of the SRD base and, after consulting them, scribbled down on the back an agreed date and time for Tom's visit.

After he had gone Mary looked long and hard at Tom. She guessed what he was thinking and wasn't happy. She didn't want to lose her husband of only a few years so soon but knew in her heart that she would never be able to persuade him to give up the germ of an idea that was clearly written on his face. Nonetheless she gave it a try.

'Please don't consider returning Tom. I don't think I could live with the worry. Think of the girls if not me. What could I tell them if anything happened to you?'

'I am thinking of you and especially Sarah and Angie. This world's their future and I want it to be a peaceful place for them to grow and live in. Can you imagine what it would be like under German or Japanese domination? I could never live with myself if there was something I could do to help end this war and never did it simply for an easy life in Sydney.'

Mary flung her arms around him and held him close. She knew that they would probably never discuss it again and she was resigned to whatever was to unfold over the coming weeks and months. He kissed her and ran his fingers through her hair and thrillingly down her back.

'Don't worry Mary; you know I won't do anything foolish.'

She smiled outwardly but knew in her heart that he probably would as he loved Kudat almost as much as he loved Australia and his family.

Tom visited the headquarters of the SRD at 39, Ackland Street in South Yarra and spent all the day poring over old maps and a few rather blurred photographs of an endless expanse of jungle. It was impossible to identify exactly what the photos showed so he soon discarded them and concentrated on verifying the accuracy of the maps from his own knowledge. One was from early in the century and of little use as it became obvious that the cartographer had not actually been to most of the places and had employed a rather large amount of what Tom considered to be educated guesswork. Some of the government maps were of more use especially those showing the railway and the layout of the towns. The lack of metalled roads meant that only areas near rivers had been mapped and there were vast tracts of land that were blank and could have held anything or nothing. It was only thanks to Tom's excellent memory that some further details could be added to make a reasonably coherent picture. The Colonel was pleased with Tom's efforts and invited him to his office for a cold beer.

'You've done an excellent job Tom. Thanks very much. I did want to ask you if you felt you had anything else you could offer in the way of supporting our little enterprise.'

Tom grinned a trifle nervously. 'I was expecting that sir. I'm willing to do anything at all to help shorten this dreadful conflict. But I guess you knew that already.'

'You're right, I did. Obviously you'll have to be a volunteer for any other work and, although working for the department, you'll not be classified as a member of the armed forces. We're a new organisation and are still unsure of the exact scope our activities will take. However, we know that we do need some people to go to North Borneo and make contact with local guerrilla groups. We want to coordinate their efforts to cause the Japanese as much trouble as possible and also prepare them to help our own troops when we liberate the island. If you're willing then your training can start next week at camp X, south of Brisbane. Please don't tell anyone other than your close family about this as a word in the wrong place could cost you your life and endanger many others. The sergeant outside will give you the details'

'I understand. I have already discussed it with my wife and, although obviously not particularly happy, she realises it's important to me.'

Tom returned home and the moment he entered the house Mary knew he was to be leaving her. She couldn't control the tears that flooded down her cheeks and for a moment Tom's resolve weakened. Again he held her close and she eventually calmed down and wiped her eyes on her sleeve.

'How soon?'

'The training starts near Brisbane next week. What I have to do is important and I'll do it as best I can. I'll also make every effort to remain safe so that one day soon we'll be back in Kudat living again as a family.'

'That would be wonderful. But only if the family still has a father. You mustn't take any unnecessary risks. We all love you so much it hurts. I don't know how I'll cope with the worry when you're away.'

Tom pulled her to him again. 'You're a strong woman. I wouldn't have married you otherwise. I know you'll manage and you have the girls to take your mind off me.'

'Just looking at the girls reminds me of you. I wouldn't want it any other way. Part of you will always be here.'

Chapter 9

During Tom's training he learned a little about the situation in Malaya, Singapore and Borneo. Some news had filtered through via various sources and a few radio transmitters continued to send signals which, although faint, were picked up by the Australian listening posts in the far north of the country. He knew all about the fall of Singapore and the Japanese bombing of Darwin but some of the new information he heard only served to stiffen his determination to do what he could to assist in driving the Japanese out of his adopted land.

The news of Japanese atrocities seemed unbelievable. One piece that Tom decided never to share with Mary was the fate of her favourite ship the Vyner Brooke. It had been in Singapore when the Japanese invaded Malaya and left a couple of days before the fall of the city. On board were a number of Australian nurses. The Captain set out on a southerly course towards Sumatra hoping to outrun any Japanese attacks but was spotted by a Japanese aircraft in the Banka Straits and within a few hours the bridge had been destroyed and the ship badly damaged. They abandoned ship and, using a variety of floatation devices, the majority of the crew and passengers reached shore safely. One party that landed at Muntok Bay consisted of sixty-four nurses and a number of the ship's officers. They set up camp and waited to see what would happen. Unarmed they only had the clothes on their backs and a small amount of food. They wondered if rescue was even a remote possibility and didn't even know if they were in enemy-held territory or not. Two days later they were discovered by a patrol of ten Japanese soldiers and one officer. The Vyner Brooke's crew were taken round a small headland at gunpoint and the nurses clung to each other as they heard a volley of shots ring out. The Japanese returned and motioned to them to wade out into the sea. When the water reached their thighs the shooting began and the water slowly turned from tropical blue to crimson. One nurse was shot in the hip but had the sense to fall as if dead and, hidden by the floating bodies of her comrades, waited for the patrol to leave. She then made her painful way to the shore and was rescued by some villagers who had heard the shots. They helped her to recover and took her to a nearby civilian detention camp for medical treatment. She never told the Japanese in charge of the camp what had happened as she thought they might well want to dispose of her as the sole witness to the murders. She related her tale to the Europeans in the camp and eventually it reached the ears of the ever-listening Australian radio operators.

Other horrific accounts of Japanese atrocities continued to filter through to Camp X near Beaudesert some forty miles south of Brisbane where Tom was undergoing rigorous training in jungle warfare skills, explosives, communications and the handling of rubber dinghies. The camp was ideally situated for such training as the area has tropical rainforest, rivers and mountain peaks similar to those found in Borneo and Papua New Guinea. When some of the stories of how the Australian and British prisoners in Sandakan, a town on the east coast of North Borneo, were treated for minor or imagined misdemeanours the men in training were rightly incensed. There appeared to be no limit to the cruelty the Japanese inflicted on their prisoners and both the service personnel and the civilians were sickened to hear of the escalating violence.

They learned about the standard punishments of beatings and imprisonment in cages open to the relentless sun. How men were driven mad by thirst and acts such as gouging out of eyes for not bowing correctly to their captors were commonplace. When British Intelligence released the first-hand evidence of a Chinese cook in the Sandakan camp telling of the method of execution of a British officer accused of stealing a pig they were united in their disgust and to a man regarded the Japanese as a cancer to be excised from the face of the earth as soon as possible. The cook, his right hand firmly clamped to his mouth, watched as the officer was taken from a tiny bamboo cage and dragged to a seven foot high wooden cross. One of the Japanese

Kempetai officers then approached carrying a stool, a knife and a hammer. He stood on the stool and raised the prisoner's left arm and drove a nail through it fixing it to the cross. Then he did the same with the right arm and hand. The prisoner wriggled and screamed so his loincloth was pulled off and stuffed in his mouth. The torturer stood back and a smile crossed his features. He admired his handiwork just as if he were viewing a fine art exhibition. Both of the prisoner's feet were then nailed to the wooden board he was standing on. The Japanese officer then stood in thought once again. After a moment's contemplation he remounted the stool and drove a nail into the officer's forehead. With his knife he made an incision down the right side of the prisoner's stomach and proceeded to pull out his intestines and placed them on a board on the ground. His genitals were sliced off and lumps of flesh were cut from his arms and legs so that his body and the surrounding ground were soon drenched in blood. These pieces of him were set out on the board like a window display in a butcher's shop and the officer then calmly informed the horrified observers that people who stole meat would end up as meat themselves. Fortunately by this time the British officer had died of the terrible wounds and the loss of blood so the Japanese could cause him no further suffering. On hearing this terrible account the trainees were more than ready to go on their various missions as soon as they could and were impatient to receive their final orders.

One morning in September 1942 Tom was called to a meeting with Colonel Stephens. He knocked on the office door and was invited in. 'Well,' began the Colonel, 'your training is now complete and I have to ask you for the last time if you are still willing to go behind enemy lines at tremendous risk to your life. Nobody would criticise you if you felt it too high a price to pay.'

'I'm more than ready sir. Nothing and nobody could hold me back from any small part I can play in defeating the Japs. I hope I'll be going soon.'

'Next week. You'll be taken by a United States Navy

submarine to a secluded bay you know well near Kudat and you'll paddle by dinghy to the beach. Your main mission is to make contact with any of the native leaders you trust and find out as much as you can about enemy troop positions and their strength. At this time you must not risk contacting any friends in Kudat itself and we want the Japanese to be totally unaware of your presence. You are not going to act directly against them even if an opportunity arises. This is purely a fact finding trip. Do you understand how important it is that you are not discovered?'

'Yes sir. But I hope that I'll be able to go back again in a more active role very soon.'

'So do I,' replied the Colonel. 'Don't fret, that time will come. We all dream of it. And now I must outline how you are to return. In exactly eighty-three days time the submarine will wait offshore at the same bay for four hours from midnight. This is for your safety as we'll drop you at a new moon when it is dark and pick you up three moons later. The submarine will return at the same time on three consecutive nights. If you do not make contact by flashing the agreed signal or rowing out to meet them then we must assume the worst. You'll not be taking a radio as they're too heavy and your calls could be intercepted, putting you and your friends at risk. We'll not know how successful you've been until you return to base. Good luck.'

Tom thanked the Colonel, turned on his heel and left the building with a whole mixture of feelings running through him. He was elated that he would now be doing something useful but was scared of what might befall him and was frightened to leave his young family for what might be the last time. He was also deeply disturbed by the level of hatred he felt for a whole nation of people he knew so little about. In all his life his emotions had never been so raw and stark. Would he be able to think clearly and act quickly if he came face to face with an enemy soldier? Was he capable of controlling the violent feelings that sometimes threatened to overwhelm him?

Tom knew that he would find out in due time and dreaded the thought that the whole experience might alter him permanently in some way and sour the wonderful relationship with his family. He returned to his quarters to mentally prepare for his coming mission by going over the plan again and again until he had thoroughly memorised every aspect of it. What he had forgotten to ask the Colonel was whether he was allowed to visit his family before departing. Tom considered this at length and decided that it would be better just to go to Borneo without them knowing. He decided to phone Mary and tell her that his training was to be moved to the north of Australia but he would be back by home for Christmas. In the meantime he would say that he would be out of contact as he would be away from any civilisation. He hoped this would save her any worries about where he really was and what he was actually doing.

Tom had misjudged her. She knew from the excitement in his voice that he was going back to Borneo. However, she decided to play along with the deception as she hoped it would help him not to worry too much about her and the girls. She kept the phone conversation on a cheery note and emphasised the fun they would have over the festivities and how the children would enjoy seeing him again. It was all rather false but both of them achieved their aims.

Chapter 10

Tom hated the submarine. The United States crew were friendly enough but Tom's size made it difficult to move around without constantly banging various tender parts on sharp corners. To add to his woes he discovered that he was mildly claustrophobic and being incarcerated in a metal box made him very uneasy. All the concerns he had about his forthcoming landing were soon dispelled by an all consuming desire to leave the vessel and breathe fresh, clean air again. At last the time came to disembark and paddle ashore in the tiny rubber dinghy that also held his minimal supplies and equipment.

For the hundredth time he mentally checked off all he was taking. He would be travelling light and in Australia they had made sure that he carried nothing that could ever connect him to the military. This was in case he was captured and he could then use a planned cover story that he had been in the interior when the Japs invaded and had hidden in the jungle since then, living off the land. He definitely did not want to be accused of spying as that would mean certain death and hoped that his knowledge of the country would enable him to convince the Japanese that he was indeed just an ordinary planter. About his person and in a small knapsack he had a waterproof poncho and bush hat, a handgun and ammunition, a knife, compass, first aid kit, fishing line, waterproof matches, a mosquito net and some basic survival rations. He also carried a fairly large amount of money to use for bribes or rewards and a garrotting wire with wooden toggles. His last, and very important, piece of kit was a large water bottle. If he needed anything else he would have to find it himself by any means possible. He was also well aware that it was very important to keep a careful check on the passing days so he wouldn't miss his rendezvous with the submarine.

The sub cautiously surfaced about two hundred yards from the beach at Bak Bak where Tom and Mary had held their first picnic. It was really dark as the new moon was shrouded in cloud. Tom strained his eyes to try to see the shore as he slipped into the dinghy and paddled as quietly as he could towards the faint line of distant trees. Silence had been maintained since they had opened the hatch and Tom, accompanied by two sailors, had ventured out on to the deck. All farewells and good wishes had been completed in the confines of the conning tower. The dinghy scraped on the hard sand with its sprinkling of broken coral and Tom gingerly stepped out to pull the boat up the beach. He froze. There was someone moving in the trees and he could hear them breathing heavily. It would be rotten luck, he thought, to be captured without even reaching dry land and his cover story would be of little use if any soldiers found him landing in a boat. Very slowly he took out his gun and dropped face down on the sand. He wriggled his way up the beach until he was partially hidden by one of the large rocky outcrops. Standing cautiously he used all his concentration to try and pierce the darkness. Suddenly there was a large snort from behind a nearby bush and he counted four legs protruding from underneath it. They were all attached to one body and to his immense relief he realised he had been spooked by a large water buffalo that was nosing around in the undergrowth. He sat down and laughed to himself thinking that he must stay cool and more in control of any developing situation. To be certain he was safe he waited a few more minutes before going back to rescue his dinghy and drag it to where he had decided to hide it until his return. He guessed that there would be no more picnics taking place for a while and that he could safely hide the boat in a freshwater well set back in the trees and covered by a wooden lid. He half deflated the dinghy so it would fit in the hole and, with his lifejacket and paddle inside, squashed it firmly down. He replaced the lid and covered it with loose earth and leaves so that it would not be discovered. He now had to move swiftly away from the coast to the relative safety of the jungle. Tom was aware that the Japanese were in full control of the entire coast although reports said that patrols were few.

They had quickly slipped into a complacent and arrogant attitude of mind somewhat similar to that of their predecessors the British. With all the Europeans out of the country they only had to subjugate the native tribes who they regarded as barely human and the Chinese settlers they viewed with disdain as another inferior race. They had become lazy and were enjoying a quiet life punctuated only by the occasional act of cruelty to keep them amused. They even tried to persuade the population that they were there to help them become part of a grand plan that would lead to the whole of South East Asia united under Japanese control. They grandly titled it The Co-Prosperity Sphere as if that gave it more respectability. The local people were not fooled and regarded it as yet another excuse for the Japanese robbery and pillage of their country.

Tom knew that so long as he kept out of the way of the larger towns and villages the chance of capture by a patrol was small. He was also aware that some of the people viewed the occupation as a chance to make money and would willingly betray him to the Japanese as there would definitely be a reward. Contacts must, therefore, be kept to a minimum and he must remain out of sight to all but his most trusted friends. This made a visit to Kudat definitely out of the question although he dearly wanted to see how the plantation was doing and to ascertain that all his workers were safe. In particular he wanted to know how Kim Bong, his loyal houseboy, was faring. Putting these thoughts to the back of his mind and focussing on making good progress away from the shore he set out on the familiar trail towards Sikuati and then onward towards the higher ground on the slopes of Kinabalu. His aim was to reach the safety of Asampit's village in four or five days where he knew he would be protected from any danger. After that he would work how he could gather as much useful information as possible before it was time to return to the submarine. Very early on in his training in Camp X he had decided that finding Asampit would be the most sensible action although he had no knowledge of how any of the Murut longhouse people had fared under the Japanese rule. He felt confident that Asampit and his family would be able to survive under any regime as they were very adept at keeping out of the way when it was politic to do so.

As he moved cautiously through the low-lying farming areas between the coast and the jungle he managed to collect some fruit and a few root vegetables from the open fields. He made sure that he took sparingly from over a wide area so that the farmers would not become suspicious. Also, he didn't want to take too much as he knew how precious such crops were to their survival. He avoided any dwellings as the dogs would soon have alerted the residents to his presence. Every family kept at least one dog and although they were fairly small mongrels and not a physical threat to Tom he knew they were capable of kicking up a tremendous racket if disturbed. He was determined to remain invisible even though this sometimes meant long detours through muddy paddy fields. At one point he had to wait for what seemed like hours but was only minutes when a light shone from one farmhouse. Tom waited until it was extinguished before daring to move on. He hoped the light had not been put out so that the farmer could watch for any movement in the darkness and was ready to drop to the ground if it came on again. It didn't so he quickly scuttled away from the farm and out of danger.

When Tom had cleared the farmland and was in the jungle he was able to make better progress and before dawn had covered a good ten miles. He sorely missed having the horse he had ridden when following the trail with Mary and knew that without it the journey would take at least twice as long. The next day he spent resting in a bivouac he made from branches and leaves. It was well hidden off the main trail and would have been impossible to spot even if you were within a few feet of it. He couldn't light a fire so the fruit he had collected was just right to assuage his hunger until the night when he could light a fire and make a simple meal from his rations to sustain him as he trekked through the jungle again. His small shelter he lined with the poncho and the mosquito net and made a bed of bracken so he had quite an undisturbed sleep until late afternoon when he stirred and made preparations for his departure. With his knife he cut a notch in the stick he was using as a staff when walking. Although he had a notebook to record the passing days he thought it would be wise to keep two records of the time he spent in Borneo. Despite his dislike of the submarine he didn't want to miss it. It was his only lifeline to connect him to Mary and the girls waiting for him in Sydney.

It was slow going travelling at night and Tom wondered if he could now risk hiking during daylight hours. He decided to give it a try as he thought he was probably far enough away from the coast to take the risk. If a Japanese patrol was in the area he felt sure he would hear them before they spotted him and he'd be able to take cover. Two more days and nights passed without incident and then Tom reached the river with the rickety bridge that had so frightened Mary. He peered out through the foliage but couldn't see the bridge. Had he taken a wrong turn? He felt sure it was the right place so he cautiously made his way down the slippery bank to the water's edge. His biggest fear was that a Japanese boat patrol might suddenly appear and he would be totally exposed. Tied to a tree and trailing in the water he spied one of the large plaited ropes that had previously supported the bridge. It was still fastened to one of the trees on the far bank. He pulled it to test how secure it was and then after tying his boots around his neck he cut the rope free from the tree on his side and lowered himself into the water. As the current grabbed him he didn't try to fight it but, holding the rope tightly, let it carry him downstream. The rope stayed taut and Tom was gently swung across the river to the far bank where he caught hold of a root and made his way up to dry land. It was easy to then go back upstream along the bank until he found the trail again. He was soaking wet but in the humidity of the jungle it wasn't very different to normal conditions. After removing the small army of leeches that had attached themselves to his arms and legs Tom made a small fire to dry his shirt and trousers.

73

He then built his bivouac; ate a slab of chocolate; made a mug of tea and then settled down for the night. Again he slept well and woke refreshed. He was cheered by the thought that he should be near Asampit's village by the end of the next day and would meet up with his old friend. There had been no sign of any human life or activity since he had left the coast so he was reasonably confident that he was away from any danger. He set off along the trail swinging his knife and eventually passed the place where the old longhouse had been so he knew he was reasonably near to the new one. The small river where they had fished came into view and he suddenly realised the longhouse had gone again. He sat down at the edge of the clearing on a fallen log with his back resting against the trunk of a large tree. What should he do? The answer came soon enough.

Tom didn't hear the puff from the blowpipe but felt the dart as it ruffled his hair and embedded itself in the bark of the tree behind him. He turned and looked at the gaudy feathers adorning the arrow and knew that he was among friends. An enemy would not have missed him and he knew he would by now be paralysed and unable to breathe. Death would have been moments away. He clambered to his feet and held out his hands in a gesture of peace. From out of the dense undergrowth the familiar figures of Asampit and his son Enduat appeared with the equally familiar beetle nut stained wide grins spreading over their faces as they approached.

'We heard you crashing about a while ago,' explained Asampit. 'Enduat thought it must be an elephant or at least a buffalo as the noise was so loud. When we saw it was you we decided to follow and make sure nobody was on your trail before welcoming you home again. I knew you would return and help us to rid the country of these cruel invaders who offer us nothing but take everything.'

Tom wasn't at all surprised that they just accepted his return so easily. He knew that their semi-nomadic way of life meant that they quite happily accepted the disappearance and reappearance of friends as the normal course of events.

'What happened to your longhouse?' Tom enquired. 'It was still new when I was last here. I was worried that there might have been a death.'

'No. We're all fine but we moved to confuse the Japanese soldiers. It has meant moving away from the river to a stream that is too shallow for them to use their boats to come and take our rice and animals. It's only a short walk from here. How long is it since we saw you last?'

'Almost exactly three years. A lot has happened since then. Luckily I was in my mother country when the invaders came. And I am now a very proud father of two.'

'Boys?'

'No, girls, but they are really beautiful.'

'Well, never mind, I'm sure you will manage to make a boy before too long,' Asampit laughed. 'Anyway, girls will always look after their father.'

They set off for the longhouse at a brisk pace with the familiar and this time reassuring bulk of Mount Kinabalu rising up in the background and soon arrived in the clearing where the building stood. The nearby stream was much smaller than the river they previously lived on and Tom wondered if this one was suitable for fishing. Asampit must have read his thoughts for he told Tom that they were missing fish from their diet but felt it a small price to pay if they could keep all their other crops and livestock. This time there was no noisy welcome and it seemed to Tom that there was a certain sombreness among the inhabitants as if their previously sunny nature had been partially extinguished. Of course there was the welcome sip of *tapai* and a hearty meal but no gongs were played and the women didn't dance. Asampit filled Tom in with what had happened in the last three years and it wasn't a very cheery tale. It appeared that the Japanese had left them alone for nearly two months while they dealt with the Europeans. They had then turned their attentions to the native population as they were in need of supplies to feed the troops. Their method of acquiring rice and other produce was simple. They just marched into a village and threatened to kill all the young men and rape the girls. Under such duress hidden caches of food were soon revealed and the villagers were left with only what they could scavenge in the jungle to feed their families. A few longhouses had attempted to stop the soldiers but these acts of defiance had swiftly and severely been put down with the occupants murdered and the buildings razed. It soon became clear that face to face confrontations were pointless and it would only be through stealth that they could hope to succeed against the relatively well-armed Japanese army. Asampit's village had made the decision to move when the news of the other longhouses had reached them but were still unsure as to how the conquering forces would view their action if they managed to find them. They lived in both fear and hope. Fortunately the absence of any roads outside the main towns was in their favour and they reasoned that the Japanese would be unlikely to send out small patrols as they could easily be picked off by the native warriors with their silent weapons. There was always the outside possibility that the army would attack in force if they were severely harassed but as the pickings would be slender that was unlikely.

In this state of limbo the village attempted to carry on their daily lives with some degree of normality. Crops, including tobacco, were regularly planted with some of them a distance from the longhouse to limit the risk of discovery. Pigs, chickens and buffalo were kept as before and occasional clandestine visits were made to Kota Belud to barter for salt and other essentials they couldn't supply themselves. These visits were kept to a minimum and were usually in the late evening when the soldiers were occupied carousing and off their guard. This was interesting information for Tom as it meant he could find out more about the enemy troop numbers and the weapons they possessed. From his discussions with the elders and the men who had visited the town he realised that the Japanese were slowly becoming more relaxed and, apart from the odd atrocity they perpetrated for fun, the local people were largely ignored and left to themselves. They had no fear of any opposition and now just enjoyed running a country by force as they were confident of their innate superiority in all matters. This was exactly what Tom wanted to reverse. He wanted the Japanese to be the ones living in fear and always watching their backs. But that would have to be for the future as his orders were that he should only gather intelligence and not make the occupying forces aware of his presence. Acts of sabotage were strictly forbidden as were any direct action against the troops. But before he left he wanted to do something that would in some measure restore Asampit's fierce pride. He would have to be very subtle if he was to cause harm to the invaders without arousing their suspicions that any fatal incidents that occurred were planned.

He spent the next few weeks collecting and collating as much information as he could without causing any alarm. The deployment of the Japanese forces and their composition was of great interest to him and he was surprised to learn that nearly all the crack assault troops used in the invasion had now left North Borneo and been replaced with Korean conscripts. He mapped out where they were all based and their approximate numbers. It was more difficult to accurately ascertain their level of armaments but he was able to hazard an educated guess extrapolating from the known figures in Kota Belud. He used the longhouse men to explore how experienced the soldiers were in jungle craft and wasn't surprised to find that they were quite naïve and made many elementary mistakes when travelling, as they thought, stealthily through the thick rainforest. But it was when he found out about one of their recreational activities that an idea sprang to mind.

Asampit told him that the Japanese soldiers liked nothing more, apart from visiting the army brothels, than a few days relaxing in the hot springs at a place called Poring. These hot springs were about a three day hike from the longhouse. They could be reached by following a river up to its source near the top of one of the ridges leading up to Mount Kinabalu and then going downhill following another river to Poring itself. The hot springs and the waterfall were supposed to have healing qualities and the bathers also drank the sulphurous water to supposedly cleanse their insides. He told Tom he had heard all of this from a neighbouring longhouse and added that the Japanese soldiers visited the hot springs regularly.

Tom asked Asampit, 'How does the water get to the baths?'

'The hot spring water comes from the ground but it's too hot to drink or bathe in so it's mixed with water from the nearby river that leads down from the mountain. The river water is channelled through bamboo pipes and is combined with the spring water before reaching the baths and the drinking fountain. When I last saw it the mix was about half and half.'

This information gave Tom an outrageous idea.

'Asampit,' he asked, 'Could you find me some of that *tuba* root you use for fishing? I would like to use it to try a few experiments.'

'Certainly, I'll send out some of the youngsters to gather a basket of it tomorrow. Are you thinking of taking up fishing to pass the time?'

'Sort of,' grinned Tom, 'But I hope to catch some bigger fish than you've ever managed to spear.'

The *tuba* root duly arrived and Tom set to pounding it to a pulp. The women of the village watched in amazement as this was not regarded as suitable work for a warrior and definitely not for the white *tuan*. As Tom wanted to carefully monitor the amount of root he used each time and the length of time he spent pulverising it then it was important that he did all the work. If others had made the drug then the various batches might not have been consistent and his planned experiments would be a total waste of time. When he thought the roots were sufficiently ground into a smooth paste he put different quantities in small baskets that he suspended separately over earthenware jars. Measuring out a quantity of water he poured it over the first batch and watched as the milky liquid percolated out into the jar. A similar amount of water was then poured over the next basket which contained exactly twice the quantity of crushed root. A third held double the amount again and a fourth, double the third, completed the line of pots. When all the drips had ceased Tom removed the baskets and looked into the jars to see if he could spot any differences. To the naked eye they seemed much the same but the liquid in the pots that had passed through greater amounts of the *tuba* felt thicker when he trickled it through his fingers. He called for Enduat to come and help him with the next part of the experiment. Knowing that during their fishing the drug had proved to be effective even when heavily diluted in the river water he wanted a way to test its effectiveness in the various strengths he had prepared.

'Enduat,' Tom asked. 'Do the fish ever recover from the drug if they remain in the water?'

'Only if they're a long way from where the *tuba* is put into the river. Those near to the source are so drugged that they're unable to use their gills and they drown.'

It was clear to Tom that the *tuba* milk was very powerful and would have to be handled with great care. He wanted to know how much of it would be needed to put into a river and how far upstream so that it would paralyse a man to the extent that his breathing would stop. Tom considered trying out on himself but calculated that the risk was too great. He asked Enduat if he could buy a buffalo from the village to use it to test the drug. If the animal died, as he hoped it would, then his plan could be put into effect.

Enduat went to his father and explained what Tom required. Asampit readily gave his permission and pointed out that if the buffalo lived then no harm had been done and if it died they would have to stage a feast. He liked the whole idea and the money would be useful in his dealings with the Chinese traders.

Tom knew that the experiment was not particularly scientific as it would be impossible to measure how much the buffalo actually drank from the stream. All they could do was limit the time it was allowed to drink and then watch for any reaction.

Tom paced out a distance upstream of about a hundred yards and, using the pot with the weakest concentration poured it into the water. At the same time he signalled to Enduat and a group of interested onlookers and put a small wooden model boat into the stream. The idea was that when the boat reached Enduat he would let the buffalo drink up to a count of five. Tom hoped that the drug would reach the buffalo at roughly the same time as the toy boat. They all watched expectantly as the buffalo lapped up the water. It shook its mighty head as if to toss away some annoying flies and then just looked around at the assembled crowd with its usual bemused expression. Tom decided to continue the test but not for an hour to give the beast time to recover from any residual effect of the drug. They all wandered off for lunch and then returned for part two. This time Tom decided to go straight to the most potent mixture and see how it fared. Again the signal was given, the liquid poured in and the boat released. The buffalo drank again, looked around and shook its head. Slowly its legs buckled and it sank to the ground on the bank. A tremor ran through its body and without a sound it lay still and Enduat could see it had stopped breathing. It was most definitely dead. Tom ran down to the animal and checked that all life had gone.

'That's just what I wanted to know,' he told Enduat. 'If the *tuba* can kill a buffalo from a hundred yards away then a man would stand no chance. We must prepare more as an additional medicinal treat for the Japanese soldiers. I think we can do them some harm without their realising that it was the hand of man that caused it.'

Tom had been worried about taking any direct action as he had been expressly forbidden from such a course but he reckoned that the Japanese would blame the source of the water and not connect it to any subversive activity. As such he reasoned that it must be indirect action. Another bonus would be that the Japanese wouldn't impose any severe reprisals against the local population which usually happened if any soldiers were found killed. They would quite happily murder the men, women and children of a whole village if they suspected them of any anti-Japanese deeds.

The next week was spent collecting and pounding the roots to make the lethal dose which was again stored in large stone jars. It would have to be carried through dense jungle and up and over some steep hills so a secure method of transportation had to be devised. Tom was also worried that it might lose its potency if left for too long in the jars so he wanted to use it as quickly as possible. Eventually Asampit's wife came up with the answer to the carrying problem. She made large *bongons* from bark, leaves and lianas that were big enough to carry a jar safely. These *bongons* were rather like rucksacks with shoulder straps but also had a built in headband to help spread the load. They were quite tall and round, tapering towards the base and had a cleverly devised bark back plate to allow the air to circulate and keep the carrier comfortable in the steamy conditions. Another advantage was that they could be broken up with the jars when the mission was completed and the men would be able to travel back swiftly without any encumbrances. They had four jars prepared and Tom had tested the first batch prepared to ensure that it was still effective. This time a pig was used as the unlucky subject as it was to be slaughtered anyway and they knew from experience with the fish and the buffalo that its flesh would not be affected by the drug. As well as Tom, Asampit and Enduat another four of the native warriors were selected by the village council to help carry the jars and the rations they needed for the six day expedition. They took some cooked rice wrapped in leaves, dried meat, a couple of skins of water and some flat bread made with rice flour. These meagre rations would have to be sufficient although, if they made good time, they could supplement them with fruit and wild birds foraged for as they went. Asampit knew the route well and, carrying his spear and blowpipe he led the group in single file away from the village and towards the hills. Enduat was at the back and stayed some way behind the main party so that if they were followed he could give an agreed signal to the others to watch their backs. He would also ensure any enemy would then be caught between them and they could easily be dispatched.

The Murut men were extremely fit and Tom struggled to keep up with the pace. They didn't vary their speed even when marching uphill and rarely stopped for a breather. Tom's heavy boots and western clothes were not as practical in the stifling jungle heat as the loincloths and bare feet of his companions. It was to his great relief when Asampit eventually stopped by a clear stream and signalled that they would camp for the night. Before they set up camp and lit a fire one of the men continued along the track for about half a mile to make sure that the way ahead was clear. When he returned then they relaxed and bathed in the cool water before making a meal. They sat and smoked afterwards and chatted about their lives and hopes for the future. Tom told them about his house in Australia and they were pleased to hear that it was near to Mary's parents as they put a great store on family togetherness. They had no real concept of where Australia was and the notion of a vast ocean was totally perplexing. Few of them had ever seen an aeroplane and Tom could tell they thought he was not being totally honest with them when he described their flight from Singapore. Even when he drew a picture of a plane on his small notepad they still remained unconvinced that such a machine could go such great distances. Asampit then talked about his ancestors and related some of the tales of their bravery and strength. All listened spellbound as he told the story of how his great grandfather had fought the Bajau pirates when they had tried to raid the longhouse by sneaking up the river in the night. He promised Tom he would show him the heads that had been collected during the battle. It was a great pity, he added, that they would not be taking back any Japanese heads to add to their collection but understood how important it was to keep their mission a secret.

The next morning was even tougher for Tom and even Asampit seemed to be feeling the strain as they forced their way through the vegetation up the slopes of the foothills to the east of the mountain. By mid-afternoon they had crossed the top and reached the source of a stream that was a tributary of the river leading to the hot springs. It was this river that fed into and mixed with the supposedly health-giving spring water. This was where the Japanese enjoyed their leisurely baths and drank the water to cleanse them inside and out.

They followed the stream for a couple of miles and noticed how it slowly grew in width and depth as they descended until it became too wide for them to jump across. They now had to make a decision before crossing would be too difficult. Asampit recommended staying on the right hand bank of the stream as he knew that when they reached the river they would be on the correct side. The stream met the river coming from the left so to be on that side would have meant that they would be stranded at the junction and unable to follow the river. This was particularly useful advice as the main baths were also to the side of the right bank. They decided to camp early that afternoon to remain well away from the Japanese. An early start would see them arrive near Poring by noon giving them ample daylight to put as many miles as possible between them and any enemy soldiers if by bad luck they were spotted. They had no idea if there would be any patrols or sentries to guard the bathing area so it seemed prudent to expect the worst and move slowly and silently as they approached.

Just after dawn they continued down the bank until thy reached the point where the stream merged with the river. They knew that they would be now be within a mile of the springs and must take extra care. Two of the party stayed hidden at this point so that they could take out any patrol coming from behind and also to give covering support if the other five had to make a hasty retreat. They also left one of the jars behind so that two of their number would be able to move more freely with one at the front and the other at the rear. Very slowly they edged their way down towards the baths until they could hear loud shouts and even laughter. No guards had been seen so they hoped their escape route was clear. By the intensity of the noises coming from the bathers they reckoned they were roughly within the hundred yards that Tom calculated would be the right distance to unload their lethal cargo. Enduat hoped they'd be nearer as he dearly wanted to see the effect on the enemy but Asampit told him just to listen as that should tell him if they were successful. He wanted the chatting and laughing to stop completely and if it did they might then venture a little closer to view the results of their handiwork.

Giving the other four the thumbs up Tom gently removed his jar from the protection of the *bongon* and took out the plaited grass stopper. The other two jars were also opened and at a signal the contents were poured into the water. Tom thought it wouldn't take very long for the drug to reach the carefree bathers whose joyful yells still disturbed the surrounding jungle. He had no idea how many would be actually drinking the water at any given moment but hoped that it would be more than one or two.

Asampit had been wrong. Suddenly it became noisier and the cries were no longer of jollity but of panic. Obviously something was happening to cause such a commotion and they lay still desperately wondering what was occurring out of their sight. Asampit beckoned to Tom and then wriggled through the undergrowth towards the now rising noise. Tom followed closely and they soon came to a vantage point where they could look down and see what was happening. It was an amazing sight with at least six Japanese lying half in the water with another dozen or more others frantically trying to revive them. It was clear they had no suspicion of foul play as they had not called up any guards and made no attempt to protect themselves in the event of an attack. Asampit and Tom grinned victoriously at each other as they made their way back to the waiting men. Then they quietly told them of the outcome and they swiftly made their way back up the river to the waiting sentinels and then the whole party set off jubilantly towards their longhouse. The return journey seemed much quicker to Tom. This was possibly because he now knew the route and had lost his heavy burden but more likely it was because he was buoyed up with elation at having actually done something positive to help win the war.

Two days later it was a very cheerful group that arrived back in the village. Despite not having any heads to display as trophies they were in the mood for a party and the *tapai* was immediately produced. After a night of celebration and the telling and retelling of the raid until its outcome became grossly exaggerated they staggered off to bed and the longhouse fell quiet for an hour or two until the cockerels sounded their early morning wake-up call.

The village returned to normal for the next few days as life followed the well-worn routine of hunting, gathering and basic farming. Tom wondered if there would be another opportunity to cause grief to the Japanese but reluctantly had to admit to himself that any further action would be too risky for him and his kind hosts. His careful reckoning of the days in his notebook and on his staff told him he now had only a few weeks before it was time to return to the coast and hopefully meet up with the American submarine. The whole expedition had so far been a resounding success and he had a wealth of information to take back to his unit. There was only one thing he needed to clarify before he left and that was to check if the rumours were true about a Chinese group based in Kota Belud that was willing to support any action against the new imperial masters. Tom knew the Chinese had suffered greatly since the invasion as they were regarded as the enemy by the Japanese. They had taken the brunt of most of the sadistic acts performed on the civilian population and were most unhappy with the situation. But how willing would they be if it came to a fight to the death and did they have any weapons to help them overcome the enemy? He needed to know before he departed so he asked Asampit if he could arrange a meeting with one of the Chinese, preferably their leader if they had one. Asampit was doubtful as there were only rumours about the plotters and the Chinese kept very much to themselves. He said he would send a couple of men to Kota Belud to buy some salt and oil and try to find out more about the secret group if it really did exist. Tom was worried that their questioning might reach the ears of any sympathisers with the Japanese who would betray them for a reward. He discussed this with the village elders and they decided that, although there was a risk it was more important to make contact with any Chinese men willing to join forces with them. They added that the people in Kota Belud did not know where their new longhouse was situated and would, therefore, be unable to give their position away to the Japanese.

The following day two men and, to allay any suspicions, a woman with a small child, made their way down the stream to the river where they had hidden a couple of canoes that would take them down to the town. They took some tobacco and woven baskets to trade with the shopkeepers and a small amount of Tom's money to purchase a few pots and pans. The problem was how to broach the subject of possible rebellion without appearing too eager or be accused of scaremongering. Tom had told them to try and find a Chinese man who could read English and had given them a note explaining what he was doing in the country without being too specific or identifying him and the longhouse. He had added the names of some of the Kudat Chinese community he thought they might know to prove he was genuine and that it was not a trick by the Japanese to flush out insurgents. There remained the element of risk but Tom reasoned that he had to show some of his hand first or everyone would just deny all knowledge of any organised group. At worst he would be captured and, if his story held up, interned with the other civilians in the Kuching camp. He was well aware of the consequences if they didn't believe his story. He waited impatiently for the shoppers to return.

In Kota Belud the small group did the trading and chatted generally to the shop owners about the current situation and how life was becoming more difficult for everyone. Their comments were received with sympathy and a general agreement that something would have to be done if it became worse. The woman carrying the child said that she hoped the men would not allow any harm to come to the females in the community and this brought a very positive response. The shopkeeper asked if their village would be willing to stand up to the invaders and was answered in the affirmative. One of the men then asked the shopkeeper if he could read English. He couldn't but was able to tell them of someone who could.

'I think you should go and see David Wong in the medicine shop,' he said. 'He speaks and reads English well. You might learn something from him. Tell him Phu Kong sent you.'

The shop was only a few doors away so they wandered towards it and pushed open the door. David Wong was standing behind the counter and was somewhat surprised to see Murut people in his shop as they rarely used, or could afford, his medicine.

'How can I help you?' David asked politely. He didn't want to cause any offence as they might prove to be a new source of business.

'Are you David Wong?' asked one of the men. 'We have been sent here by Phu Kong. He said you can read English.'

David was rather taken aback by the way the conversation was going but decided to go along with the visitors. 'Yes, I learned to read and write English as a boy in China. Why do you ask?'

'We have a note from a good friend of ours and he has written it in English to give to any Chinese man who is willing to assist in seeing the Japanese invaders defeated.'

David was shocked with this remark as it would be a certain death sentence if the Japanese found out. He knew his visitors must be very brave to risk being betrayed and felt that he had to try and find out more.

'Let me read the note.' They handed it over and he read it carefully. He realised that it was almost certainly genuine as it contained many references to people and places of which the Japanese would have no knowledge. It seemed fantastic that there was a white man who had the courage to return to occupied North Borneo and who actually wanted to build up a network of contacts to indulge in subversive activity. His curiosity aroused, he decided that he would like to meet with this insane man and find out if it was a realistic possibility to work together.

'I will meet with the man who wrote this note. I suggest we meet at night in a village away from the town. It would be possible for me to go up the river to the next *kampong* and meet him there. How soon can it be arranged?'

They fixed a date for five days time and the group swiftly melted away leaving an over-excited David to break his usual routine and have a cigarette at least two hours before normal. This managed to calm him down somewhat and he pondered for a long time about whether he had done the right thing or not. On reflection he thought he might have been too reckless but argued with himself that if it was a Japanese trap then they would already have the evidence against him so he had nothing to lose. Not that they actually needed any evidence anyway. He would take with him one of his closest friends Luther Kiong and tell his wife they were going to visit a patient who was unable to travel to his shop. Luther was everything in looks that David was not. He was tall and well built with strong arms and a thick thatch of coal black hair that stood up in spikes. It had earned him the nickname pineapple at school. They were, however, very alike in temperament and equally determined to guard and protect their precious families and their way of life.

The tale of the Murut's outing was related to Tom as soon as they returned and he was overjoyed to find they had been able to make contact with a Chinese sympathiser. His time in Borneo was running out so he had to set out the next day to travel to the *kampong* sited by the river and meet with this David Wong they had told him about. He also hoped that it wasn't a trap but was determined to go as it might lead to a more unified resistance against the oppressors. Asampit insisted that Enduat must accompany Tom to give him some protection. That their efforts would shorten the war he was doubtful about but he preferred to be doing something rather than sitting around waiting for others to solve the problem. David Wong felt exactly the same.

They met in the back room of the only shop in the small *kampong*. David had arrived first and was very nervous. He couldn't sit still and was constantly looking around him. Luther Kiong waited outside hidden in the bushes to warn David if any soldiers appeared. It might give him a few seconds to escape. The few days of waiting had done nothing to calm David's nerves and he was in a state of high tension. The unknown was soon to reveal itself and he felt totally out of control. It was a huge relief when the door opened and he saw the tall white man. He had partly expected a Japanese bayonet to greet him. He recognised Tom as the man he had seen with his wife outside his shop and had said such complimentary things about his medicine. This was much more than he had expected at the time as his dealings with the English had not always been cordial. Then he remembered that the man had told him he was Australian.

'How is your wife?' he enquired. 'I hope her pregnancy ran its course smoothly. Is she back in Australia?'

Tom looked closely at the man behind the table and recognition slowly dawned.

'You!' he exclaimed, 'the man who knew I was to be a father before I did. Well, I'll be damned. We've a lot to discuss but we must both be well away from here before dawn.'

Now that they knew they were both safe they called to Luther and Enduat and invited them in to join the discussion. Tom and David preferred to use English for communication and this meant constant translating by Tom for Enduat and David for Luther. Despite these language difficulties they all managed to understand what was discussed and they sat and talked for over an hour and outlining how each thought they could best hamper the Japanese war effort and hasten the end of the conflict. They were in agreement over most things and the talk was warm and productive. Tom stressed that direct action must be avoided whenever possible and they must rely on devious means. As an example he told David about the poisoned water at Poring and had him and Luther laughing about the antics of the Japanese futilely trying to revive their comrades. Both were concerned that any action which could be attributed to any particular group might result in severe reprisals and agreed that any acts of sabotage must be disguised as accidents. Tom told David he would contact him again when he next returned and they worked out coded signals so that each would be sure that any message was genuine. This was in case one of them was captured and the Japanese tried to flush out the other rebels by taking their identity. They parted with warm handshakes and both felt much more confident in what the future might bring. There were now two groups working together under Tom's leadership. Tom felt his mission had been a success and now he had to prepare for the return to the beach at Bak Bak and another ride in a foul submarine.

Asampit was reluctant to let Tom go as he thought he might never see him again. Tom also wondered if he would ever again enjoy the hospitality of these people he had grown to love and admire. Neither of them spoke about their concerns but both had an idea what the other was thinking and preferred to keep the parting light and talk about meeting again very soon. Tom left the parcel of money with Asampit for safe keeping and in case it was required to bribe any informants. He packed his small rucksack and, accompanied by Andaman, who was Asampit's younger son and had recently been elevated to the status of warrior, set out on the journey to the coast. Andaman stayed with him and helped him cross the river and down towards the farms on the coastal plain. Here they parted and Tom bivouacked until darkness descended sufficiently for him to make the risky move through the farms to meet the submarine. He hoped that his dinghy was still in its hiding place and was in a fit condition to carry him out to the off-shore rendezvous. Moving as quietly as he could and staying close to ditches that he could use for cover if he spotted a patrol Tom eventually arrived at the well where the boat was concealed. To his relief it was undisturbed and he soon reinflated it sufficiently to transport him to the sub. He now had to wait for the signal light flashing over the calm black sea telling him that it had arrived to collect him. A couple of hours passed and he began to wonder if his rough calendar was accurate. Had he missed a day or two? The lack of moonlight at least pointed to the fact that the moon was new and when it appeared through the light clouds it didn't look as if it could get any slimmer. Nevertheless Tom remained nervous and peered out into the gloom with intense concentration. The only sound was the gentle rushing of the waves as they lapped up the beach. Even the farm dogs remained silent which comforted Tom as it indicated that no one else was around in the night. He also worried about falling asleep and missing the signal so he deliberately sat on the most uncomfortable tree root he could find. At last he thought he saw a glimmer of light in the distance. Submarine or fishing boat? Again the light shone but this time it was steadier and was flashing the prearranged signal. Tom rushed to launch his dinghy and paddled out towards the light. He was soon next to the solid metal bulk of the conning tower and willing hands helped him aboard then pulled up his boat and swiftly hustled him into the depths so that they could submerge and be safe from enemy patrol boats that plied up and down the coast. A hot drink and a welcome bar of chocolate soon had Tom relaxed to the point where he totally forgot his fear of being in a large tin can. All he wanted to do now was sleep for a week and wake up next to his beloved Mary with their two girls curled up beside them.

Chapter 11

With the submarine safely berthed Tom was taken to see Colonel Stephens to outline what he had achieved. The Colonel realised that Tom was more than eager to go to his family so he intended to keep the meeting as short as possible knowing they could fill in all the details over the following days.

'You're looking fitter than ever,' was his initial greeting. 'The jungle life seems to suit you. How did it go? Was it worth the risk?'

'Apart from having to travel in that awful submarine it all went fairly smoothly,' Tom replied. 'I managed to stay with my old friend Asampit in his longhouse and made contact with the leader of an embryonic Chinese resistance group based in Kota Belud. A few Japs unfortunately met with a bathing accident while I was there but otherwise all was peaceful. I've collected the information you wanted about the numbers and deployment of enemy troops as well as their state of morale and the level of weaponry and any transport they possess.'

'Great! You can give us all that next week. First you must go to your family to reassure them you're still in one piece. I did go and see Mary after you'd left to reassure her but realised immediately that she had already guessed where you were and was determined to stay cheerful and give the children as normal a time as possible.'

'Thank you sir. It was good of you to do that and I'm certain Mary really appreciated your visit. I hadn't actually told her the truth about where I was going but, like you, realised she'd worked it out for herself. I'll leave immediately if I may.'

'There is transport waiting outside to take you home straight away. I'll expect you back on Monday at eight o'clock sharp. Now move.'

Tom needed no second bidding and gathered up his few belongings and rushed out to the car.

Mary, having been 'phoned by the Colonel to expect Tom

very soon, was waiting on the front lawn with the girls beside her when his car stopped. He ran to her and lifted her off her feet to whirl her round whilst at the same time trying to smother her with kisses. The girls watched shyly with the youngest, now walking, holding on tightly to her sister's hand. Tom left Mary's embrace to pick them up and then held them close to him as he included Mary in a family hug. Before they knew it they were all laughing and crying at the same time as the relief of being together again sank in and all the worries that had plagued Mary through the lonely nights evaporated.

'It's so good to have you home. And in one piece,' Mary spluttered through her tears. 'I never stopped thinking about you for a moment. Will you be able to tell me much about what you did?'

'I don't see why not,' Tom answered. 'The Colonel didn't swear me to secrecy and I'm sure you won't pass on to anyone anything I confide in you. It'll do me good to tell someone apart from the army about what happened so I can have some feedback from an ordinary person to hopefully reassure me that I'm doing the right thing.'

'Ordinary person!' Mary exclaimed. 'Since when have I been ordinary? You'd better not say that again.'

'Sorry love, I meant someone removed from the military who still has a human perception of events.'

'Have you any news of our friends and the estate workers?'

'I'm afraid not. I wasn't allowed to go too near to Kudat in case someone saw me and reported me to the Japanese hoping for a reward. I spent nearly the whole time with Asampit in his longhouse. I did meet one other person you know and that was the doctor who spotted you were pregnant with Sarah when we visited Kota Belud. He's now involved in organising the local Chinese resistance.'

'Yes, I remember him. He was very perceptive.'

'I found out his name is David Wong. He's only small in stature but is a very brave man. He took a great risk in meeting me as it could have been a Japanese trap.'

'Well, you can leave all the fighting to them now. You've done your bit and we can be a family again. I'll check with Dad to see if you can return to your job. I'm sure he'll agree.'

'Not so fast,' interjected Tom. 'The war isn't anywhere near over. I may still have a job to do.'

'You mean you're going there again? What about me and the girls? Don't we mean anything to you?'

'Of course you do darling but remember there are many Australians who are prisoners in Borneo who would dearly love to return to their families. If I can help that happen more quickly by working behind the lines then I have to. Surely you understand that?'

'I do understand but the uncertainty is very hard. If anything happened to you while you were away then I would probably never ever find out the truth. I know I'm being selfish but you and the girls are my whole world.'

'And you are mine but I couldn't look at myself again in a mirror if I refused to fight. There's some danger but think of the greater risks we take by doing nothing. Australia could become a Japanese colony.'

Tom held her close again as she had started sobbing. He felt a bit confused as he knew he had to continue the fight but was fearful of the damage it could do to his family. All he wanted was reassurance that he was doing the right thing but Mary seemed unable to let him go with her blessing. He wasn't sure what to do for the best so resolved to put the dilemma to the back of his mind until he was able to think it through more clearly. His immediate concern was to enjoy family life again and then relate to the Colonel all the information he had gathered and find out the future plans. It might turn out that they didn't need him again and Mary could relax at last. In his heart, however, he knew that was a forlorn hope as his task was nowhere near finished. At least he had the weekend to spend with his wife.

Monday came far too quickly for both of them and Tom found himself back in Colonel Stephens' office first thing in the morning. He had with him his notebook so that he could give the Colonel all the details about the enemy that he had collected in the three months. The Colonel ordered coffee and via the intercom invited a couple of intelligence officers to join them. After a few pleasantries Tom stood and moved to a large blackboard to give them the information they desperately needed to help plan for future action.

'The enemy troop levels in the whole of Borneo number around thirty thousand of which only five thousand are experienced Japanese soldiers. Most of the men are concentrated in Sarawak and the Dutch East Indies sectors of the island. In North Borneo, where they feel more confident and secure, there are only around two thousand soldiers and few of these are well-trained Japanese troops. The remainder are Korean conscripts who are not particularly keen on fighting or even being in the army. They don't have the same attitude as their Japanese masters and only stay loyal through fear of brutal punishment. If they show any weakness to the local people then they are badly beaten themselves so they have to act as cruelly as their masters. I would guess, however, that they would be unlikely to fight to the death if they saw they were in danger of being overwhelmed by our forces. The Japanese army don't seem to have any organised supply lines and mainly rely on food, shelter and transport that they can scavenge on the ground. Only small quantities of ammunition and some replacement weapons seem to be coming by air from Japan to the new landing strips they've built at strategic points. In many respects they're left to their own devices and this seems to suit them as they can swagger around as conquerors and do as they please.'

'What about the transport and weapons?' enquired one of the officers.

'They have a few cars and motorcycles that they've commandeered from the local population but these are only used by the top brass and the Kempetai. The ordinary soldiers have to go on foot or use bicycles to patrol the coastline. Some trucks taken from the plantations are also used to transport troops around. They have boats to go up the navigable rivers but they don't like travelling too far into the interior as it is hard going and there's always a chance that they could fall foul of a local tribe. They're well aware that the native people are skilled and silent killers who leave no trace of their deeds. Weaponry is mainly light with rifles and machine guns. They've a few mortars and have been seen practising with these but no heavy artillery or anti-aircraft guns. To sum up: only the coastline is defended and then only in a perfunctory manner as they are confident of their control of the air and the seas.'

'You mentioned a Chinese insurgent. What can you tell us about him?' asked the Colonel.

'That's David Wong who lives in Kota Belud. I met him briefly before the war and we had a profitable meeting while I was staying in the longhouse.' Tom took out a map and pinned it to the blackboard so he could show the Colonel and the officers exactly where the places he mentioned were situated.

'David is a Chinese doctor with a large family and he is committed to sending the Japanese back to their islands for good. Many of the Chinese community feel the same as they moved to Borneo to escape the Japanese menace in China itself. They are eager to take action but I warned them about the dangers of possible reprisals by the Kempetai. With great foresight before the war they stockpiled a quite large collection of guns including pistols, shotguns and hunting rifles. This was relatively easy under the British rule and they added to their armoury a good supply of ammunition as well as some explosives from the mines. It is all well hidden in many different places. The Japanese have no suspicion that they are plotting to overthrow them and have, so far, left them alone. David is waiting for the signal that we'll be invading and then he'll mobilise his men and attack from behind the Japanese lines. Meanwhile they hope to make life for the invaders as uncomfortable as they can without attracting too much attention to themselves.'

'And the bathing accident you spoke of?'

Tom told them all about the poisoning of the water at the hot springs and they were hugely impressed by the tale. When Tom related the way that the panic had spread they laughed out loud and shook him vigorously by the hand. The Colonel clapped him on the back and, despite a nagging worry that his orders had been flouted, expressed his delight at Tom's initiative.

'I knew you were just the sort of man for this unit,' he enthused, 'I hope that our other operatives have similar success and are equally devious.'

After answering a few more questions about the terrain and the deployment of the troops it was time for Tom to return home. Before he left he asked the Colonel about the future.

'No idea,' came the reply. 'We're operating from day to day until the powers that be decide on a definite course of action to liberate Borneo and free our captive troops. I'll keep you informed but don't expect to hear from me again this side of New Year.'

With that welcome news ringing in his ears Tom departed with a much lighter heart to pass it on to Mary. He felt sure she would be pleased that nothing definite had been decided and they could enjoy a real family Christmas. Mary and the girls were waiting for him on his return and she could read from his expression that all was well. She was hardly able to conceal her emotions and when Tom confirmed her thoughts she felt overjoyed and overwhelmed. At last she could start to plan for the festivities with a lighter heart and was determined to make it the best Christmas ever.

The weather was beautiful and they decided to spend part of Christmas Day on the beach. This was great news for the girls as they loathed being cooped up indoors when it was hot. Mary's parents and her brothers were naturally invited and the small party spread out a picnic and broke open some bottles of beer that had been kept cool in a box of dry ice. Mary was careful not to make a big deal of only her relations being present as she knew Tom would be thinking of the family he'd lost as a young child. She needn't have worried though as he was so happy just to be with her and the girls. It was a fabulous day and in the evening Tom and Mary sat on the veranda without feeling the need to speak as they knew their thoughts were as one. Sarah had kept her eyes open for as long as possible but eventually succumbed to all the sun and excitement and had been carried by Tom to her bed where he kissed her tenderly on the forehead as she slept.

The festivities of the New Year of 1943 were rather muted as so many young Australians were away and families were reluctant to conspicuously enjoy themselves. Some had been served with bad or distressing news about their loved ones and these families turned in on themselves until they returned to work or school. Mary was desperately upset to hear that both her brothers had volunteered but was consoled by the thought that they would probably remain in Australia until the time came to liberate south-east Asia from the clutches of the Japanese. One had joined the army and the other the air force and they were waiting to be called for their basic training to begin. She knew that they had volunteered after hearing some of Tom's tales but she didn't blame him as she felt sure that they would have joined up eventually without the added push.

Near the end of January Tom heard again from the Colonel and was summoned to the headquarters. He arrived early and met one of the intelligence officers that had attended his debriefing. The officer told him that more stories of Japanese atrocities had leaked out of Borneo and that there was a growing determination at government level to take action when the time was right. Tom wondered if there would ever be a right time but held his tongue and waited for the Colonel to appear. He soon did and they went into his office. The Colonel looked tired and Tom realised that the war was taking its toll on all those involved. He sat down and waited for the Colonel to begin.

'Some bad news I'm afraid. Of the eight operatives we sent to Borneo only two of you have returned safely. We've no idea of the fate of the others and probably never will. Such a high failure rate makes it difficult to justify any further operations and questions have been asked at ministerial level. What do you think?'

'I think that it means we need to continue with our work. To stop now would be an insult to those who may have given their lives and I'm sure they would feel the same if the roles were reversed. We must continue or we'll never defeat the enemy. Our actions behind the lines could help save many lives when the invasion occurs and our presence in the country is a real boost to the morale of the people and makes them feel they are not alone in their struggle. In any case there might be some better news soon.'

'Thank you for that,' the Colonel replied. 'I agree with you but you can understand the reluctance of the powers that be to send men on missions that are almost a certain death sentence. Is it possible your contacts are more reliable than those of the others?'

'I've no idea. You kept us all separate during training so we wouldn't have anything to divulge if we were captured and tortured. All I know is that I can trust my Murut friends with my life and they'll always help me if I ask them. They do this from real friendship and not for any reward. All of them are trustworthy and good men that I'm immensely proud of.'

'Do you think you could go back reasonably safely?'

'Yes,' Tom answered firmly. 'I've every confidence that I could return if there's a job for me to do.'

'There is. We need to drop some supplies in the jungle to be stashed away ready for the future. No date has been set for the liberation but we need to be prepared. The plan is for you to identify and accurately map a site to drop the goods. It must not compromise your friends by being too near to their village but be reasonably accessible to them so they can visit it regularly, collect any cases and destroy the parachutes. The Japanese must have no inkling that we are doing this so, just like your equipment, it will all be unmarked and untraceable back to the Australian forces. Do you consider this possible?'

'I do. There are a number of places I can think of that might fit the bill. I know the headman Asampit will be happy to help and if he hides something then it will never be found by accident or design. He's very clever. It would, however, be a nice gesture if you could include some food and tools for his village in the crates. They're good people but don't have much and any extra supplies would help them tremendously.'

'An excellent suggestion. I'll mention it at my next meeting with the top brass. Leave it with me and go back home. I'll be in touch before too long.'

Tom returned home to find Mary waiting apprehensively. He told her there was no definite news so she visibly relaxed and busied herself preparing dinner. Tom wondered if he should tell her about the latest plan but decided that it would be soon enough to do that when he had his final orders. Meanwhile he had a family to father.

February 1943 passed without any contact and Tom and Mary settled comfortably into a domestic routine that involved little effort and even less thought. They rarely spoke about the future and this seemed to suit them both as they concentrated on bringing up the girls and delighted in all their small successes in growing up. Sarah was definitely becoming a forceful character and at four years old knew exactly what she wanted. She had started at a private nursery school and the teacher was always telling Mary how Sarah organised all the other children in games and play. Angela was much quieter, probably because her sister was so strong minded, but even at only fourteen months she could hold her own when crossed. The age difference made it difficult for them to be real playmates yet so Sarah often took on the role of surrogate mother when Mary was busy. All in all they were a source of genuine pleasure to their parents and grandparents. Their large and noisy uncles were also always welcomed by the girls who loved the boisterous way they played with them; throwing them high up in the air and catching them or swinging them round and round until they were dizzy.

The peace of these days was eventually shattered in March when Tom was again called to see the Colonel. He knew what the summons meant and tried his best not to let Mary worry but she picked up on his anxiety and guessed correctly that he would soon be leaving her on another mission. She had been hoping that the war would end before Tom was wanted again but it appeared to continue unabated and no end was even vaguely in sight. She shared her concerns with her ever supportive parents but there was little they could do or say to allay her fears that she would never see Tom again.

Tom received his orders and they were much as he had anticipated. He was to be dropped at the same spot as before and make his way to Asampit's village as quickly as he could. There he had to find and mark a drop zone for the planes to find and deliver their valuable cargo of food, arms and ammunition. This time he would only be there for one lunar month so he had no other objectives to fulfil during his stay. In all probability he would have returned before the first drop so it was important that Asampit was fully prepared about how to store the armaments safely. Tom now knew that the food he had suggested was also to be included and would prove to be very useful for the villagers to eat or use for barter with neighbouring villages and in the town. At Tom's request the food had been packaged to look as if it had been made pre-war and hoarded by the villagers rather than coming fresh from Australia. Final preparations were made and Tom said his farewells at the end of March and once again set off to board the submarine.

Chapter 12

The sea was rougher this time and Tom struggled to paddle the tiny dinghy to the shore. The waves made it dangerous to go too close to the rocks and he feared that the fragile craft would be punctured before he reached the relative safety of the beach. He knew he could make it to land without the boat if it came to the pinch but then he would have no means, apart from a long and hazardous swim, of reaching the submarine at the end of his mission. Fortunately one of the waves carried him over the outer coral reef to the quiet water in the small bay and he thankfully dragged the boat up the sand to stow it safely away in the disused well behind the bushes. There was no welcoming beast this time and all was still among the trees except for the incessant night noises of various frogs and reptiles that become so familiar to people who live in tropical areas to the point that they no longer notice them. Tom waited for over an hour to make sure that his landing hadn't been observed and then cautiously moved across the track at the back of the trees to the ditches that surrounded the fields. These were his main means of staying low and out of sight as he passed the farms on the fertile plain. This was the most dangerous part of his journey and it was worth moving slowly to be certain of avoiding detection. There were no lights in any of the buildings and no sign of Japanese patrols so it was with a mounting sense of relief that he entered the now familiar friendly embrace of the jungle and headed towards the hills and the isolated Murut people.

Naturally they found him before he had an inkling they were near although he knew that unless they had been forced to move on again it wasn't far to their longhouse. Everything was exactly as he had left it and old friendships were renewed and sealed with *tapai* drinking late into the night. Tom explained his reasons for the visit and the villagers were very excited at the prospect of receiving gifts from above. Since Tom's last visit they had seen more and more planes above the treetops and now accepted them as part of everyday life. Tom told them what he required and they eagerly discussed possible sites for the drop. Asampit fully appreciated the need to have it at some distance from where they lived so that the village would not come under suspicion if the goods were intercepted by a Japanese patrol. He suggested that it should not be close enough to reach in one day and be far away from any major river to make it even safer. Tom explained that the plane would be flying quite low so they must avoid places with any nearby hills or large rock features but there must be some way of identifying the drop zone from the air. This was clearly a problem as a river would have been the ideal flight path to follow but ran the high risk of being used by enemy patrols. They pondered for hours but found no solution so they decided to retire for the night and think again with clearer heads the next day.

It was Asampit's young son Andaman who eventually came up with the answer. He knew a part of the jungle a safe distance away where there had been an open cast copper mine and the land had been cleared. The vegetation had grown back over the years to cover the worst of the scarring but was still much lower and less dense than the more mature surrounding jungle. Even the track used for transporting the ore to the nearest river had long since disappeared from view. It was difficult to see the difference at ground level but he reckoned that it would be readily visible from the air and would make the ideal place for the crates to be parachuted down. Tom wanted to go there immediately but Asampit wouldn't let him go until Andaman had revisited the area to ensure it was still as he remembered it and free from any unwanted activity. Reluctantly Tom agreed and Andaman left with his brother Enduat to check all was as he had said. Tom and Asampit settled down to discuss how the arms would be hidden and who would be using them when the time came to rise up against the oppressors. He also asked if there was any news of David Wong.

'He's fine,' Asampit assured Tom. 'Some of the women

from our village were in Kota Belud only a week ago and made contact with him. He asked about you and, obviously, they had no news. Will you be seeing him this time?'

'No, this is only a brief visit. I don't want to take any unnecessary risks. But please tell him I was here and I'll contact him as soon as there's any definite news of action. Also please remind him to take care.'

'I don't think we need do that. David's well aware of the consequences if he's found to be plotting against the Japs. I'm sure he always takes every precaution to avoid detection. The Chinese are a close knit community and it would be very unusual for one of them to deliberately betray a fellow tradesman.'

'Yes, you're right. I'm just rather twitchy about the whole enterprise and want it to succeed without any unnecessary complications and especially without any deaths. I know that there'll be casualties when we eventually openly come out and fight but we must minimise these as best we can. If we're well organised and catch them by surprise then we might be able to quickly overcome any opposition.'

'That's unlikely,' replied Asampit. 'The Japanese will fight to the last man and they are certain to fight ferociously. Our main hope is to prevent them coming together as a single force and pick them off in ones and twos as they try to join their comrades. The Korean troops will be no trouble. They will lay down their arms and surrender as soon as it's clear that we're winning.'

'Good. Let's hope it happens soon. I can't wait to return to normal and have my family living peaceably again in Kudat as we did before this whole mess blew up.'

With all the necessary plans made they could only wait until Asampit's sons returned. The message they brought was a good one. The jungle hadn't been disturbed since Andaman's previous visit and it was far enough from the nearest river to be of little interest to the Japanese. All Tom had to do was visit the place and take as accurate bearings as he could to help the planes find it. They set out again the next day armed with paper and a compass. Tom needed to find other likely features that could be used to guide the pilots and act as location markers. When they were near to the site he noted carefully all the streams and small hills in the surrounding area to build up an aerial picture that could be followed by sight. The actual drop zone was exactly what was required. It stretched for at least three hundred yards and was around a hundred yards wide. It was not a uniform rectangle but had a narrowing in the middle like a waist so Tom called it the hourglass. He hoped that from the air it would be very distinct. Taking a range of bearings including one of the top of Mount Kinabalu and some of the lesser peaks he felt confident he could provide them with a useful map when he returned to Australia. The task completed they made their way back to the longhouse.

Tom was worried that when he returned to the coast he would have to carry the rough map and the notes of the compass bearings he had made. If he got caught they would be a real giveaway and could cause untold problems for Asampit and his people. He decided to try to think up a way to disguise the information so that no one else could decipher it. After much thought he came up with an idea that had distinct possibilities. He reversed all the bearings in his notes, cut up the map and then rearranged it in a different pattern so that it looked totally different and stuck it to a piece of cloth. Kinabalu was now in the opposite direction and the drop site appeared to be on the other side of the mountain. He then folded the map as small as he could and sewed it between his back trouser pocket and the trousers themselves. An old map of the whole of North Borneo was put in the pocket to distract any investigator from the important one. In another day or two he would be leaving again and was determined to meet the submarine on the first night it appeared to rescue him.

Goodbyes were made and he set off confident that yet again he had been successful. He made such good time on the return journey that he had to stop on the edge of the jungle to wait for nightfall before going on his careful zigzag route through the paddy fields. It was warm so he just lay down leaning against a tree, having first checked for any ants, and drifted asleep.

He woke suddenly and realised someone or something was kicking his right foot. Opening his eyes he looked straight down the barrel of a rifle with a Japanese soldier at the other end. Nervously he rose to his feet and was suddenly knocked back when the soldier whirled the rifle round and hit him in the mouth with the butt. Blood poured down his throat and he spat out at least four teeth. He remembered what he had been trained to do and bowed as low as he could only for the rifle to now clout him on the back of the neck sending him sprawling on the ground again. He was angry and jumped up but his arms were suddenly held from behind and he realised the soldier was not alone. They dragged him towards a track where a vehicle stood and bundled him in the back. It seemed vaguely familiar and then he realised it was his own truck from the estate. They must have taken it to use for their patrols along the coast. With the gun firmly stuck in his guts they lurched along the track to the dirt road that led to Kudat.

The truck eventually stopped as darkness fell and Tom was roughly manhandled into the police station. There was an army officer there so he bowed low again and tried to look bemused. The officer spoke a little English and asked him who he was and what he was doing out of the internment camp.

'So far so good,' he thought, 'they reckon I'm an escaped civilian and not a soldier.'

He gave his true name but no other details. The officer consulted a list.

'Your name is not on my list as having escaped. Why are you not with the other Europeans in the camp?'

'I never escaped. Months ago when I saw your soldiers in the town I ran and hid in the jungle. I've been hiding ever since and living off the land. Your soldiers caught me just before I went into the fields to take some fruit and vegetables to eat.'

The officer looked at Tom's dishevelled appearance. He did look and smell as if he had been living rough for months

106

which gave some credibility to his story. Two of the soldiers came in with Tom's belongings, bowed and spoke in Japanese to the officer. He searched through them himself and held up the compass.

'What do you have this for?'

Tom replied quickly. 'I am often working away from home on other plantations and have a fear of losing myself in the jungle. I carry that to guide me if I am unsure of my route.'

The officer signalled to his soldiers who held Tom while he searched his clothing. He found the map in the back pocket and Tom's tobacco. Fortunately the tobacco was rough and obviously local as Tom had been given it by Asampit so as not to cause any suspicion. Tom worried about the map but the officer seemed to find it of little interest. Presumably he thought it was what you would expect to find with a compass and, therefore, not unusual. The Australian Service Reconnaissance Department had done a thorough job and nothing in Tom's possessions could link him to the military in any way. He was relieved when the officer barked an order to the men and they dragged him off to one of the cells and threw him in so violently that he hit his head on the far wall, fell on the hard bed and blacked out for a moment.

When he came to he gingerly rubbed the rapidly developing bruise and assessed his plight. It seemed that the officer believed his story and had no proof that he was anything other than what he said he was. One problem might be if they inquired about him at the plantation and found he had left the country months prior to the invasion. He hoped they would think that too much trouble and just send him to join the others in the internment camp in Kuching. His optimism was not to be proved right.

The next morning he was again taken to the officer who this time introduced himself formally as Captain Kasya and told Tom that he was to be shot as a spy. Tom protested his innocence but the Captain was adamant and said he couldn't believe Tom had been living in the jungle without support for over a year. He told Tom that if he gave details of the people who had helped him then he would be able to spare his life. Tom knew that this was simply a ruse to gain information about his friends and also realised that if he didn't then the next step would be extremely painful. He was sure he wouldn't be leaving Kudat alive. The officer gave him one day to think about it before, as he put it, he took further measures to help Tom remember.

Back in the cell Tom did as he was bidden and thought. He wasn't sure how well he could withstand torture and worried that he would break and implicate Asampit and David Wong. Suicide was one option but he felt this was wrong when he still had the slightest chance of getting free. He must either escape or die in the attempt. If he could get away then there was still time to meet the submarine that night. There were two guards on duty, both Korean, and Tom considered what he could do to disarm them. One idea was to feign illness and cry out loudly but this would bring both the guards to his cell and he wasn't confident he could take them on at the same time. He needed a plan to deal with them separately. He surmised that they would bring him food and water at some time in the evening and pinned his hopes on only one guard bringing it in. Tom had his bush hat with him and fingered the hat band with its two little wooden toggles as decoration. He lifted the band and slid out the hidden wire attached to the toggles. He knew the guards always peeked through the small peephole in the cell door before entering so he had to make it look as if he was lying in the bed. An old schoolboy trick might just work. By using his hat at one end and his boots at the other he put the pillow in the middle as his body and rucked the blanket over it to make a passable human form. It would be good enough to survive a cursory glance. Tom would have to be quick as the second guard would come to investigate if he heard anything untoward. He stood close by the side of the door and waited. His heart was pounding and his palms were sweating. He stood with his arms held forward. The toggles were firmly grasped in his hands with the wire running between his finger joints.

At last the key scraped in the lock and the door swung open as the soldier entered the cell. He moved towards the bed and put a bowl of rice on the floor. As he straightened up Tom silently crept forward put his fists above the guard's right shoulder with the right fist on the top, looped the wire round the guard's neck with his right hand as he had been trained and in one swift movement pulled hard on both the toggles at the same time. There was no sound as the soldier's body went limp and Tom lowered him to the floor. Tom was shocked at the amount of blood pumping out from the body. The wire had actually cut through his neck, sliced open his windpipe and then on to sever his carotid arteries and jugular veins and kill him immediately. Tom had been protected from the worst of the gore as he was behind the lifeless body but wiped some the blood from his hands on the soldier's tunic. He put on his boots and cautiously went out of the cell. The second soldier was sitting at a table side on to Tom. He turned as soon as he heard footsteps and leapt to his feet when he realised it wasn't his comrade. His rifle was leaning against the wall out of reach and Tom saw a look of uncertainty in his eyes. Tom took the initiative and charged forward giving him an almighty blow with a balled fist to his stomach. As he doubled up Tom brought his knee crashing under his chin and the guard fell to the floor motionless. He kicked him hard in the head. Knowing that he had to finish him off to gain sufficient time to get away he completed the job by strangling the unfortunate man before he could regain consciousness and raise the alarm.

To his great fortune one of the guards had left a bicycle leaning against the fence outside so he jumped on it and pedalled as fast as he could along the road to Bak Bak and, hopefully, safety. He had no idea if there would be any patrols on the way and kept listening intently for any engine noises. It was his plan to cycle straight into the storm drain down the side of the road at the slightest hint of danger. Bak Bak had never seemed so far from the town as it did now and it appeared to Tom that it had been moved at least ten miles further than his memory told him. The road remained deserted and with an audible whistle of relief Tom turned down the track back to the beach. His watch had been confiscated but he calculated that it must be around nine o'clock and the submarine wasn't due for at least three hours.

Tom retrieved the hidden boat and hid in the undergrowth as best he could and waited. He guessed that a patrol would soon find the dead guards and would be scouring the area for him. Luckily they couldn't know the direction he had taken and, hopefully, wouldn't think he would return towards the place where he'd been caught. He might be safe at least until daylight if the submarine failed to show. This was the second of its potential three visits to pick him up. Would they bother coming as he hadn't been there the previous night? Just like the distance he had cycled seemed longer, time appeared to slow down to a crawl. He'd almost given up hope when he saw the flash of light over the water. With an involuntary cry of joy he pulled the dinghy into the foam and paddled frantically for safety.

Once aboard and under way Tom's whole system collapsed. He shook uncontrollably and the medical officer gave him hot sweet drinks to combat the shock. They'd been unable to get a coherent sentence from him and were worried he was losing his mind. At last he calmed down and the shaking was replaced by silent weeping. This continued for over an hour until he was able to tell them something of his ordeal. Initially it all came out in a rush and events were jumbled up so he took a couple of deep breaths and started again. His story had the officers on the edge of their seats and when he got to the part where he killed the guards he broke down again. It had been the first time he had killed anything with his bare hands and he was sickened with himself that he had done it without compunction and with no compassion for his fellow human beings. The submarine Captain reassured him that he had done the right thing and had probably saved the lives of his friends in the longhouse. But Tom couldn't shake from his mind the thought that the two men might have had families like his own who would never see their father again.

By the time the submarine docked Tom had largely rationalised his thoughts and was nearly back to his normal, confident self. He was taken directly to the Colonel but this time was not allowed home immediately. The submarine Captain had sensibly conveyed his fears about Tom's breakdown to the Colonel and it was decided to keep Tom under observation for a few days. They told him they urgently needed the information about the drop zone he had identified so he wouldn't realise they were concerned for his mental welfare. First though, he was checked out by the medical officer and given some emergency treatment to his teeth by the army dentist.

One of the officers who sat in on the sessions over the next two days was, unbeknown to Tom, a psychiatrist. His brief was to assess the state of Tom's mind to see if he was fit for further duty abroad. They did not want to risk his health breaking down completely or, more importantly to them, jeopardise the success of any future operation. After the second day he was sure that Tom had recovered and had even been toughened by his experiences. He told the Colonel he considered there was no cause for concern.

The Colonel and his senior staff realised that Tom was now a marked man in Borneo and if he was captured again would be shown no mercy. They decided to only use him again when there were definite invasion plans and his local knowledge and contacts could be employed to the full. Tom was duly informed that he was to go back to his family and wait for developments. He was told that it would probably be quite some time before he returned to Borneo and that he should take up his job again and enjoy family life. None of them guessed it would be two years before Tom was needed again.

This time he arrived home without Mary being given any prior warning. He just walked in the door to the kitchen where she was preparing lunch for herself and the two girls. When she saw him her hands flew to her mouth and she started to sway.

Tom rushed to her and held her arms to prevent her collapsing to the floor. He helped her to the sitting room and lay her down on the sofa. All the colour had drained from her face. After a minute she sat up and stared at him.

'Your face!' she exclaimed. 'What happened to it?'

In the excitement of returning home Tom had forgotten that his injuries had not fully healed and that the bruising was now showing all the full range of hues from purple to orangey yellow. He realised he looked a mess and smiled at Mary.

'Your teeth!' she gasped. 'Where are they?'

'Somewhere near Kudat. We parted company during a little argument with a rifle butt. The dentist said that I can have some nice new ones once the swelling has gone down. I'll probably look even more handsome than before.'

'No chance,' she laughed at last. 'That would be an impossibility. I'd better warn Sarah before she sees you. You'll give her nightmares otherwise. She'll be home soon. Mum's taken Angie and gone to pick her up.'

'At least I have some news you'll like. I've been stood down for the present as it's too dangerous for me to return until the invasion is definitely going to happen. You'll have to put up with my ugly mug for quite some time.'

Mary looked very relieved. That was exactly what she wanted to hear. Even though it was likely Tom would be going off again she could bear it better knowing he would not be alone next time. She looked at him again. Somehow he had changed. He seemed more serious and some part of his infectious joy for life had diminished. She wondered if he would ever be able to tell her what had happened or would he hide behind the line that the mission was a state secret. In truth, she wasn't sure she wanted to know all the details anyway but somehow not knowing was even worse than the bald unvarnished truth. She decided not to press him but try to make everything as normal as she could and hope he would open up if and when he felt ready to confide in her.

'I must see your father soon,' Tom said. 'The Colonel told

me to go back to work and forget Borneo for the time being. He stressed that I would not be needed again for many months. It will be great to return to being an ordinary worker and family man again.'

'And I will also find it wonderful to have my husband back with me. The girls will be overjoyed to be able to play their silly games with you and I will enjoy our own private games as well.'

'I don't know what you mean,' Tom formed another gappy grin. 'How long before your mother returns with the girls?'

'Long enough for a quick game.' Mary took his hand and pulled herself up from the sofa. Grabbing his belt she dragged him uncomplaining to the bedroom and quickly stripped him naked before shaking herself out of her dress and, almost falling over in her haste to remove her slip and panties, joined him on the bed. She kissed him very gently on the mouth as she was worried it might hurt but he kissed her back with such force that she knew it was alright. They continued with stroking and kissing each other and Tom followed the old routine that Mary enjoyed so much but never tired of. His fingertips and tongue wandered all over her body, lingering on her nipples and descending down to her warm belly where he traced patterns on her skin that sent quivers of joy coursing through her whole body. When he reached her sensitive inner thighs she was almost ready to orgasm and she quickly pulled him to her closely so he entered her and she felt whole once again.

'You don't know how much I've missed you,' she whispered while they lay back satiated from their lovemaking. 'I couldn't continue living without you. I pray you won't be asked to go away again as I'd find it impossible to go through all the worry again.'

'As I said, I'll be home for a long while yet,' mumbled Tom through her hair. 'Let's just get on with living our lives to the full and enjoying watching the girls grow up. Like you, I wish this war was over and we could head back to the plantation and check up on all our old friends.'

Tom thought it was likely many of their friends and acquaintances were dead and that life in Kudat could never be the same again. It was pure fantasy to think the last few years could be wiped out and life would pick up as before and without a hitch. He also wanted to find out what had been happening but part of him was fearful of finding out that everything he had worked for was destroyed and that there was nothing left. Knowing, even the worst, was preferable to ignorance so he just determined to put such thoughts firmly to the back of his mind and deal with the truth when it happened.

His father-in-law James took him on again as his assistant in the engineering factory. They were still quite busy with government orders for military equipment. All the production was geared to helping the war effort and the workers took great pride in the feeling that they were doing something constructive. James worked long hours to keep the factory at full stretch and was glad to have Tom's help in organising and maintaining production. Although Tom didn't have an engineering background he had developed excellent man management skills on the plantation. These were invaluable in coaxing the extra mile from the workforce and James was pleased to have him on board again.

Their life in Australia was to continue in a regular mix of work and domesticity for two years during which time their first son was born. He was named James Joseph after Mary's dad and the father Tom had hardly known. Naturally before long he was always known as JJ. The girls thrived and Tom almost forgot about his frightening last visit to Borneo. Mary's brothers were still safely in Australia as there was nowhere to send them on active service. The liberation of France had yet to start and the Americans had still to gain a foothold in South East Asia although they had started to win the war in the Pacific following their victory at the battle of Midway. Since that event they had started to capture Japanese outposts such as Guadalcanal and Rabaul. While Tom waited for news about his future deployment the Japanese navy and air force were further decimated by the American attacks on all fronts and their resources were now in short supply. They had started to lose ground in all areas round New Guinea and towards the Philippines. It was making them very twitchy as the ignominy of defeat became a distinct possibility and those who were in command in Borneo felt they might soon be isolated from the rest of their forces and be open to attack from the air and sea. They knew they would fight to the death but defeat was still an unspoken spectre on the horizon.

Chapter 13

In1943 life for the Chinese in Kota Belud had taken a turn and not for the better. The first hint of a problem came when a notice was issued by the Japanese High Command setting out exactly how they felt about the Chinese migrants in North Borneo. It stated: 'The Chinese have maltreated, oppressed and denounced overseas Japanese. Such anti-Japanese conduct is intolerable. They have behaved as our enemy by helping our enemies (the British and the Dutch). Let the Chinese remember that the power of seizing them and putting them to death rests on the decision of the Japanese High Command. Although the Chinese are now allowed their freedom, it is only temporary to enable the Japanese to watch their movements. Now let the Chinese reflect deeply, and come to their senses before the issue of another notice.'

On reading this notice David Wong and his friends were incensed and frightened in equal measure. They decided to make even greater efforts to recruit more to their cause and become better organised. They raised money from the wealthy Chinese traders with the intention of setting a bounty on the heads of the Japanese soldiers and to purchase arms and ammunition from farmers and some of the Korean conscripts who were grateful for the extra money to help supplement their abysmal pay. At the outset it was to be based on passive resistance and they named their society The Overseas Chinese Defence Association. Its objective was to prevent people from collaborating too closely with the enemy forces. They had worked out that any assistance given to the Japanese was harmful to the Allied cause.

By now most of the Chinese community were aware of the society and David received a note from Jesselton asking him to meet an old friend. He knew it couldn't be Tom as he wouldn't dare be seen in the town so he puzzled as to the sender's identity. Although it was a risk he went down to Jesselton with his friend Luther to the address given and in a small smoky back room once again met Lo Vun Lip who had recruited him years earlier. From Vun Lip he learned that there were other organised pockets of resistance, some of them from outside Borneo. One in particular was mentioned and Vun Lip explained to an astonished David how it was operating on an island off the coast of North Borneo towards the Philippines. The rebel group consisted of some local people, the Sulu pirates, together with the remnants of the Filipino army who had never actually fought the Japanese as their country had surrendered before they had the chance. They were waiting to strike the Japs wherever it might hurt most. The island was called Tawi-Tawi and the leader of the group was Lieutenant Colonel Nonez the ex-commander of an infantry regiment of the Filipino army. Vun Lip's contact was one of the leaders of the Sulu pirates named Taganam who was masquerading as a trader but in reality was a fierce opponent of the Japanese. He'd been recruited by Lt. Col. Nonez in Tawi-Tawi. Vun Lip went to the door and said Taganam was waiting to speak with them. He opened it and beckoned a waiting figure into the room.

David and Luther looked in awe at the imposing figure filling the doorway. He had a long black beard streaked with grey and his hair was pulled back in a ponytail. He was dressed in black from head to toe apart from a yellow scarf tied around his waist. It didn't take much imagination to add in a cutlass, eye patch and large boots to make him look like a typical storybook pirate. He strode forward and sat next to Vun Lip at the table and glared at David and Luther.

'Who are these Vun Lip?' he growled. 'You said I would be meeting the leaders of the Chinese resistance and not a couple of shopkeepers.'

'Don't be deceived by their looks Taganam,' Vun Lip commented. 'They are brave men who, even before the war started, had the foresight to collect a useful armoury together so as to be in a position to take action when the time was right.'

Taganam still looked unimpressed but grudgingly admitted that they needed support on the mainland as their capacity to

117

strike from the island was limited. He invited David to his island to discuss tactics with the Lieutenant Colonel. A time was set for him to board a boat for Tawi-Tawi.

It all happened so quickly that David had no time to consider if he had any options. To make contact with a regular army force was an important step and he knew that to have any success against the Japanese he would need all the help and expertise he could find. His mind made up he sent a message to his wife explaining that he had been delayed and was waiting for a batch of herbs to be delivered. This, he thought, should pacify her for a short while but then he knew she would start to worry so he wrote out more notes to be sent at intervals of a few days by Lo Vun Lip to make everything seem normal. He would be away for about a week at the most so his absence would not be noticed or remarked upon as he was often in Jesselton on business.

Luther returned to Kota Belud with the first note for David's wife as David made his way to the wharf just off the main street in Jesselton. The layout of the town was rather similar to Kudat but on a larger scale. At the back of the main road was the neat, whitewashed Post Office and behind this the land rose up to a small hill on top of which sat the detached houses where the government officers had lived before the invasion. A few miles out of town was Tanjung Aru which was famous for having a yacht club and a lovely clean white sand beach. It was also the marshalling yard of the only railway line in North Borneo. This line wound its way south west down the coast through Papar and Kimanis and on to Beaufort. The first part of the route was through the muddy, fertile paddy fields that supplied most of the area with rice. At Beaufort it turned at right angles and headed south east to Tenom through a break in the Crocker Mountain Range and then took another ninety degree left turn to its final destination at Menlalap. It was a single track for most of the way with passing places at strategic points although so few trains used the line that they rarely met. Before the war it had carried passengers and freight to the isolated outposts of Empire and the rubber plantations nestling behind the mountains. The Japanese used it mainly to reach the town of Beaufort, one of their few military bases away from the coast.

David arrived at the wharf and was hailed by Taganam from a rather dilapidated looking boat tied up at the end. It was small and in need of a coat of paint with a wheelhouse about one third of the way back from the prow. It may once have been a fishing boat but was now loaded with various lumpy sacks and some wooden crates. David went aboard and was directed to a bench behind the wheelhouse. As they made ready to depart two Japanese soldiers appeared on the wharf and signalled for them to cut the engine. David was in a state of panic and felt sure they had come for him. His insides felt as if they had liquefied as he waited for the soldiers to seize him. When they boarded they ignored him completely and went straight to Taganam who, to David's surprise, greeted them warmly and gave each of them a small package. They clapped him on the back, turned and clambered up to the wharf where they wandered off talking animatedly and obviously in high spirits. David looked enquiringly at the unconcerned pirate.

'Opium,' was all he said as the boat puttered out to sea.

Once out of sound and sight of the town the boat suddenly leapt forward and was streaking across the waves at a high rate of knots. Obviously it had a much more powerful engine than David had expected to find in such a decrepit looking craft and was soon eating up the miles to Tawi-Tawi Island.

Taganam laughed. 'I saw the surprise on your face when we picked up speed. We can outrun nearly all the Japanese boats. We changed the engine for one that used to be in a large truck. It's a petrol engine and has greater power than the small diesel one it replaced.'

'But where do you find the fuel to run it?' David asked. 'We're very short of petrol and those few vehicles we've managed to keep away from the clutches of the Japanese can only be used occasionally.'

'We've quite a large supply in a fuel dump that the Filipino army set up on the island when they thought they could hold out and then mount an offensive against the Japanese. When you return to Jesselton you can take some cans of fuel with you so you'll be more mobile when the real fighting begins. The Japanese never check the boat when we return as they think we are only trading down the coast and the empty sacks we bring back help support that story.'

'That'd be a great help. We need to be able to move quickly when we receive news of American or Australian landings. Having the fuel will enable us to drive towards Jesselton and attack the Japanese from the rear.'

After a few hours David started feeling decidedly queasy then the boat, to his enormous relief, sailed in through a narrow gap in a coral reef surrounding the island and stopped at a short wooden jetty. A group of Filipino soldiers met them and helped unload the cargo. The sacks were opened and upended releasing a variety of objects including scrap iron and pieces of wood on to the beach. The sacks were then neatly folded and put back on board. The crates were given similar treatment and also returned to the vessel.

'What do you tell the Japs you are trading in?' David enquired.

'We tell them its spare parts for motor boats and construction materials. All they see is the metal and wood and these are of little interest to them. They are after more valuable cargoes to line their own pockets. They suspect the Chinese of smuggling out gold and valuables to prevent them being seized. These days they rarely check the load as we give them occasional sweeteners but we have to keep up the pretence just in case we meet a Japanese officer who insists on playing it by the book.'

David was led by Taganam into the trees lining the beach and along a rough track that followed the path of a small stream. They reached a clearing that had some wooden huts round the edge and a number of tents scattered haphazardly on the tough grass. It didn't look particularly well organised to David who was rather alarmed as he thought that all armies were disciplined and orderly. On reaching one of the huts David was told to wait outside and Taganam went in. David could hear a number of voices in the hut, some sounding angry. After about ten minutes a soldier came out and David was ushered into the darkness. It took a few moments for his eyes to adjust from the searing midday sun but he soon registered that there were four soldiers seated round a table made of a plank of wood perched on two ammunition boxes. One of the soldiers was noticeably fatter and older with silver hair and a uniform with a multitude of colourful decorations on it. David had already guessed this was Lt. Col. Nonez before he introduced himself and asked David to sit. They questioned him in great detail about his work, his family and what his association had done so far to thwart the Japanese invaders. David answered truthfully but was a little concerned at giving a stranger so much detail about his organisation that, in the wrong hands, could have catastrophic consequences for his family and friends. It was clear that they were as suspicious of him as he was of them and he surmised that the argument had been about him being brought to their camp without prior discussion. He knew they would have no hesitation in killing him if they thought he was an enemy agent. Luckily his contact with Lo Vun Lip that stretched back before the war gave him credibility for the time being. After the inquisition he was taken by the soldier to another hut and given some food and a mug of water. He was left alone in the hut and was relieved that the soldier didn't lock the door as he left. At least he wasn't being treated as a prisoner.

By evening David was becoming more and more concerned. Nobody had been to see him and he wondered if he dared to go outside and find out what was happening. He calculated that as he was not locked in then nothing bad would happen if he ventured out. With a pounding heart he slowly opened the door and stepped out onto the grass. He had expected to be challenged by a guard but, to his astonishment, the camp looked deserted. There were no signs of life and no sounds you would expect to hear in an army base. Not even a plume of smoke was visible. David walked further towards the centre of the field and turned round slowly to view the camp from all angles. Still he heard and saw nothing. He went to the first hut where he had been interrogated and pushed the door after first knocking on it. It was empty. Even the makeshift table and chairs had vanished. A perplexed David left the hut and wandered round the perimeter to see if there was a path leading to another sector. He rounded a large tree and suddenly found himself face to face with the pirate Taganam.

'You can now come to the proper camp,' he said. 'This one is a decoy for any stray Japanese planes that might cross the island. We deliberately left you here to see if you would try to signal in some prearranged way to the enemy. As you made no such effort then we feel we can trust you a little, at least for the time being.'

'This trust all seems to be one way,' complained David. 'How do I know I can rely on you to deliver me safely back to Borneo?'

'You don't. We hold all the cards. You'll return once the Colonel is fully satisfied that you are exactly who and what you claim to be. A reliable contact would be very useful to him and could make a great difference to the outcome of any battle. If we attacked from the sea then an attack from the land behind them would take the Japanese completely by surprise. You must do your best to convince the Filipinos that you're reliable.'

This time it was a much longer walk through the jungle and David's shirt was soon soaked with sweat as he wasn't really used to physical exercise. He told himself that when he returned he would do something to improve his fitness as it could possibly save his life. It wouldn't do the rest of them any harm either. He chuckled at the mental picture of some of his fellow shopkeepers and businessmen doing exercises on the *padang* each morning and even playing in a football match. Their opponents, he fantasised, could be the Japs. They would, of course, let them win to prevent them taking offence.

They reached the real headquarters of the army deep in the jungle. There was no clearing to alert the enemy from the sky and it was all well concealed beneath the thick green canopy. This was a much more orderly establishment with all the huts neat and tidy. David noticed a strange tube fitted to the roof of one of the huts and then realised it was taking away the smoke from the open cooking fire into some sort of filter that appeared to be made from leaves. Only a thin plume of white smoke was escaping and that soon dispersed in the branches before it could emerge and signal their position to any plane flying overhead. As a man of science David was impressed.

Lt. Col. Nonez was waiting for him and after a brief chat with Taganam beckoned David to go into his hut. Inside the hut was a Filipino woman and the Colonel introduced her to David as his wife Rosa. She looked very tired and drawn with dark rings around her eyes and she shook hands with him listlessly. They sat down and discussed a range of possible plans. Most of them sounded a bit too far fetched to have any chance of succeeding but David listened patiently and made his own points concisely and intelligently. He was in favour of the Colonel's troops landing away from any of the towns and getting into defendable positions before making any attack. The Colonel preferred a head on assault to make the Japanese panic and run. After more discussion it was decided that both plans could be utilised with some of the Filipinos in hiding and others, with the Sulu pirates, attacking from the sea. David's guerrillas would be used to prevent the Japanese escaping. David liked his association members being referred to as guerrillas and thought they would also be pleased. He decided to call them The Kinabalu Guerrillas as he felt that would bring in the power of the mountain on their side.

The Colonel's wife sat silently throughout the talking and when it finished she rose to get some refreshments. As she stood her knees buckled and she fell in a faint to the floor before anyone could reach her. David rushed to her side, took her pulse and checked her breathing. He reminded the Colonel that he was medically trained and, when she regained consciousness, gave her a thorough examination and questioned her about her health. By pulling down her lower eyelids and seeing white instead of a healthy pink he knew she was suffering from anaemia. This he could treat with a few suggestions to improve her diet. He explained the condition and its remedy to the Colonel who was visibly pleased and warmly pumped David's hand. His wife looked very relieved as she'd thought she was suffering from some terrible incurable illness. David felt that at last he'd been accepted by this motley rebel gang.

That evening, in the flickering light of a coconut-oil lamp they planned the first moves of the only rebellion the Japanese were to face in all the territories they had occupied although the Colonel was destined not to be a part of it. It was decided that David would return to Kota Belud and carry on his normal lifestyle without raising any suspicion and wait until they communicated with him again. Lt. Col. Nonez gave David a document stating that he was now in the services of the United States Army Forces in the Philippines in the Sulu Sector. It went on to appeal to all patriotic citizens to help David financially to purchase military supplies to destroy and exterminate the common enemy. It added that all money loaned would be backed by United States dollars to be collected after the war. David was inordinately proud of this document and packed it away very carefully.

Arrangements were quickly made for David's return and the same boat that had transported him to the island again took him back home. As well as his letter he had a United States Army Lieutenant's uniform to wear when the rebellion began. It was to give him authority and to show his guerrillas that he was a legitimate combatant. He also optimistically considered that it might mean he would be treated better if he were captured.

The return boat trip was uneventful and they saw no other craft as they rounded the northern tip of Borneo and back down the coast to Jesselton. David was pleased with his expedition and it gave him confidence to know his small group were not alone in the struggle. He went to see Vun Lip and told him all about the Island and its inhabitants. Vun Lip was delighted that David had made a good impression on the Colonel and his officers. All his dangerous and secretive work to inspire a rebellion seemed to be coming together in a most satisfactory manner.

On his return to Kota Belud David went home and contacted Luther to show him his new uniform, the cans of petrol and his letter from Lt. Col. Nonez. They talked for a long time about how to approach more rich Chinese merchants in other towns whilst avoiding the ever-present possibility of being denounced to the Japanese as traitors. They had been told that a number of the poorer Chinese had been recruited by the Kempetai to spy on their compatriots and would willingly turn them over to the secret police for a few dollars or a bag of rice. Quite a number of these spies were known to the Chinese community and they were tolerated because to do otherwise would only have meant reprisals. They were kept isolated and rarely found out anything of value for their masters so David and Luther felt reasonably safe in their work.

Some of the money they raised was used to buy clothing and medical supplies that were clandestinely sent by fishing boat to Lt. Col. Nonez and his troops on Tawi-Tawi. The rest was used to swell the bounty fund for the head-hunters and to buy more guns and ammunition.

Chapter 14

The Japanese had heard whispers about Tawi-Tawi. A spotter plane had been seen the fake camp and reported back. They decided to send a small expeditionary force to the island to find out what was going on and occupy it but they had an unexpectedly hot reception as the Sulus and Filipinos had been forewarned by friends in Jesselton. The Japanese landed but never even left the beach as they came under such fierce opposition and withering fire. They had expected a few local rebels and not an army complete with machine guns and mortars. After three fruitless days the Japanese had to withdraw and return to North Borneo leaving behind thirty-one of their men. These were captured by the Filipino force and handed over to the local Sulus who had no intention of keeping any prisoners so they loaded them onto boats and took them out to sea. Here they were beheaded and their torsos tossed into the water.

When the news filtered through to Jesselton it gave a great impetus to anti-Japanese feeling and inspired in the Chinese a desire to become more militant. They also wanted an active role in fighting the enemy. The Defence Association which they had formed gained support from nearly all the Chinese to rid the country of the oppressors. David was becoming a little too well known and decided it was time to leave Kota Belud and set up a military camp in the interior. He chose a remote rubber plantation up the Tuaran river about equidistant from Jesselton and Kota Belud and a dozen miles from Mount Kinabalu. He told the thirty men in his force that they would be safe in the embrace of Kinabalu's shadow. David had by now forgotten or at least put to the back of his mind, the instruction from Tom Field not to act until he was contacted about the liberation force. Here they waited impatiently for news from Tawi-Tawi. None came but another event overtook their plans.

The Japanese issued instructions in the autumn of 1943 that

all male Chinese youths would be conscripted into the Japanese army and be sent to fight wherever they were needed. This was a practice they had followed in other occupied countries such as Korea and also in Malaya where they had recruited disaffected members of the Indian Army who wanted home rule and had been abandoned when the British surrendered. They said they wanted at least three thousand youths who would be given a course of intensive and rigorous training in Jesselton before being deployed overseas. These were the very youths that David had hoped to recruit to his resistance group the Kinabalu Guerrillas.

The next piece of news forced them into immediate direct action. The Japanese next announced that they also intended to seize the daughters of local Chinese and use them as comfort girls for the troops. This was a step too far. The Chinese had always protected their daughters from predatory males, even those of their own community and certainly from the Japanese whom they regarded as being sex mad. Japanese and Korean girls were already housed in brothels in various buildings including the rectory of All Saints Church in Jesselton. Another, for officers, was in the Basel Mission School. These were not kept a secret from the local inhabitants as the Japanese could not think of any reason why they should be. To them it was a normal part of military life. The Chinese regarded their plan with disgust and viewed it as a most frightening threat.

David and Luther conferred at length. Who could they rely on for support? Most Chinese were behind them but they were unsure about what the reaction would be from the diverse tribes of the native population. Tom had deliberately not given him any clue as how to contact Asampit in case David was captured. The Bajaus in Kota Belud would certainly enjoy a battle but the support of the other tribes was doubtful. He knew he could call on the Filipinos on Tawi-Tawi but that would take time and he couldn't wait in case the Japanese put their plans into action before Lt. Col. Nonez could respond. They had no idea when the Australian liberation force would arrive and no way of contacting Tom.

'Luther,' implored David, 'we must act now before all the girls and boys are rounded up. It'll be too late once they've gone and we'll never see them again. I can't bear the thought of my sons being brutalised and my daughters defiled. We must agree on a date to give the Japs a shock they won't recover from.'

'You're right. In a few days it'll be the tenth day of the tenth month. That'll be a very good day to overthrow the invaders.'

The tenth day of the tenth month is a particularly auspicious day and of great significance to the Chinese. Known generally as the double tenth it was the anniversary of the establishment of the New China under Chiang Kai Shek. It was the day of liberation when the despotism and tyranny of the old dynasty were replaced by a more democratic regime.

A message was sent to Tawi-Tawi informing them of the uprising and begging them to come and support the Kinabalu Guerrillas by attacking from the sea. A rough plan of attack was conceived and, dressed in his US army uniform, David led his armed band of men towards Kota Belud. They had the benefit of surprise and took the small garrison of Japanese troops with ease, killing every last one of the enemy. Quickly they cut the telephone line to the capital so that they retained the initiative. The police, who hated their new masters, opened up the armoury for David and gave them their pick of the guns inside. Next they repossessed six of the trucks used by the occupiers and set off at high speed towards Jesselton. More men had joined their force in Kota Belud, including some of the local police, and they now numbered around fifty; all of them armed with rifles or handguns. Their shotguns were discarded in favour of the more accurate rifles but they did take the explosives they had hidden before the war. David's idea was to set large explosions along the waterfront in Jesselton so the Japanese would think they were being attacked by heavy fire from warships out to sea. If they could panic the Japanese into fleeing inland away from what they thought was an invasion force then they might have a chance to fight them on more equal terms in small groups in the jungle.

David and Luther knew that it was going to be a fierce fight for the capital of North Borneo but had no other option open to them. They knew that once the fighting started in Jesselton they would have to continue until the end and there would be no way back. If, and it was a big if, the Filipinos arrived in the next few days then they might drive the enemy from the country. What would happen after that was not considered.

To their relief there was no welcoming party for them as they entered Jesselton. All seemed very peaceful and calm as the drove the trucks to the godowns at the north end of the wharf. The few soldiers they saw never gave them a second glance and presumably believed they were delivering goods to be put on board the ships. Once they were hidden from the road they entered one of the large sheds which was owned by a businessman based in Kota Belud who had given them the keys and waited for the cover of darkness when they would set their explosive charges to detonate just before dawn.

The waiting was tense as they couldn't be sure that there hadn't been any of the troops from the Kota Belud garrison out on patrol when they had attacked. If any had been out then they would have returned to their base by now and could be travelling down to Jesselton to raise the alarm and ruin the surprise element. This would certainly make their task much more difficult and give the Japanese a distinct advantage. There was nothing to do but hope and the men tried to sleep for a while. Some of them went out in pairs to forage for food and fill up the water bottles. They returned with varying degrees of success. One couple came back with a large sack of rice they had liberated from a shop and another pair brought a sack squawking and squirming with its contents of two outraged chickens. Most could only find a few scraps thrown out as rubbish but at least they all brought back water to last them a few days.

Once the town was quiet and deserted the group of men

with knowledge of explosives crept out and placed the charges well hidden from any curious eyes. They inserted the fuses and then hid a distance away from each one ready to light them at a prearranged signal. Again, the waiting started to put them on edge and it was with great difficulty that some of the men kept calm. A few were actually sick with the tension. As the first streaks of light showed in the sky the sound of a whistle blown twice galvanised them into action. The fuses were lit and they returned swiftly to the godown where David was waiting. Just as they arrived the first charge exploded with a tremendous bang and this was soon followed by the others making the sky turn orange and debris rain down on the town. The effect was just as they had desired. They could hear great shouts from the town's inhabitants and then the Japanese troops came streaming down the road from their barracks. They were not in any formation or even keeping under cover so the guerrillas were able to pick them off with ease. When the troops following the first arrivals realised the fate of their comrades they turned and ran back towards the other end of town. David led his men in pursuit to prevent them digging in and defending from any position of strength. They caught up with most of them and despatched them with bullets and knives. There was still the problem of the Kempetai who lived in the Sports Club so Luther led a party of twenty heavily armed men straight there and put the building under withering fire. The secret police were forced to evacuate and were mown down as they came out.

With the Sports Club and the barracks taken it was time to take stock of their achievements. They were in complete control of the town and any Japanese soldiers still hiding were slowly winkled out. Some had been seen leaving towards the railway station but David had insufficient men to cover all the escape routes. He knew it wouldn't be long before they would be under attack from the soldiers who had fled and others who would join them from towns and villages all over the region once it was known that Jesselton had been taken. They calculated that they had killed at least a hundred and fifty soldiers and had taken no prisoners. Possibly a hundred had escaped the slaughter and would be regrouping outside the town. It was time to set up road blocks and take control of the railway line. David still hoped the Filipinos would land to boost his force and give them a far better chance of holding Jesselton and even breaking out to take other areas. He knew that without reinforcements they would have great difficulty pushing the Japanese out of the country and taking full control.

While waiting for the expected attack they destroyed the Japanese radio communications centre housed in a local church and released all the prisoners from the police station cells. The prisoners were given the choice of fleeing or joining David and his men. The police did nothing to stop them and some of the policemen joined the guerrilla group as had their colleagues in Kota Belud. Again the armoury was opened and they found they were in possession of more rifles as well as some mortars and a couple of machine guns. They were quite well armed but their numbers were still too few to mount any decisive action outside the town.

The first attack came at the railway station that was defended by Luther and his select band of twenty men. The Japanese came by train and stopped short of the station. They got out and using the train as cover moved slowly towards Luther's men. There was a fierce exchange of fire and there were casualties on both sides. Luther had the advantage of a machine gun he had set up to the side of the station and used this to rake the Japanese soldiers with a hail of bullets. The Japanese realised they needed more reinforcements and greater firepower and the train slowly backed away from the station, picking up the remaining soldiers and then departing down the narrow track. Luther had lost four of his best men and sent a message with a runner to David explaining what had happened and that the Japs could soon return with more soldiers and heavier weapons.

It was a difficult problem and David did not want to have his group destroyed little by little as they attempted to hold the town. He decided that without immediate support from Tawi-

131

Tawi it would be best to disperse and renew the attack at a later date. In fact he could probably have held out as the Japanese force in North Borneo was smaller than he'd estimated. Also he didn't know that Lt. Col. Nonez had already set out to join him. With their radio communications gone and the Kempetai eliminated the Kinabalu Guerrillas and the reinforcements could probably have taken the whole of the West Coast and even held it until the Australian liberating forces arrived.

But the decision had been made and the order was passed on to his men that those who had recently joined should return home and his own group comprising the original rebels would go back towards their base in the rubber plantation up the Tuaran River to await developments. Using the trucks they left the town before the local population knew what was happening. Before leaving, David posted a proclamation in prominent places declaring that he and his men had taken up arms to liberate the people from the tyranny of the occupying forces and asking for the full cooperation of the populace. He warned that all Japanese spies were known to them and would be dealt with harshly when the time was right. He accused the Japanese of great cruelty, reducing the people to poverty and the disgraceful treatment of women. He vowed to right these wrongs and to fight to the death to drive the Japanese from the country.

On the way back towards the base camp they met small groups of Japanese soldiers who were unaware of what had happened in Jesselton. These men were summarily executed so they couldn't tell their officers in which direction the guerrillas were going. It wasn't the wisest of decisions as the trail of dead soldiers gave the Japanese a good idea as to where they were heading. The guerrillas burned some of the bridges they crossed by soaking them in oil and then setting them on fire. This was to delay any pursuit but again they marked their trail. Eventually, still buoyed by success, they decided to set up a camp on the other side of the Tuaran River and wait.

In Jesselton the few Japanese soldiers who had fled

when the fighting started or were stationed outside the town cautiously re-entered along the roads and the railway to find their opponents gone and the streets deserted as the civilians cowered behind shuttered windows and barricaded doors. With no idea where or why their adversaries had disappeared the Japanese went on a rampage around the town and rounded up a hundred men at random to torture so as to find out who the rebels were and where they had gone to. The men were herded onto the *padang* and told to sit on the coarse grass. Ten were then taken and tied to the fence surrounding the green. In full view of their friends and neighbours their eyes were gouged out with bayonets and their stomachs cut open spilling their intestines on the bloody ground. The Japanese then called on the ninety remaining to save themselves by giving them information they required. A few called out that they knew nothing about the raid but a number had seen and recognised some of the rebels including David Wong and, thinking to save themselves, told their captors what they knew. Luckily none of them were aware of the whereabouts of David's headquarters. Their hope of salvation was in vain as the Japanese proceeded to either shoot them in the back of the neck or decapitate them with their swords. The *padang* was soon totally quiet and the murderers moved off to leave the families to claim the corpses of their loved ones.

Similar atrocities were committed in Kota Belud and in other villages and towns the Japanese thought might have information to help them capture the guerrillas. On the thirteenth of October, three days after the rebellion had started the Japanese forces eventually reached the final bridge over the river that had been destroyed by fire. They came under sniper fire from the opposite bank and took cover. Heavy machine gun fire raked the jungle and David's rebels were forced to retreat. On the following day more Japanese troops were brought up to the river and David retreated further to take up a defensive position near to the base camp. The Japanese now sent aircraft over the area and the guerrillas had no defence against this. Large areas of the forest were bombed and strafed causing many innocent villagers to be killed or wounded. They bombed any house that looked a likely target and followed up by sending foot soldiers to mop up any survivors.

There was now no alternative for the guerrillas but to retreat right back into the foothills of Mount Kinabalu. They were reluctant to move too far from the coast in case the Filipino army arrived by sea and they could then resurrect their original plan but this was now more difficult as the Japanese were again in full control of the coastal strip. Using binoculars and from a high vantage point they were able to catch a glimpse of the sea and they searched daily for any sign of an invasion force. Many argued that such a force would come at night and they were wasting their time. David remained optimistic although it was obvious some of the rebels were losing heart. Supplies were a constant problem. Lower down the mountain slopes they had been able to live off the land, gathering coconuts, stealing maize and fishing in the river but higher up the pickings were sparse and the men were hungry. Each night they sat by their small fire to keep out the chill of the wind and talked about the future. One by one they asked if they could return home to their families and David had to let them go. Eventually Luther also returned home and this left David without his trusted deputy and only a dozen men. These were mainly youngsters who were out for adventure and had no wives and children of their own. David realised his great plan was in tatters and faced failure.

Those who returned home were quickly rounded up by the Japanese as a price had been put on their heads and village spies soon turned them in. Under torture they were forced to mention more names until the Japanese had a full list of the remaining rebels and where they lived. To try to find more information they began to systematically question whole villages. The occupants were rounded up and herded on to the *padang* where the men were left in the sun to bake. The women and children were forced into the District Office in overcrowded conditions.

Men and women were repeatedly beaten to try to extract information from them. They were given a handful of rice each as a ration. When the torturers felt they could get nothing more of use from them they were released and could return home. Often they found that in their absence their belongings had been ransacked and homes burnt to the ground. None escaped the ordeal as more soldiers were drafted in from other parts of Borneo and the Chinese, Bajaus and Kadazan people were all taken. Some villagers fled when they saw the soldiers approach and this was taken as a sign of guilt. They were hunted down and shot. If a whole village was found to be deserted then it was torched. Old and young were mercilessly beaten as a reprisal because the Japanese already had the information they needed about David Wong and his band. A price was put on his head of five thousand dollars with smaller amounts of two or three thousand dollars on other rebels still at large. It was still only two weeks since the taking of Jesselton.

The Japanese formed two parties of Kempetai, soldiers and native police. One, mainly comprised of the police, was to search for the bodies of Japanese soldiers and the other to hunt down the guerrillas. More and more proclamations were issued threatening various punishments for any citizen who withheld information about the guerrillas. By the fifth of November the thirteen names on the list were still at large. They remained in the foothills trying to keep their spirits up but the stories of the atrocities in the towns and villages reached them and they began to feel guilt that they had caused so much suffering by their raid on Jesselton. They questioned themselves as to whether it had been worthwhile. The Japanese had executed around ten of the populace for every one soldier that the Kinabalu Guerrillas had killed. On the twelfth of November, the birthday of Dr Sun Yat Sun, the founder of the Chinese republic, they hoisted the national flag and sang patriotic songs and their national anthem. By now they were hunted men and their position worsened day by day. They made the joint decision to return to the coast and hide among friends.

135

Although appearing outwardly calm David's mind was in turmoil. He loved his family above all else and had never really considered that he might never see any of them again, watch them grow up, marry and give him a host of grandchildren to spoil and enjoy. The thought of his faithful and, to him, still young and beautiful wife made his heart ache and he couldn't see any way out of the corner he had pushed himself into. The only hope was that the army from Tawi-Tawi would somehow miraculously appear and rescue them and then they could regroup and start the offensive again. It was just as well he didn't know that the Filipino army had already landed down the coast and had been informed that David's rebels had been destroyed. It was a formidable force of specially chosen men armed with the latest American machine-guns and ammunition. They also brought thousands of dollars in cash. But without David's local knowledge of the land and the Japanese troop deployment it would have proved impossible for them to fight with any degree of success. So they had boarded their boats and sailed back to the island.

The guerrillas headed at night to a village of Northern Chinese people who had supported them with funds for the Tawi-Tawi resistance forces. These were trustworthy and, although their village was rather too near to the main road to Jesselton for complete safety, wouldn't betray them. They were hidden in the gravedigger's hut in the local cemetery and he was to bring them food and water in his wheelbarrow as he went to work. It was in an isolated spot on a hillside and no one passed that way unless there was a funeral. They hid for a week until their hiding place was given away.

The gravedigger was an inveterate gambler and drinker and the money David had given him to buy supplies for the fugitives in the cemetery was soon gone in a card school in the local bar. He explained to his fellow gamblers what the money he had lost was actually for and loudly asked them to give back some of their winnings so he could supply the much needed food to the cemetery where they were hiding. His pleas were overheard by a passing villager who happened to be employed by the Japanese as a spy. This man realised that he could soon be rich and ran to tell his masters where they could find the guerrillas.

The Japanese Command was overjoyed with the news. At four o'clock the next morning on the 19th December 1943 a hundred strong force of crack troops and Kempetai surrounded the cemetery. They called for David to surrender saying they would spare any of the villagers who had helped him if he came out without a shot being fired. Bravely but foolishly David decided to sacrifice himself for his friends and trusted the Japanese to keep their promise. He put on his American Lieutenant's uniform and walked slowly out of the hut with his arms held high. The rest of his group followed his lead and they stood fanned out in a chevron behind him. They moved down the hill to the road where the enemy waited. Some of them had expected to be shot as soon as they appeared but the Kempetai had other plans for them and didn't want them to die quickly. If they had come out firing at the massed troops they would have been mown down and had a much easier death. The soldiers tied them up and bundled them roughly into lorries to be taken with all haste to the Kempetai headquarters in the now repaired Sports Club in Jesselton. Here they were mercilessly tortured.

Over the next few days the prisoners were subjected to the very worst forms of torture the twisted minds of their captors could devise. David attempted to commit suicide but failed. He steadfastly refused to answer questions and would only state that he was solely responsible for the double tenth revolt. He didn't succumb to the torture and never gave away the names of any of his accomplices or supporters. Others from his group were not so strong and soon the Japanese had a long list of names that had been extracted under extreme duress. Many of the names were just friends and neighbours of the accused and had not been directly involved in the action but the prisoners gave their tormentors any names they could think of in the vain hope it would alleviate their suffering.

The list soon numbered over four hundred.

All of these were rounded up over Christmas and into the New Year of 1944. The fact of their arrest made them automatically guilty. They were held in terrible conditions in the town jail that had been built by the British to house no more than fifty prisoners. Their plight was desperate and a number committed suicide rather than give the Japanese the satisfaction of torturing and then killing them. There was no sanitation and very little food or water provided. With the heat and overcrowding the smell was horrendous and the Japanese decided that the time had come to end the chapter. This was not a humanitarian decision but because they wanted revenge and decided to hold a massacre of all the prisoners beside the railway line a couple of miles past Tanjung Aru where it crossed the Petagas River by bridge. Deep trenches were dug in the sandy soil and no traffic allowed along nearby roads for three days leading up to the killings. On the 21st January the prisoners were led from the jail and each one photographed holding a card bearing their name and a document that they had signed admitting to their complicity in the rebellion. As the documents were in Japanese then they had no idea what they had signed and few of them cared. There had been no trials so this action was presumably to make it look as if they had all pleaded guilty.

The prisoners were herded into six covered trucks at the halt outside the prison. These six trucks were in the middle of the train. At the front were carriages for the Japanese civil and military officials. No one wanted to miss the day's sport. To the rear of the train were some open trucks filled with soldiers of the Imperial Army. On arrival at the river the train stopped and the prisoners were pushed out and forced to walk in the direction of the prepared graves. They were surrounded by the Japanese soldiers and the officers then selected some of the men for special treatment. In this group were David Wong and Luther Kiong together with other senior members of the Kinabalu Guerrillas. They were photographed as a group and then beheaded. The other prisoners were shot and all the bodies were shoved unceremoniously into the ready made grave. Not all of them were dead and their cries could be heard in nearby villages for hours after the slaughter. No one dared to go to their aid as they feared they would suffer the same fate and eventually all was silent. The next day a working party was sent to fill in the grave and, they thought, conceal the evidence of the massacre.

Ah San, David's wife had heard the news of her husband's death and was trying her best to comfort her younger children. The man who had given her everything in life was gone and she had no idea how to continue without him. She had known little of his guerrilla activity until he had told her about it before he left for the hills. Her elder sons vowed to take revenge for what had happened to their father but Ah San just wanted the family to slip into obscurity and keep her sons away from danger. It was a difficult time for them as they had lost the only breadwinner and now the older children would have to forget the great hopes their parents had held for them and go to work in menial jobs just to stay alive.

In Jesselton Lo Vun Lip, who had been the original driving force behind the revolt, was incensed at the brutal reaction of the Japanese and planned another uprising. He still held nearly a quarter of a million dollars that had been raised from the community and wanted to use it to finance another resistance group. He plotted with some of his friends but they were being closely watched by the Japanese who deliberately gave them time so that all those involved could be identified. They kept a watchful eye on Vun Lip's movements and all who visited him. For a few weeks they did nothing to arouse his suspicions and let him think his plans were coming to fruition. When they felt they had all the conspirators in the bag they acted.

It was at a dinner party at Vun Lip's house for all his prominent business friends that the Japanese chose to arrest him. They wanted it to be dramatic to show his associates that they were in complete control and to oppose them would be suicide. It would give a message to the whole Chinese community. Lo Vun Lip was taken to the prison where he was held while they rounded up all the known members of the resistance movement.

Once again the Kempetai threw themselves with evident pleasure into their main sport of torture. They decided that Vun Lip should have alternate wet and dry torture. The dry torture was to hang him from the ceiling by his thumbs and burn him with coals from a charcoal brazier. This was followed by the wet torture which consisted of him being forced to drink two buckets of water and then they would stamp on his stomach until the water burst out of all his orifices. After twelve days of this he confessed to his involvement and named more of the conspirators. The torture stopped and all that remained was to try a novel method of execution for their delectation. It was to be based on a Chinese method of execution thought up by the First Emperor of China in his efforts to subjugate his new country. The Japanese felt it would be a rather symbolic gesture for the Chinese in Borneo to appreciate. Two buffaloes were brought to the prison compound and with the other prisoners lined up to watch Lo Vun Lip had a buffalo tied to his feet and the other to his hands. They were then driven off at speed in opposite directions. The remaining prisoners were left to view the gory remains before being taken back to their cells to await their own fate. A number of them managed to thwart their captors by committing suicide but the majority were beheaded a few days later. The Double Tenth revolt had ended and the Kinabalu Guerrillas were no more.

It had not been as much of a failure as David Wong had thought during his last hours. The Japanese had always wanted a quiet time in Borneo and the uprising had given them a lot of work as well as many dead soldiers. If they were to enjoy their time away from the battle that was raging across the Pacific then they needed to avoid any conflict that would bring them to the attention of the Supreme High Command in Tokyo. The plan to enlist the young Chinese men into the army was dropped and they also decided to leave the Chinese girls alone and not take them as sex slaves for the troops. Even taking local people for forced labour was abandoned and they used Javanese labourers shipped in to do the work of completing the airstrips and building defences. They decided that it would be a more productive policy to woo the native people and try to win their support. It was far too late for that to happen but they were arrogant enough to think they could succeed. This arrogance was to play a part in their eventual downfall.

Chapter 15

News of the fate of the Chinese rebels reached Asampit in his longhouse and he was deeply saddened despite not knowing any of the guerrillas particularly well. He had heard nothing from Tom for over a year and wondered if he would ever see him again. The expected drop of arms and supplies hadn't happened and he worried that Tom hadn't made it safely back to Australia. His sons longed for some action, especially his younger son Andaman who wanted to prove himself as a warrior and gain the respect of the village and the young woman he wanted to impress. Enduat, Andaman's older brother, recommended caution as he had carefully listened to, and taken in, Tom's advice about keeping in the background. The stories they had heard of the massacres of the innocent villagers along the coast was proof enough that the Japanese must not become suspicious of them. It was a dilemma and needed much thought if any plan was to succeed and avoid any reprisals.

Despite Andaman's vociferous protests they decided to hurt the Japanese without bloodshed. They reasoned that anything they could do to weaken the defences would be of use when Tom's promised liberation force landed. With this in mind they considered embarking on a programme of subtle sabotage. Asampit called the village elders to a meeting.

'We can't sit back and do nothing,' he began. 'It's our duty to rid the country of these evil men and return to our old traditional lives. *Tuan* Tom is an example to us all and his bravery in returning here must not be forgotten. He saved my son's life and I owe him my complete allegiance and everlasting friendship. How will we feel if he returns and finds we have done nothing but sit around smoking and drinking while he was away?'

'But we've no idea if he'll ever return,' argued one elder. 'We might just be risking our necks for nothing. We watched the clearing in the forest for weeks but no boxes arrived from the sky. Surely it's better to stay alive and bring up our families despite the hardships rather than lose everything.'

'That's the easy way out,' retorted Asampit scornfully. 'Have you no pride? You used to be one of our bravest warriors and now you talk like a toothless old crone. I expected better of you.'

There were general mutterings of agreement as Asampit outlined some possible plans. He then put it to the vote. The outcome was overwhelming support for him and his sons. Long into the night the men of the village considered various options and the more outrageous were discarded together with the high risk strategies. Eventually they decided on three main possible actions that they could hopefully complete without implicating themselves. All of them must appear as accidents to the Japanese rulers.

The first plan was to be implemented without delay. It was the simplest and probably the most ingenious of the three. The idea was to destroy some of the railway track that the Japanese used daily to transport troops and goods to the interior. If they could totally disrupt this line of transport and communication then it would deal the Japanese a severe blow and make any escape from the coast more difficult when the Australian army landed. They knew that along the coastal route from Jesselton the underlying soil was very sandy. If some could be removed from beneath the track then it would not take a particularly heavily loaded train to fall through or tip over and put the line out of action for weeks if not months. It might, they hoped, also lead to some deaths or serious injuries. A train carrying troops would be very welcome. The problem was how to remove the sand without arising any suspicion. Various possible solutions were discussed at length and it was decided that Enduat and another warrior would go and reconnoitre the line to find the best spot and see how the deed could be done. To blend in they would dress as peasant farmers and carry *changkols*, the digging tools used in the fields. They knew that any Japanese soldiers they met would not be able to tell that they were from a different tribe to the usual Kadazan farmers they saw daily in the area and so they should be able to pass unnoticed.

They set out the next morning on the two day trek to the railway. Once they were on the coastal plain they assumed their disguise and walked purposefully to look as innocuous as any other farmers in the area going about their daily business. They hoped that they would be able to complete their task without meeting anyone as there were many informers active near to and in the main settlements and any genuine farm workers would instantly recognise them as from the Murut tribe and conspicuously out of place. They had considered going at night but that would have made the reconnaissance much more difficult and might have aroused suspicion if they unfortunately met a patrol. When they reached the railway track they decided not to walk along it but to stay to the left hand side where they were given a little more cover by the scrubby vegetation growing between the line and the sea. They kept looking for likely places to undermine the rails but all the possible sites were too close to farms and a large group of men seen digging around the railway would have been noticed without fail. There was insufficient cover to hide them from prying eyes and, in any case, a train full of armed soldiers might come along at any time and discover them in their clandestine work.

After walking for an hour or so they came to the bridge over the Petagas River where, unbeknown to them, the Kinabalu Guerrillas had been massacred only a few months previously. It looked a likely site for their sabotage as the river itself might be used to help with the undermining of the track. The bridge itself was far too sturdy to be sabotaged as they had no explosives so the only possibility they could think of was to somehow divert the river around the bridge on one side or the other and under the rails. They studied the lie of the land for a while before Enduat suddenly realised that it would be better if they followed the river upstream and looked for a place to make a dam or blockage. This could then be released sending a wall of water down to the bridge where it would hopefully wash away the sand from each side of the bridge piers and leave the track dangling in space. If powerful enough it might even destroy the bridge completely.

Enduat and his companion made their way along the river bank through the farmland until the river wound uphill into the jungle. About half a mile later they came to a bend in the river and on the other side of this it narrowed and the water was tumbling roughly through a rocky gap. Scrambling up the slope and past the pinch point they found the river opened out and was calmer as it waited to rush headlong through the rocks. This was the ideal place to make a dam similar to the ones they built when fishing but much larger and stronger as they wanted to hold back as much water as possible. It would not be an easy task and Enduat reckoned they would need at least twenty men to make a successful structure. It was time to return to the longhouse and report their findings to Asampit and the elders.

They realised that they wouldn't have to backtrack to the railway as they could now just follow the river a little further inland before branching off on to the faint jungle path they knew led towards their home. This also made the whole enterprise a lot safer as a party of twenty or more men seen walking in the paddy fields towards the railway would certainly cause alarm. Now they could approach safely through the dense vegetation that was their normal habitat and melt back into it when the job was completed. They had no way of knowing when a train was likely to come along the line as unsurprisingly the timetable strictly adhered to by the British was no longer followed. Enduat hoped his father would let him hide near the bridge to see if their plan succeeded. Bursting to pass on the good news of their expedition they made good progress back to the expectant villagers and by travelling overnight they reached the longhouse before sunset the next day.

Asampit was very pleased with their account of the river and the way it could be dammed. With the others he planned the best way to construct the dam and the tools and equipment they would need to fell trees, cut branches and move rocks.

He agreed that they needed a large number of men for the work and settled on a party of twenty-five. Two of them together with Enduat were to act as lookouts down the river and a further two with Andaman upriver to prevent them being discovered. When the dam was completed and the water had built up behind it then Enduat and his men, dressed as farmers again, would go down to the bridge and wait to see the result of the torrent pouring down the valley to the sea. Enduat was naturally delighted although this was not what Andaman had hoped for. He wanted to be the one to see the outcome and was resentful that it was his older brother who had yet again been chosen for the most exciting part. He said nothing but his father could see the hurt in his face and determined to give him a leading role in the next exploit.

There was no need to wait for a rainy season to add to the water in the river as it rained in the hills nearly every day. They could set out as soon as they had assembled all the required equipment. The group were in good spirits as they followed Enduat in single file carrying axes, *changkols*, liana ropes and woven baskets to carry spoil and rocks. They also took their knives, hunting spears and blowpipes in case of attack together with some food for sustenance. As was their custom they had a couple of men go ahead and two others follow behind the column to watch out for any enemy patrols.

Moving silently as they neared the narrow gorge that Enduat had discovered they waited for an hour or so hidden in the jungle to make sure it was safe to start. The two lots of lookouts were in place and signalled by bird calls that no one was in the vicinity in either direction. The work commenced. Firstly they felled two large trees to put in a cross formation in the river. These were wedged in the rocks on each side and had ropes attached to them so they could be pulled apart when the water reached the required level. Asampit knew that to try and pull them back upstream against the pressure of the water would be impossible but to slide them sideways would probably be manageable with the men he had. With these in place a lattice work of branches was added and some rocks and soil placed at the base of the dam to give it extra strength and prevent leakage. Soon the water level was rising and they worked flat out to try to prevent too much water escaping by plugging holes as they appeared. This was extremely dangerous work as if the dam burst while they were in the water they would be swept away through the narrow gap and hurtle to their deaths. Asampit calculated that it would take about two hours before the dam gave way under the increasing pressure or, if not, then he would give the signal for the main logs to be pulled away and the torrent would start. He sent a messenger to Enduat to tell him it was time to go down to the bridge.

Enduat and his men made their way down the river bank towards the farmland and across the paddy fields to the bridge. The river was in a fairly deep channel as it went through the fields as there was a risk of occasional floods that would ruin the crops. The amount of water used by the farmers was carefully controlled to maximise the harvest. This meant that the imminent rush of water would reach the bridge without its power being dissipated on the land. They found a good vantage point in a small stand of trees away from the bridge and up a small hill in case the rising water reached them. They could hardly contain their excitement as they waited.

Asampit watched as the water level rose until it had almost reached the top of the dam. It still held so he raised his hand and when he brought it down the two groups of men on either side of the river pulled mightily on the ropes attached underwater to the main logs holding back the water. At first nothing happened and Asampit feared that their plan had failed. He prepared to remove part of the dam wall to release some of the water and ease the pressure when there came a groan followed by an almighty cracking sound and the groups of men hauling on the ropes fell back in two heaps of tangled limbs. Almost in slow motion the stones and sticks moved towards the narrow opening in the rock and then with a crashing noise the water was released and it surged in a foaming torrent through the gap.

Enduat heard a roaring sound and looked up towards the rainforest. He could see no change in the river and, like his father, wondered if they had failed. He glanced away and then one of the others nudged him hard in the ribs and he looked again and saw a wall of muddy water carrying a collection of debris coming at speed towards the bridge. He could hardly stifle a whoop of joy as it bounded towards them. On reaching the bridge it split in three and completely washed away the sand and earth surrounding the piers and supporting the track. The line was completely taken away and the bridge now stood starkly alone in a sea of mud and water. It would be a long time before any train would be able to chug along this track carrying the men and hardware of war. The main disappointment was that it was now so obvious a disaster that the chance of the next locomotive actually being derailed was highly unlikely. They turned to go back to rejoin the others.

Enduat couldn't resist one last look and surveyed the scene of devastation from the hill. He then saw something that would haunt him for many nights. The river was now back to its normal slow pace but at the edge of the now widened bed a stinking collection of corpses had been revealed. They were all dressed in civilian clothes and Enduat realised that he was viewing the results of a fairly recent burial. He didn't know it was the remains of the Kinabalu Guerrillas but guessed that the once hidden mass grave had been concealing yet more evidence of Japanese cruelty. His companions also looked on in horror at the sight and all three committed it to memory so as to be able to tell the rest of their village what they had seen unearthed.

They quickly made their way back to the others and told Asampit the good news about the railway's destruction. Again Asampit noticed the displeasure on Andaman's face at the attention being paid to his older brother. While Asampit and his men had waited for Enduat to return they had busied themselves removing all signs of human activity. The scars on the trees from which branches had been hewn and the two large stumps of the felled trees were covered in mud. Footprints were brushed away and dead leaves strewn around the area to hide any other marks caused by dragging the logs into position. Asampit knew that the Kempetai would investigate the disaster and didn't want them to have any idea that it was anything but an accident. He certainly didn't want to give them any excuse to instigate reprisals on the innocent farmers.

When he was satisfied that the Japanese would find no evidence of their presence Asampit gestured for the men to leave and melt back into the rainforest. They took their tools and weapons and set out for home. When they arrived back they sat with the elders and recounted what had happened. Everyone was very pleased with the successful outcome and spirits were high. Enduat now told them about his gruesome discovery and the mood turned flat. They did not know that it was David Wong and his men but realised they had stumbled upon yet another atrocity perpetrated by the dreaded Kempetai. After some thought it was decided not to mention the incident again as it might cause less trustworthy people to suspect that if they had been there and seen the corpses then they might have been responsible for the wrecking of the railway tracks. It would also be wise not to go ahead with the next act of sabotage until they were certain that they were above suspicion. The second plan would have to wait a few months until the end of the year.

Chapter 16

The frame of Colonel Barry Stevens filled the Field's doorway. His neatly clipped black moustache twitched as he tried to put on a friendly smile. He was not a welcome sight to Mary who stood wringing her hands.

'Tom's still at work,' she gabbled. 'He won't be home for half an hour or more. I have to pick up the girls from kindergarten and school soon. The baby needs changing. Can you come back later?'

Mary knew she was just talking to try and gain time to compose herself. She had tried to put Tom's involvement with the military to the back of her mind. The latest news was that the Americans were making good progress in their push for Japan and she had hoped that Tom would no longer be needed. Obviously she was mistaken. Why did it all have to start going wrong just before Christmas 1944? She had been preparing for a wonderful family day with no worries and now this man had appeared on their doorstep to spoil it all. The children were so excited. The girls had been whispering furtively as they planned the surprise presents that they would make for their parents and grandparents. Little JJ was going to have the first Christmas he'd enjoy as he'd only been a few weeks old at the previous one. What had she done to deserve this?

'I know Tom's still at work,' the Colonel explained. 'My early arrival was deliberate as I wanted to talk with you before he came home.'

'What do you want with me? You know Tom will make up his own mind. He's a good man and has a strong sense of duty. Hasn't he done enough to help you end this awful war?'

'He's been of tremendous value to the war effort and particularly to my department. I know Tom thinks the world of you and it would destroy him if he felt you didn't support him in his decisions. We can not and would not try to force him to return to North Borneo but it will be easier for him to make up his mind if he knows you're behind him. We need you as much as we need him'

'What you ask is very difficult, probably impossible. Tom can read me like a book and will soon know if I'm lying to him. I'll tell him what I feel but will try not to let my emotions run away with me. It must be his decision in the end.'

'I can't ask for anything more than that,' the Colonel sighed. 'Thank you for not making this as difficult as it could have been. Tom's a very lucky man to have you as his wife.'

'And I'm lucky to have him as a husband. I fervently hope and pray that I will still have my husband when the war ends.'

'I'm sure you will. I'll come back in about an hour to chat with you both.'

The Colonel left the house and Mary felt tears welling up behind her eyes. She went to the bedroom and clutched Tom's pyjamas to her face. His smell was still on them and she inhaled the familiar male scent deeply as she cried. She knew he would be home soon and after ten minutes of pure grief she made the superhuman effort to compose herself. With her face washed and her dress smoothed down she sat and waited for him to arrive.

Tom breezed in through the door and immediately knew something was not quite right. Mary was sitting as if frozen in an armchair and didn't come to give him his expected welcome home kiss and hug. He feared the worst.

'Has something happened to the children?' he blurted out. 'You look as if the world's about to end. What's the matter?'

'There's nothing wrong with the kids. I've just had a visitor. The Colonel.'

'Oh. What did he want?*

'He'll tell you himself. He's coming back shortly.'

Tom grabbed Mary by her hands and pulled her to her feet. He wrapped her in his arms and stroked her hair. She started to cry again. Not the wracking sobs of earlier but just a quiet weeping. She buried her head into his chest and they stood in a silent embrace until the doorbell rang. Normally they welcomed the sound but now it seemed too strident and insistent. Tom disentangled himself and went to the door. Mary tried but failed to look unconcerned.

It was the Colonel again. He looked a little ashamed and abashed. They went into the sitting room and he quickly addressed them.

'I must apologise for earlier. It was insensitive of me to arrive without warning. I should have 'phoned Tom at work to prepare you for what I now realise is a most unwelcome appearance. Especially so near to Christmas. My only excuse is that I've become so involved in preparing Australia's next move that I'm blind to everything else. Can we start again?'

'It's too late for that,' answered Tom. 'The damage has already been done. But we'll listen to what you say with open minds.'

'Before you start,' interjected Mary. 'I must 'phone my mother and ask her to pick up the girls.'

That task done they sat down.

'I must first advise you that what I'm about to tell you is top secret and must not be spoken of to anyone else, not even your closest family and friends.'

Tom and Mary nodded their assent and the Colonel continued.

'We have discussed the progress of the war with the Allies and decisions have been made. America is to continue with the main thrust in the Pacific with the intention of taking Japan. The British under General Slim are to force the Japanese out of Burma and down the Malay Peninsular. Our forces are to retake New Guinea and Borneo with all the surrounding islands in the Dutch East Indies. As we only have a small air force the Americans have offered to do the softening up of these areas by bombing the coastal towns and obliterating military targets such as airfields, supply dumps and army camps. They'll try to minimise the effect on the civilian populations but some damage is unavoidable. Once the Japanese infrastructure is destroyed then our troops will attack from the sea and men will

152

be landed to drive the Japs away from the coast and eliminate any stragglers. It's hoped that the bombing will start within the next few months and the landings are scheduled for the middle of next year. Borneo should be free from the enemy by autumn.'

'At last there's now hope of an end to this war,' Tom smiled briefly then looked serious again. 'But what has all of this to do with me? It would appear that everything is already in place and the strategic bombing will make the liberation of South East Asia much easier. We now have complete control of the seas and with the American's air superiority the final mopping up operation should surely be just a formality.'

'I wish that were true,' answered Colonel Stevens sadly. 'The mopping up as you call it is spread over a vast area with many islands. The Americans have already found out how difficult it is to dislodge the Japanese troops who fight to the last man standing. Even when they are all dead there are often booby traps to kill any of our troops who do not stay constantly on their guard. There are also many prisoners of war held all over Borneo not to mention the Europeans who are in internment camps. We must ensure that these people are safe from reprisals when the Japanese finally realise they are about to lose the war. It's imperative that we have good intelligence before the attack and some sort of armed force to hinder and harass the Japanese as they try to fight off our troops. We must quickly take all the main towns and gain a secure footing before moving forward to complete the operation.'

'I can see what you are leading up to,' Mary spoke softly. 'You're about to say that you need Tom to lead this guerrilla force and prevent the Japs from regrouping away from the towns.'

'You're correct,' agreed the Colonel. 'Tom's knowledge of the country and its people is an invaluable asset in our strategy. With his help we'll know where to find any pockets of resistance and make a two pronged attack on the enemy. Tom, I know I can't force you to help but if you're willing then it'll probably save many of our soldiers' lives and also shorten the war by weeks if not months.'

'So no pressure then? You know I'm totally loyal and willing to help if possible. Can you give us a few days to discuss it and become used to the situation?'

'Of course you must discuss it. But remember to keep it to yourselves. One loose word could jeopardise thousands of lives including those of your friends in North Borneo.'

The Colonel departed the Field's house and they just sat alone in their thoughts for what seemed like hours but was in fact only a matter of minutes. Eventually Mary broke the silence.

'I don't want to say anything to make you change your mind. You know exactly how I feel. Just get on with what has to be done and we'll deal with whatever happens as it occurs. I don't need to go through all the possible outcomes before you go as I will have plenty of time to dwell on them while you're away. Just promise me to do your very best to return to me and the children in one piece.'

'I promise. But I can't guarantee I'll be in one piece. Last time I left some of my teeth behind, remember?'

'How could I forget? I won't mind a few minor scrapes and scratches so long as you appear in our doorway again with the usual silly grin on your face. Now we must prepare for Christmas and appear our normal cheery selves to our family and friends. Let's make this the very best Christmas ever for the children and us.'

Nothing more was said on the matter and they both tried to make the next few weeks as joyful as they could given the cloud hanging menacingly over them.

Christmas passed pleasurably for the children and Mary's mother who knew nothing of Tom's clandestine activities. By New Year 1945 Tom had still not heard from the Colonel. Mary's father had been informed of his possible departure because Tom needed suitable and believable reasons for being away from the factory for long periods. The other workers were told he was finding new contracts and inspecting the quality of some of the work they contracted out to other factories. Mary started to think that the war might end before Tom was required to go but knew in her heart it was a forlorn hope. Despite the fact that they felt prepared the call came as a shock. The Colonel wanted Tom to attend an intensive training programme to build up his fitness again and to familiarise him with the new weapons and technical wizardry that had been developed since his last taste of action. In late January he set off again to the camp and was soon following a strict routine of exercise, unarmed and armed combat, communications and survival techniques. The days flew by and it was soon time for him to go. He was summoned to the Colonel's office.

'Well Tom, you've completed all the training successfully which is brilliant considering your age.'

'Is that a compliment sir? Or should I be considering retirement?' Tom laughed. 'Why is it that when you're over forty everything you do is qualified by a reference to your advanced years? Just telling me I'd passed would have been quite sufficient.'

'I take your point. But you are our oldest operative and we're very proud of your involvement. You realise this is the final mission and that there will be no submarine coming to bring you back. The next time you return will be for the victory parade with the rest of our troops.'

'Yes, I'd worked that out. Will I be taking one of the new long range lightweight radios?'

'Of course. And you'll also be in uniform this time. It wouldn't do for our boys to shoot you by mistake as one of the enemy. You'll be well armed and in constant contact with our invasion force commanders once their ships are in range of your radio receiver.'

'When's that likely to be? It's April already and the Pacific war seems to be won.'

'We hope to land after the American bombers have softened up the towns a little more. The first landing is planned for June on the island of Labuan which I'm sure is familiar to you. From there we will work our way up the coast to Jesselton and then down to Beaufort. When the coast is secure we will have to move further inland and destroy any of the enemy still causing problems. As we land we need you to lead some actions against the Japanese to make them wary about retreating into the jungle. If possible we will try to wipe them all out on the coast. We hope that when they realise there are armed groups waiting behind them then they'll be reluctant to venture far away from their usual defensive positions.'

'So I'm to make some trouble am I? I think I can manage that and I have the men who will revel in it. The Japs won't know what's hit them. But we'll still try to be subtle in our approach and minimise the danger to ourselves and the civilian population. I meant to ask, did you ever use the drop zone I found on my last trip?'

'I'm afraid not. After you had been caught we thought it would constitute too great a risk to your friends so we knocked it on the head.'

'We could resurrect the plan now couldn't we sir?' asked Tom. 'It might be useful to have some extra weapons and ammunition dropped in.'

'I'll think about that. Now all that remains to be done is for you to take a few days to see your family and then be off again. This time to the front line.'

Tom made his way out of the camp and returned to his home where Mary was waiting for him. All she seemed to do these days was wait and it didn't come any easier with practice. When Tom returned after this mission she vowed never to let him out of her sight so that she would never again know the empty feeling inside that accompanied the eternal waiting. She was determined to remain cheerful in front of Tom and the children so that he would not find leaving too difficult. He was welcomed home with the familiar kiss. They sat down and Tom outlined the job that was ahead of him. He stressed the fact that he would be in uniform and part of a large force. It was much safer for him he told her and there was every chance he would return within a couple of months and they could put the whole war behind them.

'Will we return to Kudat?' Mary asked. 'I'm not sure I could face all our friends and hear about the troubles I'm sure they must have endured whilst I was safe and well fed in Australia. Some of them mightn't have survived the war and that'd make me feel really guilty.'

'I've no idea love. Whatever we do we'll do together. I'd like to pick up where we left off but I don't know if it would work out after all that's happened. I'm sure that any of our friends and neighbours still there will be very pleased to see us and the kids. Just like us they'll be happy to have lived through it and survived. And now they'll have to call me Captain Field.'

'You're a Captain?' Mary saluted and giggled. 'That was the most rapid promotion I've ever heard of. A couple of months ago you weren't even in the army. Wait till I tell my brothers! They'll be green with envy.'

'Sorry dear but we must keep that to ourselves. As the Colonel said to us before Christmas we must not let anyone know what's happening. This invasion is very hush-hush and could be jeopardised by any talk. People know where I worked before the war and could draw some accurate conclusions. Once again I'll be leaving on company business.'

Three days later Tom was on his way back.

Chapter 17

'Now to put our second plan into action.' Asampit looked around at the assembled warriors. 'This one will take a great deal of stealth and nerve as it is hitting at the headquarters of the evil Kempetai. It will only need three men to achieve it but they must be able to blend in with the ordinary workers in the town. Any of you who look like seasoned warriors wouldn't last a minute so we must send young men who could pass as fishermen. I've decided that my younger son Andaman will lead the group and I'm sure he won't let us down.'

Andaman was expecting Enduat to be chosen again so wasn't really listening to his father. When he realised everyone was looking at him he guessed he was involved in some way but wasn't sure how. He had a puzzled expression on his youthful face.

'Didn't you hear me?' asked his father. 'I said you were to lead this next raid. But if you're not concentrating then maybe someone else should be in charge.'

Andaman gulped as he saw the opportunity slipping away. 'I was listening,' he rattled off quickly. 'I was just taken by surprise that you chose me. Of course I'll be the leader and you can trust me to complete the mission successfully. Thank you for having such faith in me.'

'I have faith in all my warriors,' Asampit pronounced. 'You must now pick two other young men to accompany you and then we will discuss exactly how you are to carry out the plan. I know you are longing for action but this raid needs patience and careful observation if it is to work.'

The other men departed to their own hearths and the four men sat and talked about how the plan would unfold. A fire was to cause the destruction of the Kempetai's headquarters. The three men were to go to Jesselton wearing local fishermen's clothes consisting of three-quarter length trousers, brown shirts and colourful scarves wound around their heads. Dressed like

158

that the Japanese would see them as visiting sailors from one of the islands and pay them scant attention. Jesselton thronged with such men along the waterfront and in the local cafes and bars so it would be easy to blend in. The headquarters was in the Sports Club which was only a short distance from the wharf and was next to the playing field which had trees surrounding it to give them good cover until they struck. For a few days they would watch the local workers coming and going to see if they could ascertain a pattern of movement. They had to discover where the kitchen was as that was the obvious place for a fire to start. They hoped it would have an outside door so that access would be easy and a safe escape possible. If not, then they would have to rethink their plan on the spot. Andaman was confident they could manage to find a way into the club without detection. He decided that he would be the one to set the fire and his face flushed with pride at the thought. Returning triumphant to the longhouse would be the finest moment of his young life.

With their disguises packed in rattan bags the trio set off confidently. They carried no weapons apart from their *parangs*, the knives that all men carried for everyday use. It would appear strange if they didn't wear knives going about their daily business. When they neared the town they changed into the fishermen's outfits and strolled down to the waterfront where David Wong had caused such consternation and panic with his explosives. It was fortunately quite busy again with small fishing vessels and some trading boats. Life was carrying on relatively normally despite the constant threat of American bombing raids. Andaman and his two accomplices nonchalantly looked at the various craft and into some of the godowns to see the range of goods being imported and exported. There didn't seem to be very much in the way of copra or rubber which was hardly surprising as the plantations had been neglected for three years and yields were now very low. Having reached the end of the harbour they retraced their steps to the other end near to the Kempetai's headquarters. Here they paused and lit hand-rolled cigarettes before moving round the *padang* to find a suitable vantage point where they could observe the comings and goings of the Kempetai and their native workers.

Andaman was eager for action and it took all his self-control to remain still and inconspicuous among the trees. They sat in a triangle facing inwards so two always had their backs to the headquarters and the third watched between them and reported what he saw happening. From a distance it looked as though they were playing some sort of game such as cards and not at all interested in any outside events. The two storey building they were watching was rectangular in plan with a balcony at the first floor level. This stretched round three sides. They learned that the Kempetai always came and went through a large centre door with five steps leading up to it. The ordinary soldiers appeared to use two other entrances; one to the left hand side of the main door and another out of sight at the far end of the building. The only other door they could see was set at the corner of the headquarters nearest to them. After over two hours watching nobody used that door to come or go. They decided they had been in the same place long enough and might attract attention so they moved to another position where they could watch that particular door even more closely. As they were now round the side it would also mean that they were no longer visible through the front windows and anyone who had seen them before would think they had gone for good. This time they stood and smoked whilst pretending to be deep in an animated conversation. Again they took it in turns to observe.

It was nearly dark when they left and they were still none the wiser as to the function of the corner door. It was solid wood with a narrow ventilation gap above it but no window nearby so even a closer inspection would reveal nothing. They went away despondently to find a safe place to spend the night. As they were dressed as fishermen they looked for a boat that was deserted and eventually found a small fishing vessel pulled up on the beach for repairs. It had a tiny wheelhouse and they crammed themselves uncomfortably into this and spent an unsettled night waiting for the dawn. At first light they moved out before any workmen appeared forcing them to make some lame excuses. Again they wandered through the town until Andaman reckoned it was time to resume their boring watch. To their surprise the door on the corner was open when they took up their position in the trees. They wondered if they could safely go any closer but before they had decided a figure came flying through the door followed by a fierce looking man with a greasy cloth tied round his waist. He was brandishing a meat cleaver at the unfortunate fellow who had preceded him and was now lying on the grass.

'If I catch you with your filthy paw in the rice sack again I'll cut it off,' roared the angry man who was obviously a cook. 'Now get back inside and carry on with what you were meant to be doing.'

The man rose from the ground and warily made his way past the chef and through the door. He was swiftly followed by the cleaver wielding cook who slammed the door behind him. The watchers strained their ears to hear if the door was being locked but heard no sound.

'We seem to have found the kitchen,' Andaman said softly. 'Now we need to know when it is unmanned.'

Ituk, who was a tall, thin youth, suggested that they could take it in turns to watch the building as three of them constantly together were more conspicuous to a casual onlooker. They all agreed it was a good idea and Andaman added that they should go into town and find some other coloured pieces of cloth to tie round their foreheads so that they appeared to be different men if glanced at from a distance. They were worried that they were becoming too familiar a sight in the neighbourhood. The shopping completed they worked out a rough rota and continued with their watch.

That evening they got together on the shore to compare their findings and discuss the next move. Now that they knew what the cook and his assistant looked like then they had been able to work out when they left. It seemed that they came and went through the doors used by the soldiers and the kitchen door, if that was what it was, stayed firmly shut all day. They wondered if it was usually kept locked. Perhaps in his anger the cook had neglected to lock it. There was only one way to find out.

Naturally Andaman took responsibility for this. The others urged caution and said that they should wait and watch for one day more. Andaman was unwilling to agree and wanted swift action as he desperately yearned for the approbation of his father and the quicker the undertaking was completed the sooner he could bathe in the praise and plaudits of his family and friends. It was nearly dark and many of the lights in the building were extinguished. They watched as soldiers returned to their barracks and the Kempetai to their large houses that had previously been the dwellings of the Europeans now festering in prison camps in Kuching. A few lights stayed on indicating that there were some Japanese on the premises but these lights were on the top floor and away from the kitchen. All the windows on the ground floor were in darkness. There were no permanent guards outside any of the doors but there was a regular foot patrol of two soldiers that marched around the area in a set pattern. If Andaman could gain access through the outside door then it would be a simple task to start a fire, escape back through the door and make a dash for the safety of the trees. The main risk entailed crossing the fifty yards of open grassy space between the trees and the headquarters. If he was seen by the patrol in the open near to the building he would be challenged and probably shot without question.

They had timed the patrol a number of times and it was clear that their routine didn't vary. There was a time gap of nearly four minutes when they would be out of sight round the other side and this would have to be long enough for Andaman to complete his task. He had a bundle of rags and paper scavenged during their wanderings along the waterfront and also a box of matches purchased in a general store. It was probable that the cooking was done on a kerosene stove so there would be plenty of fuel to make a decent blaze. The building was predominantly made of wood and would soon catch alight so the fire would rage uncontrollably in a matter of minutes.

Crouching down behind the tree nearest to the door Andaman watched the patrol disappear round the corner. He counted in his head until they reappeared at the far end and continued past the main door and back to the corner again. After checking their movements three times he found that each time he could count to two hundred before they appeared again. He thought he had long enough to enter the building without being detected so it was now time for action. His heart pounded high in his chest as he waited for them to turn the corner and then he took a deep breath and made his dash for the door. It was unlocked and he swiftly pulled it open and went inside. Even though his eyes were accustomed to the dark it was difficult to make out what was in the room. After barging into what seemed to be a metal table he risked striking a match and quickly took in the layout. The large cooking stove was against the far wall with the tank of kerosene alongside on the floor. He punctured the tank with his knife and the pungent fluid spilled out and spread rapidly over the stone flags. Spotting a large drum of cooking oil he wrenched off the metal cap and added this to the mix. With trembling fingers he struck a match and lit his bundle of tinder. It flared up immediately and he threw it onto the floor. The effect was startling as a wall of fire leapt up in front of him. He turned quickly to escape but slipped on the oily floor and fell to the side hitting his head with a sickening crunch on the corner of the metal table. He was out cold and knew nothing as the fire took hold and licked up his legs setting his clothes on fire and then igniting his hair.

Ituk and the other youth watched from the safety of the trees and saw Andaman go through the door. They heard the whoosh as the kerosene and oil exploded and waited for their friend to reappear. First a plume of smoke and then flames came through the small gap above the door. There was no sign of Andaman. They saw the patrol appear round the corner and heard their cries as they saw the blaze now taking hold of the building. The two soldiers ran to the kitchen door and one of them yelped when he touched the metal handle. There was nothing they could do to quench the fire so they shouted loudly to warn the occupants and after a short while a trickle of sleepy looking Japanese stood bemusedly on the grass outside the main door. Soon the whole structure was engulfed in flames and the sky lit up and glowed orange and red as the fierce fire reflected off the rising smoke. The two silent observers suddenly realised they were now exposed by the firelight and, realising that Andaman was not returning, made their way despondently through the trees and away from the roaring and crackling of the doomed Sports Club. Their assignment had been a triumph but at such a great expense and they wondered how they could break the difficult news to Asampit and his family.

Many people had come out from their homes to see the blaze and this made their escape much easier than if the streets had been deserted. They mingled with the noisy throng and, despite their sadness, were cheered by the comments they heard about the fate of the dreaded Kempetai headquarters. Most of the feelings expressed were of joy and many added that they hoped some of the enemy had perished in the fire. There was nothing left for the two men to do but quietly and unobtrusively leave Jesselton and head home.

Two days later they were close enough to the longhouse for the people to know they had returned. It was immediately noticed that Andaman was missing but nobody commented on it as Asampit had to be the first to receive any news, good or bad. The two young warriors slowly mounted the notched log leading to the main meeting area and sat in the shadows. Asampit came out of his door and sat before them. He knew something had gone wrong and steeled himself for their explanation.

'My son is dead,' he pronounced as a matter of fact and not as a question. 'I want to know all the details so I can start grieving.'

'He died bravely after fully completing our mission,' answered Ituk. 'All we know is he started the fire without being seen and although we waited until the building was fully ablaze he never emerged from the fire. Something must have gone wrong as he had enough time to escape.'

'Is it possible he was caught and is a prisoner?'

'No, we saw all the men who came out of the building and Andaman wasn't among them. He perished in the fire. It was so fierce he would have died quickly.'

'That is some small consolation,' Asampit reasoned. 'But more importantly he must have known that he had triumphed before he died. That thought will keep him in good spirits as he makes his journey to meet our ancestors. Thank you for your work and now please let me sit and remember his life. He was a fine son.'

The two left him alone with his thoughts and went to relate their tale to the other villagers. Enduat was angry with them and accused them of running away and deserting his brother when they could have saved him. They explained again that they were too far away and that the fire took hold much quicker than they had expected but he was not to be appeased. He stalked off to the jungle harbouring thoughts of revenge against both them and the cause of all the trouble, the Japanese. Later he calmed down and went to comfort his mother and father in their section of the longhouse. He voiced his concerns about the two who had survived but was swiftly put down by Asampit who told him that he fully believed their story and felt they had suffered almost as if Andaman was their own brother. He sent Enduat to apologise to them which he did, albeit rather reluctantly. It was only out of a deep respect for his father that he forced himself to take back his harsh words.

When Andaman had been suitably mourned the elders called a meeting to discuss the third plan they had devised to sabotage the Japanese cause. Firstly they talked about whether or not the plan should go ahead in the light of what had happened in the fire. Asampit was adamant that nothing had changed and that he was actually even more determined than ever to fight the invaders cruel grip over the country. Enduat, of course, agreed and wanted swift retribution. With that decision made they set to working out the details of the next plan but this one was destined never to be carried out.

Chapter 18

'Never again,' vowed Tom to himself as he boarded the confined space of the submarine. 'If I live to be ninety-five I'll avoid this particular form of travel torture. I like to see where I'm going and not just trundle along blind in an oversized cigar case.'

The sub was to drop him off as near to Kota Belud as possible so he would have a relatively short journey to Asampit's longhouse. This time there would be no need to find a safe place for the dinghy to be stored as it wasn't needed for his return. He was dressed, as had been promised, in combat uniform and armed with the latest M3A1 version of the Thompson submachine gun and an M1911 pistol as they used the same .45 ACP ammunition. A lightweight radio, water bottle, first aid pack and some emergency rations completed his kit. The arms, ammunition and radio meant that he was not travelling as light as on his previous missions but the fitness training in the camp had hardened his muscles so he was able to carry the extras without any problems. 'And all this despite my advanced age,' he thought with a wry smile.

It hadn't been possible to make the landing coincide with a new moon and there was little cloud cover so it seemed very light when Tom emerged from the conning tower to leave for the shore. There were no lights twinkling in the trees behind the beach and no sounds reached the men as they helped Tom into his little craft. Tom didn't know the area as well as he knew Bak Bak near Kudat so he was a little apprehensive about what he might encounter when he landed. His hand gripped the handle of the large hunting knife tucked in his belt and it gave him some comfort and confidence. It had been a present from his father-in-law who reckoned it might prove useful in the jungle. He was immensely proud of Tom and had supported him throughout his clandestine missions into enemy territory. In fact he wished he were younger and could join Tom in his exploits. But he still worried that his beloved grandchildren could end up fatherless.

The waves were small and Tom soon reached the shore where he beached the dinghy. He slashed the rubberised fabric with his knife to deflate it and buried it quickly in the sand. He knew it might be discovered eventually but by then it would be too late to cause him any problem. Moving swiftly away from the beach and into the deep shadow of the moonlit trees he waited to see or hear if anyone had witnessed his arrival. All remained quiet but he stayed unmoving for a further ten minutes or so just to be sure. His previous encounter with the occupying troops had made him extremely wary and he had no intention of a repeat meeting even though he was fully armed this time. The main thing was to reach his old friend undetected and then the action could start. No precise date had been finally set for the Australian landing so Tom hoped his radio would continue functioning in the humid conditions long enough for him to receive the much anticipated signal. He would then, with the Murut warriors, be able to give them the necessary support from behind the enemy lines. But before that occurred he had another idea to discuss with Asampit.

He gave the town a wide berth and was soon on familiar ground at the place where he had met up with David Wong during his first return visit and knew the way from here to the longhouse. At least to where the longhouse had been two years earlier. He knew very little about what had happened in his absence including the result of David Wong's rebellion. Tom still thought the Chinese would be joining him and Asampit to harass and fight the invaders. Nor did he know of the death of Andaman that had happened only a few weeks prior to his arrival. He felt sure he would receive a warm welcome from his old friend and was looking forward to meeting him again even if it meant another night drinking *tapai*. Buoyed by the thought he made good time in his hike towards the hills. As he walked he occasionally looked up to see the black hump of Mount Kinabalu ever present in the distance.

A small hunting party spotted him and came out from the jungle to bid him welcome. He knew some of them by sight so he was confident they would take him to Asampit. This they did and the two men were soon embracing. Each of them had a great deal to tell the other and they were both impatient to start swapping news. But first the formalities of greeting an honoured guest had to take precedence and this was done with almost indecent haste, or so thought some of the more conservative elders. Next the large *tapai* jars were brought out and the time honoured ceremony of getting drunk was soon enthusiastically underway. Good news was swapped at the start and Asampit was delighted with the news that Tom now had a son to carry on the family name. He told Tom how successful the sabotage of the railway had been and that the Japanese never suspected a thing and regarded it as plain bad luck. His face went solemn when he recounted the details of the fire in the Kempetai's headquarters. The loss of his son still gave him great heartache and Tom realised the sacrifice that had been made to carry on the fight. He was almost as sorrowful as his friend as he remembered Andaman as a proud yet friendly youth who desperately wanted to impress his father. Next Tom was told of the double tenth rebellion and its aftermath. He heard of the initial successes in Kota Belud and Jesselton and was astonished at the bravery of the Kinabalu Guerrillas in taking on a regular army. The account of David Wong's capture and execution saddened him considerably as he had liked the man immensely and decided that he would do what he could to make his sacrifice worthwhile. Enduat then told him of the chance discovery of the corpses buried near the river that they had unearthed when destroying the railway bridge. With the bad news out of the way it was time to plan for the future.

First they admired Tom's weaponry and all the warriors had a try holding the submachine gun, feeling its cold metal and weighing it in their hands to assess its balance. They were suitably impressed although some of the elders thought that guns were no improvement over their traditional hunting and fighting methods. They considered guns too noisy and inaccurate.

'The date for the landing of the Australian troops has not been set,' related Tom as he showed them his radio. 'I will be tuning in at regular intervals on a set frequency that will put me in contact with the approaching ships when they are in range. When we know they are close to the landing beaches then that will be our signal to move towards the coast and attack the Japs from the rear.'

'How soon is it likely to be?' asked Enduat who was eager to avenge the death of his brother.

'Certainly some time in June. That's about six weeks away. We'll have a few days notice of the landings so there'll be plenty of time to get into position. Until then we must cause as much trouble as we can. After four weeks we can throw caution to the wind and start openly attacking Japanese patrols to capture their guns and be better armed for the final battle. There'll also be an air drop of guns and ammunition at the place we identified last time I was here.'

'That'll be difficult to find now because the jungle will have claimed even more of it,' explained Asampit. 'But I'll send a group of workers to cut back and burn the vegetation so it's again easily spotted from the air.'

Enduat then smiled, 'I look forward to the day we strike against the foe *tuan* Tom. We've spent too long hiding and acting in secret. It'll be good to stand up as men to these invaders who have killed so many of our people purely for their own pleasure. Not one of them will leave our country alive.'

'We still have a third act of sabotage planned,' said Asampit. 'Will we still be using it?'

'What's the plan?' asked Tom.

'The idea is to contaminate the fuel stored in large tanks near Kota Belud so that when the Japanese try to use their vehicles they won't work. It's a dangerous task as the fuel dump is well guarded but we might be able to disguise some of our men as mechanics and gain access to the site.'

'I think it's too risky,' mused Tom. 'If you were caught the Japanese would be merciless and it would put them on their guard. In any case the Americans will soon be bombing all the fuel dumps as well as the coastal towns and any supply lines such as the railway. However, I've an idea to make them suffer through friendship.'

'What do you mean?' one of the elders asked. 'How can we cause them any grief by befriending them? It doesn't make any sense.'

Tom outlined his plan to organise a feast for the Japanese officers. He knew they were probably now worried about what might befall them if the unthinkable happened and they lost the war. He hoped it would make them receptive to friendly overtures from the local people. Asampit and three of his elders were to go to Jesselton and give the Japanese an invitation to a feast. They were to make up some story about it being a particularly important day in their village with a tradition that they had to invite all the local headmen and that, of course, would include the ruling Japanese soldiers. Asampit worried that they might not believe the tale and just arrest him but Tom convinced him that the Japanese were now only too grateful for any support and had no reason to fear the native population. They had only ever considered the Chinese and the Europeans to be a threat. He was sure they would fall over themselves to be invited to a feast.

For many hours the elders talked about how to arrange the feast and where it should take place. There were many suggestions made and they all became quite excited at the idea. Some were in favour of having music and dancing but others voiced concerns that the girls might be abused if it went wrong. Asampit was adamant that he would be there with his wife to make the event seem normal. The idea of constructing a mock longhouse was Enduat's and everyone was delighted at the audacity of the plan. For it to work without raising suspicion it was decided that Asampit would go to the town with another longhouse chief who was already known to the Japanese as he supplied some of their rice. The date was set for the feast giving them just four weeks to construct a longhouse in a virgin piece of forest and prepare the meal.

It was good for Tom to be involved in the preparations as he was impatient for action and he helped the other men cut wood and make bamboo flooring. It had to look fairly old so they rubbed the wood with a foul mixture of mud, ash and animal droppings. It would not only give it an authentic look but an authentic smell as well thought Tom amusedly. Every evening he strung the wire aerial for the radio between the trees and tuned in to the pre-arranged frequency. All he heard was static and the villagers soon tired of joining him in anticipation of some news. A couple of men were constantly watching the now cleared drop zone in the jungle in case any supplies arrived. Nothing happened for days and Tom started to wonder if the invasion had been called off for some reason. He knew that to act prematurely would be disastrous and fretted that all was still on course.

After three weeks the men watching for the airborne supplies rushed into the longhouse and excitedly told the others that a plane had just flown over and a number of wooden boxes had fallen to the ground on parachutes. They had quickly hidden the crates and the parachutes and come straight back to the village with the news. A larger party of men and youths immediately set off to retrieve the goods and bring them back to the longhouse. There was a buzz of anticipation as the long awaited boxes were carried to the open ground outside the house and noisily unpacked with a great splintering of wood as the men used their knives to prise out the nails. As each rifle was freed it was held up like a trophy for everyone's inspection. In all there were thirty rifles with ammunition, some hand grenades, first aid equipment, camouflage clothing and the long awaited food for the villagers. One of the cases also contained a tin box with Tom's name on it. Inside he found letters from his family, photos of the children and a cake supposedly made by Sarah his elder daughter. He shared this with Asampit and his family and they dutifully pronounced it to be excellent. Tom had hoped for possibly a mortar and definitely another submachine gun but had to make do with the rifles. He wasn't sure how the Murut tribesmen would take to the camouflage trousers as they rarely wore anything but a loincloth. The first aid supplies were very welcome as they would be useful in the village even if there were no casualties from any fighting. A few of the warriors had some experience of using guns but these were usually shotguns or ancient hunting rifles. None of them had seen a hand grenade before never mind thrown one so Tom embarked on a swift training programme to make them a more effective force. Naturally he expected them to continue using their own deadly weapons as these were silent and could completely shred the nerves of the enemy waiting for a poisoned arrow to reach its mark. Tom was well aware of the psychological advantage to be gained by encouraging the enemy's fear of the unknown.

The training had to be extremely basic because Tom expected to hear from the Australian Navy any day. The rifles were simple to use as they were the pre-war Lee-Enfield bolt action version made by SAF Lithgow in Australia. It only took a few days to make the men proficient in the use of the rifle and many of them became excellent shots as they had been trained from birth to aim accurately at small distant targets such as birds and monkeys and had a very steady grip. The hand grenades were a different matter. Tom demonstrated with one live grenade to give them an idea of how long it took for the grenade to explode after removing the pin. He then had them practise with stones from the river that were similar in size and weight until most of them seemed to have understood the routine of pulling the pin, drawing back the arm, tossing the grenade and then falling face down to avoid any of the blast. A couple of the men had trouble with the arm action and others experienced difficulty with the timing of the release. Eventually, worried about accidents, he decided that he would only give the live grenades to the ones who were confident in the whole process.

As Tom had thought, the camouflage clothing was not well received. They found it cumbersome and hot as well as not being particularly useful in helping them blend in with the rainforest. As Asampit pointed out, they had many years experience travelling unseen through the jungle and their brown bodies were camouflage enough. All of them were supremely confident that they would be able to approach a Japanese patrol and kill them without ever being spotted. Most of the clothing was returned to its crate to be used after the war in a number of highly imaginative ways by the women of the village.

Asampit had meanwhile managed to make contact with Kiyo Konno the senior Japanese officer in Jesselton. He had forced himself to bow low to the soldier and to ingratiate himself to him by many flattering comments translated by a rather bemused local fisherman who had worked on a Japanese boat before the war. He also gave the officer presents of knives and spears from the longhouse and some of the finest of their *tapai* to drink. Eventually he told Kiyo Konno about the planned feast and asked if he would like to attend with his fellow officers. Kiyo was delighted as it was the first time any local people had invited him to anything and he also felt that Asampit could be a useful contact if the fortunes of war turned against them. The day was agreed and Asampit told Kiyo that he would send a man to help them find their way to the longhouse.

All the carefully made plans for the feast swung into action and the villagers transported all manner of goods through the jungle to make the imitation longhouse appear to be lived in. They even took a few pigs to put underneath to add their distinct noise and aroma to the place. The elders decided against taking any children and hoped the guests would not notice their absence. The dancing girls were an important part of the plan as a diversion for the soldiers and to put them at their ease. It was planned that the girls would leave well before the final action commenced. All the necessary food and dishes were prepared in advance so that there would be a minimum of cooking done on the day. Many jars of *tapai* were carefully carried along the jungle paths and placed to the side of the main eating and entertaining area.

The trap was set.

It was a huge success.

Not a single guest survived the feast.

Chapter 19

Captain Yukina Matsai sat at a desk in his humid office situated in the centre of the administration block of the largest prisoner of war camp in North Borneo. It was on the other side of the country from Jesselton near the coastal town of Sandakan. He was squat figure of a man with a big face that seemed larger because he had no discernable neck as rolls of fat seamlessly joined his head to his sweating chest. Squirming to get comfortable in his cane chair he looked out of the window and viewed with distaste and annoyance the few prisoners he could see toiling in the camp flowerbeds. He ruminated on the problem that confronted him. Most of the prisoners in the camp had been captured at the fall of Singapore and were brought to North Borneo to work as slave labour on a variety of projects including building a military airport. In 1942 there were around two thousand Australian and seven hundred and fifty British prisoners incarcerated under Captain Matsai's strict regime. When those works had finished in 1944 a surprising number had survived and 2240 were still alive. His problem was that they no longer served a useful purpose and he had to decide what to do with them.

After some thought he concluded that it would be a good idea to reduce their numbers and make his job easier. Their rations and Red Cross parcels could then be diverted to his troops or sold to the local population who would pay good money or even trade gold for extra food and medical supplies. There would be no need to tell his superiors that the numbers had dropped. At least not for a while. He hoped to be a rich man whatever the outcome of the war. With his soldiers and the Kempetai he then embarked on a systematic plan of starvation and punishment that killed the inmates as successfully as if they had been shot. Many would have preferred that fate. Medical supplies were stopped and even the sick were regularly flogged and beaten for the guards' amusement. He designed a punishment cage to incarcerate prisoners who annoyed or offended him. It was just over four feet high and wide and five feet long so a man couldn't lie down properly. They were given no blanket or mosquito net so they suffered terrible bites to add to their hunger and thirst. Men were kept cramped up in the small space with the sun burning them and no food or water for days on end until they lost consciousness. Soldiers would take them out of the cage and revive them only to return them to it for further punishment. Captain Matsai thought it all good sport and spent his slothful days enjoying their suffering and dreaming up new and novel tortures.

An Australian former teacher, Lt. John Watson, was dragged before him one day charged with trying to communicate with the local people. There was no proof but Matsai pronounced him guilty as he wanted to try out another torture to see if a man could survive it. John was to be his guinea pig.

The Kempetai had lost patience with him as he refused to name any of his supposed accomplices and were on the verge of executing him when the kind Captain rescued him from their clutches to subject him to a terrifying form of punishment. He smiled at John when he was standing before him.

'Are you hungry?' he enquired solicitously.

'Of course,' replied John defiantly. 'We're all hungry. We are always hungry.'

'Well, we'll soon do something about that. Guards, bring him some rice and water.'

The guards had been briefed in advance and went out smirking to fetch the food and drink that John so earnestly craved. They returned quickly with a sack of raw rice, a spoon and a hosepipe.

'Now you will eat your fill,' smiled Matsai.

The guards forced open John's mouth and spooned the rice down his throat. To avoid choking he had to swallow until his stomach was full. He was then laid on the floor and the hosepipe that had one end connected to a tap through the open window was forced down his neck. The water was turned on

177

and it gushed in to him until it overflowed from his mouth and he could take no more.

'There. Now you are well fed and watered,' gloated the Captain. 'Take him to the cage and lock him in.'

The cage was situated where the Captain could observe the suffering of his charges and help to while away the long days. He watched with interest to see what would develop. It took longer than he had thought and it was not for about three hours that he could see any reaction to the experiment. Then John visibly started to grow fatter. He was nought but a skeleton anyway so the swelling to his stomach was much more pronounced. His face registered extreme discomfort as the raw rice cooked slowly in his body heat and tried to take up more space than there was available in his scrawny frame. He screamed as it forced its way into his small intestine and back up his throat partly choking him. In intense agony for nearly four days the rice eventually forced its way through his system taking part of the bowel out with it. This John managed to push back in by hand. Matsai was most pleased with the outcome and added the method to his lengthening list of sickening pastimes.

Many men were summarily beaten over the next few months, often by Matsai himself. The offences cited were generally for laziness which was not difficult to prove as there was no work available anyway. Prisoners' health started to deteriorate rapidly as did their morale. The list of dead lengthened. Over three hundred died in March 1945 and then there were only about one thousand six hundred prisoners remaining.

One day in April there was a feeling of rising panic among the Japanese officers. They had heard the Americans had taken the island of Palawan, part of the Philippines which lay to the north of Borneo. They were worried it might be used to launch an invasion and decided to move some of the prisoners towards the interior to Ranau which is near the Poring Hot Springs where Tom poisoned the soldiers years earlier. It was a trek of over one hundred and fifty miles through unforgiving jungle along barely marked tracks. The twelve hundred men who were too weak to walk far were left behind in Sandakan to die of their illnesses or from the American bombing that was becoming more and more frequent. The airport that the prisoners had worked so hard to build was already totally destroyed and the town of Sandakan was disappearing fast under the heavy bombardment. It was not a safe place to be.

In nine groups of fifty the prisoners set off at daily intervals. They had to carry their rations, ammunition and even the Japanese officers' kit so each man had a load of forty to sixty pounds. Half the men had no footwear and were suffering from jungle ulcers. Many others had malaria and beri-beri so were in a very weak condition. The weather also conspired against them and the torrential rain every day washed away the paths and turned them into small rivers of mud. The prisoners were driven on by their guards and those who fell behind were shot, bayoneted or just left to die. One Australian sergeant was very weak from the effects of beri-beri and he pleaded with his sergeant major to shoot him. He wrote out an authority and the sergeant major took it to the Japanese officer who amazingly gave him his own revolver. The sergeant major shot his comrade and returned the gun to its owner without any thought of using it to try and escape. Such notions had left most of the prisoners' minds months ago and they knew they were probably too weak to survive in the jungle. Although twenty-one days had been allowed for the march most of the groups completed it in fifteen or sixteen days. The relentless pace accounted for the unnecessary deaths of many men. When they eventually assembled at Ranau in April only about one hundred and fifty men out of the original four hundred and seventy were still alive.

Once in Ranau life improved for a few weeks as they were no longer marching or working. The rations stayed as meagre as before and there was still no medical attention for the seriously ill men. There were no shelters to keep them out of the continuous rain that fell every afternoon at four o'clock as if to order. After their rest period they were again set to work on menial tasks such as building huts, thatching, fetching wood and water and within a month a further hundred had died. The remaining men were then given the job of transporting sacks of rice to a Japanese post at Paginatan. Each sack weighed forty-five pounds and the journey out took three days, mostly uphill. On the second day the killing began. Men were bayoneted and shot for walking too slowly and their loads distributed among the remaining prisoners. More were killed on the two day return journey. At the end only a few were still alive.

Now it was May and the Americans continued to bomb Sandakan. The Japanese, still in great fear of an impending invasion, decided to move all the remaining prisoners, now numbering eight hundred, to Ranau with total disregard for their physical condition. Life in Sandakan had become too dangerous to stay as rats had taken over the camp and the bombing had already claimed many lives including thirty of the prisoners. The rice ration had been stopped completely and the water supply was contaminated. Of the eight hundred it turned out that only just over five hundred were capable of walking at all and these were herded up for the march inland.

Before leaving the town the Japanese troops exploded the ammunition dumps and torched the camp. The remaining dying prisoners were left unguarded to fend for themselves. In an almost unheard of act of charity the Japanese made them a present of five pigs. These could either be eaten or traded with the remaining local people for rice, fruit and vegetables.

In ten groups the long trek started. Any men who couldn't continue were, as usual, left to die at the side of the track. The marchers kept finding the unburied remains of the men who had died on the previous march and the stench of death pervaded the already foetid air of the jungle. More and more men were unable to continue through the thick mud that reached over their knees. As they reached each hill they crawled up on all fours and then slid down the other side. At last they reached Ranau. The head count showed that one hundred and eighty-six of the original five hundred and thirty-six made it.

Events were now moving towards their horrifying climax. The prisoners realised that they were all going to die and most were resigned to their fate. They were so ill they considered death a blessed relief. Forty men died in the first fortnight and the remainder were too weak to give them a decent burial. They had heard rumours of a proposed allied landing but this only drove them deeper into despair because they knew the Japanese would never allow them to survive and relate their tale to the world. But four of the prisoners made a plan. They were going to escape. It was, they reasoned, better to take a chance of being shot on the run than the certain death that awaited them. They ran.

The four were Ted Owen, Dave Wilson, Toby Long and Frederick Johnson. They were all from the same army unit and had been firm friends since their days in Singapore. Although they had little in common either in background or appearance they had somehow bonded so well that their friendship had kept them alive through all the dark days and nights of incessant suffering. Their support for each other had been the main factor in their survival and they were not to be beaten at the final hurdle. It would not be difficult to escape as the Japanese had long since given up calling a roll and had no real idea how many prisoners were still alive each day. They just ran into the jungle and hoped for the best.

After two days without seeing a soul they began to feel safe. Then they turned a corner and met a Japanese patrol. They pretended they were still prisoners returning from delivering some supplies and were waiting for their escort. As they spoke an American bomber roared overhead and they all dived for cover. When it had gone they realised that so had the Japanese soldiers.

'That was close,' breathed Toby, the fittest of the group. 'We mustn't relax our guard until we reach safety.'

'How do we know where safety is?' asked Ted. 'We've no idea where the landings, if any, were made. We could be heading completely the wrong way.'

'Any direction away from the camp is good enough for me,' chipped in Dave the eternal optimist. 'I reckon that if we head downhill away in the opposite direction to that monstrous mountain then we'll eventually reach the coast and meet up with our troops. If we're really lucky we might find a river to follow down to the sea.'

They set off again towards the west and, they hoped, freedom.

Chapter 20

Asampit told Tom that some of the village men had been hunting near to Ranau and watched unseen as a few bearded and emaciated white men staggered through the jungle accompanied by Japanese soldiers. The hunters weren't to know that they had seen the remnants of the first forced march as they returned from delivering the sacks of rice. They discussed what they could do. It was the end of May and Tom was still waiting for his radio to crackle into speech and tell him the landing had begun.

'Asampit,' he began, 'can we send a small party of warriors back again to see if they can possibly find out more? The local people must have some idea about what is going on although they'll probably be reluctant to talk.'

'They'll talk to my men. I'll send Enduat and four others immediately.'

The group set out and later returned with the news that another contingent of white men had just arrived in Ranau from Sandakan and that they were being ill-treated by their guards and many were dying. Tom was desperate to help the men he guessed were his fellow countrymen but had no idea of the size or strength of the Japanese force he would have to overcome on order to save the prisoners. He decided to take a tremendous risk and go and see for himself. Going alone would prevent him from implicating any of the longhouse men if his scouting mission should go wrong.

Just before he left he tuned in his radio. To his intense surprise the static that had been the only sound it made had ceased and he had a clear channel of communication. He tuned it as fine as he could and spoke into the mouthpiece. After repeating his call sign a few times he got through to an operator on board one of the Australian ships. They went through the planned security checks and at last he was speaking to one of the officers in charge of the liberation force. It was a Colonel from the 9th

Division and he told Tom that they were to be landing on the island of Labuan on the ninth of June, only a week away. He asked Tom to give them as much assistance as possible as they moved towards Jesselton by harassing the retreating Japanese. Tom was ecstatic and promised to do as much as he could with his small army of Murut warriors. The Colonel added that three days before the landing there would be a parachute drop of a couple of dozen commandos at the same place where the guns had previously been delivered. He wanted Tom to join up with them to make an even more effective fighting force.

Asampit was also delighted with the news and Enduat wanted to go out immediately and kill as many of the enemy as he could. In all the excitement they had quite forgotten about the plight of the prisoners of war in Ranau. When they eventually calmed down and started thinking things through Tom realised that there wouldn't be time for him to go to Ranau and try to free the men and at the same time join forces with the commandos. He hoped that their Japanese captors would flee when they realised that the island had been reoccupied by the allies and leave their prisoners unmolested to be rescued later. Tom had a touching faith in the innate goodness of mankind that was not to be upheld. In the meantime they had to prepare for battle.

One group of well armed men was to go in position outside Jesselton to give covering fire to the troops as they landed and to kill any Japanese who tried to leave the town and join their comrades in the interior. These were under Enduat's command and Tom made him wear one of the Australian camouflage jackets to show he was a friend. Tom's orders were not to attack until it was clear that the invasion had commenced and the Japanese were in disarray. When most of their officers had mysteriously disappeared after going to the longhouse feast the remaining men were even more jittery. It would not take much to throw them into complete and utter panic making the operation much easier.

A second group of older men armed with their native

weapons was to camp out in hiding along the few jungle trails that the Japanese were known to use and pick off any of them who tried to escape that way. These men grinned widely when told of their task and set about enthusiastically sharpening their headhunting knives and checking their blowpipes and poisoned darts. It was going to be a hunt to remember and would be told about in drinking sessions for generations. They could hardly wait.

Tom and Asampit were to lead the third group to the drop zone and wait for the commandos to parachute in. They would then show them the way to the coast via Kota Belud and help them with surprise attacks on any of the remaining pockets of resistance. Tom had unfinished business with the Japs who had dealt so harshly with David Wong and his brave guerrillas. The time for retribution had come.

Preparations were completed and everything double checked. They all met together for one last drink before going their separate ways when they heard one of the village women scream. Rushing out of the longhouse to see what the problem was they were confronted by the sight of four white scarecrows minus their straw stuffing standing at the edge of the clearing. The four didn't see Tom at first and just stood there holding out their hands in a pleading gesture. One of them, Ted, dropped to his knees, covered his face with his hands and started sobbing loudly. It was all too much to escape from the Japs only to walk into a crowd of savage head-hunters. They had heard tales of the ferocity of these jungle men and were now at the end of their endurance. Tom stepped forward from behind the others and they looked at him in amazement. His shock of blond hair and his size made him unmistakeable as being of European origin. When he spoke they realised that he was not only white but an Australian.

'Where on earth have you come from?' asked Tom.

'We could ask the same about you,' chirped Dave. 'The last person I expected to meet in this fucking awful jungle was another Aussie.'

Ted still couldn't believe what he saw. 'Tell me it's not

another dream,' he pleaded. 'It would be too much to have to wake up back in the camp again.'

'The camp?' queried Tom. 'Do you mean the camp at Ranau? We had heard that there were some prisoners there and had hoped to rescue some before we received news that the liberation was about to start. Now it seems that you have come to us. What about the other prisoners?'

Ted started crying again. In between sobs he managed to say, 'It's too late. We are probably the last ones alive. The few we left behind wouldn't have lived more than a day or two.'

Tom stood stonily at this news. He asked them how many had been in the Sandakan prison camp and was shocked almost beyond belief when he heard the death toll. It was unbelievable and after a moment, when it truly sank in, his eyes filled up and he joined Ted in his weeping. Asampit brought them back to the present.

'We must give them water and food immediately. Tom, look in the first aid boxes and see what there is to help them. They look close to death and are probably suffering from many diseases.'

The men were helped to the shade of the longhouse and given good clean water to drink and small amounts of food. They were obviously near death from starvation as well as having beri-beri, malaria and probably dysentery. Tom was no medical expert but knew they must try to take them to a hospital as soon as was feasible. Slowly the full horror of their tale came out and Tom learned about the random cruelty and harsh conditions in the Sandakan camp. The details of the death march to Ranau and the random slaughter of nearly all their comrades made everyone extremely angry. When he next made contact with the Colonel onboard the ship he told him their story and asked if he could retell it to his troops before they landed. He wanted them to know exactly what they were fighting for and to be aware of the horrific way their fellow soldiers had been treated as prisoners. The Colonel readily agreed.

The four men would have to be left with the village women

to feed and nurture them back to a semblance of their former selves. Unfortunately one of them, Frederick Johnson, died that night as he was too weak to eat and totally ravaged by disease. With the help of the villagers the remaining three buried him with as much dignity and military honour as they could. They vowed he would not be forgotten.

The next morning the three groups set out with the common purpose of totally and speedily destroying the Japanese in North Borneo before they could cause any more unnecessary deaths.

Tom and Asampit, together with their band of warriors picked because of their prowess with the rifles, left first as they had to head inland to meet the parachute troops before turning back with them to the coast. It was a familiar and easy march to the clearing where the Australians would soon be dropping in from an American plane. Tom wore his captain's uniform and most of the men had a few bits of the camouflage clothing on but had adapted it to their own ideas of battle style. Some had cut it up to make loincloths and others had fashioned rather fancy head or neck scarves. Asampit refused to wear any of the clothing and kept faith with his ancestors by dressing in traditional style befitting a chief. His colourful armlets and feathered headdress gave him an air of authority that no western uniform could possibly emulate as he stood proudly next to the others.

They arrived at the clearing and waited patiently hunkered down in the undergrowth around the edge. If the plane did not arrive as planned then they would wait for one more day before carrying on with their planned mission without the additional support. They were confident that they would be undisturbed by any of the enemy as by now the other two groups would be in position and would stop any patrols coming in the direction of the landing zone. It was boring for them as they were all fired up and ready for immediate action. Tom knew he could rely on the men to fight to the last in defence of their families and way of life. He hoped he would not be found wanting in the forthcoming battle as it was only a few years since he had broken down after his previous encounter with the Japs.

187

His resolution had been strengthened by the meeting with the Australians from the death camp and he kept the haunting picture of their skeletal frames in his mind as a spur to keep him focussed. Asampit and his men had been brought up as warriors from an early age and regarded fighting as the usual way of life. They had no fear of death as to die in battle was a great honour and they would be held in high regard by the rest of the village for many years. Those who had families knew that if they failed to return the rest of the village would look after any children as their own and their surviving wife would be well fed and protected.

Alone in their diverse thoughts they continued to wait. At last the droning of an aeroplane intruded on their quiet contemplation and they looked up to see a twin-engine Douglas C–47 break through the clouds and release its human cargo earthbound. The parachutes opened and the men whirled and twirled their way down to the rough grass of the clearing. They landed one after the other and quickly jumped to their feet and gathered up their parachutes to bury them in the soft earth. Tom called to them.

'Hey! To save you time we've already dug holes to conceal the parachutes.'

They moved towards him a little warily as he was surrounded by an odd collection of bizarrely dressed men clutching an assortment of modern and traditional weapons. Naturally they had been briefed that they would be met by a local guerrilla force but assumed they would be dressed similarly to themselves.

'Welcome to Borneo,' added Tom. 'We hope you enjoy the experience. We were told that there would be a couple of dozen of you and it's great to meet you.'

A tall, athletic Lieutenant stepped forward.

'Hello Captain Field. I'm Lieutenant Roger Harris and I'm very pleased to meet you as we have no knowledge of the country and will rely on you and your men to guide us to the Japs. All our training has been in Oz so this is our first taste of action. My men are ready and very keen to start pushing them

188

from the island. It looks as if you've a pretty formidable set of fighters under your command.'

'They're not my men,' replied Tom. 'This is Asampit who is their chief and a great friend of mine. They take their orders from both of us. We've always worked well together.'

Tom gestured to Asampit to move forward and greet the Australian Lieutenant. This he did and clasped him by both hands as he looked into his eyes. He seemed satisfied with what he saw and welcomed the Lieutenant in Malay.

'I hope what he said was favourable,' joked Lieutenant Harris. 'I wouldn't like to get on the wrong side of him. That knife looks pretty formidable. But I see you are also armed with rifles and handguns. Do the men know how to use them?'

'Of course. And they have other much quieter but equally deadly weapons. Watch.'

Tom asked one of the warriors to show his proficiency with the blowpipe. The Australian soldiers stood spellbound as he primed the long wooden tube with a feathered dart and moved slowly towards the edge of the clearing. He stopped motionless for a second or two and stared up into the trees. The blowpipe was raised and with a barely audible puff the dart was expelled. Next came the crashing sound through the branches and down to the undergrowth. The warrior strolled over and returned carrying a large macaque monkey by the tail.

'That's certainly impressive,' allowed the Lieutenant. 'Presumably the tip of the dart is poisoned. Is it powerful enough to kill a man?'

'There's no doubt about that,' Tom replied emphatically. 'It's strong enough to kill one of the much larger orang-utans. The formula has been handed down for generations and is extremely potent.'

The combined party then made their way to a nearby river where they would rest for the night and discuss exactly how they would approach the next phase of the operation. Half of Asampit's men built shelters and lit a fire whilst the others went out hunting for food. The Australian men watched with admiration the quiet efficiency of their hosts. They had with them some rather unappealing rations of their own but Tom told them to save them for a real emergency. They would, he explained, probably eat a lot better if they let the experienced Muruts do the cooking.

When the hunting party returned with a selection of feathered and furry animals for the pot it was almost dark and all the men were ready to eat just about anything they could chew and swallow. It didn't take long to prepare the meat and, with some cooked rice and a few jungle vegetables, a veritable feast was soon demolished by the company. The Australians contributed chocolate and coffee to end the meal and with the warm feeling of camaraderie that followed Tom was confident that there would be a successful outcome to the enterprise. Afterwards Tom, Asampit, the Lieutenant and his Sergeant sat apart from the others to make plans. Tom acted as interpreter and, as the senior officer, took charge of the meeting. While they had their discussion the other men settled down in their makeshift huts and bivouacs for the night and prepared themselves mentally for the coming struggle.

'We have to hit them hard,' Tom emphasised. 'This must not turn into a fight comprising of a few occasional, unplanned skirmishes. We must act decisively to show that we mean business. The Japanese will otherwise just melt into the jungle and dig in making our task even more difficult. They have to be stopped in their tracks before they realise the strength of our force. The Korean conscripts will be no problem but the Kempetai and the Japanese soldiers won't be so easy to defeat. They're battling to save their country as well as their honour and will never surrender. We'll almost certainly have to kill virtually all of them to make the country safe. I suggest we storm Kota Belud and take the small garrison that is situated in and behind the police station. If we are quick enough and surprise them then we should gain our first victory without much loss of life on our part. For the Japs it will be a totally different outcome. They will never recover and, apart from a few men out on patrol, the town will be ours in a matter of minutes.'

'How far is it to Kota Belud?' asked the Sergeant.

'Not far in miles,' replied Tom. 'But about two or three days hiking across the hills and down a river to the side of the mountain you must have seen when you dropped from the plane. We'll make it there just as the main force land along the coast to the south and take Jesselton.'

'We certainly saw the mountain you mentioned. I'm glad we won't have to cross over the top. It looked quite daunting. Do you have any idea of the strength of the Japanese force in the town? There are twenty-five of us and you seem to have a similar number of men. Is that sufficient to overcome the opposition?'

If we attack at dawn then we should have no problems. The garrison was strengthened after David Wong's attack and now holds around a hundred men but only about twenty of these are crack troops who will give us any sort of problem.'

Tom kept Asampit informed of the plan and he nodded his approval. He liked the idea of a proper battle and not skulking clandestinely behind trees and picking off the enemy one by one. It was a long time since his longhouse had been involved in a real fight. It would be good for his warriors and it would do no harm to his own standing as the headman of the village. The meeting ended and they went off to join the others as they slept.

Once alone again with his thoughts Tom turned over the events of the past years. His time in Kudat; meeting Mary; the children; the start of the war; his unexpected involvement in the fighting; Asampit and his sons; the Japanese. Just as Mary had wished before he left he thought that maybe the time had come to turn back the clock and return to the old times. He pictured the house in Kudat but now with his three children laughing and playing on the veranda. Mary pottering in the garden in her thin cotton frock with the sun shining through it. His friends on the estate and the neat little town bustling with the trappings of trade. All it boiled down to, he thought, was his memories. Was that what he was fighting for? Did it really matter? Even if the past couldn't be recreated the possibilities of the future could be relished. He was suddenly absolutely sure what he was doing was right and felt calm and in full control.

Chapter 21

Well before Enduat and his men were near to Jesselton they could hear the bombers coming in over the sea and the crump of the deadly cargo being delivered on the town. In the distance they could see a rising column of black smoke tinged with red on its underside as it fanned out forming a thick cloud. They moved to a vantage position at the back of the town on a small bosky hill where they could watch unseen. The devastation they saw both astonished and pleased them. It seemed that every building was burning fiercely from the wharf to the commercial centre and out to the suburbs. Even Kampong Ayer, the village on stilts over the sea, was ablaze and they could see small figures running about in panic trying with little effect to dowse the flames. They felt sorry for the innocent people who were losing their lives and homes but realised that the airborne operation was necessary if the landing was to be a success. There must be no places left for the Japanese to hide and slow the progress of the incoming Australian troops.

There was nothing they could do but stay hidden and wait for the softening up process to be completed and then, when the landings began in earnest, put into action their plan to harass and confront the retreating enemy. They wanted to cover the two main routes they calculated the Japanese would use to leave the town. The railway line, now operational again, was one of the quickest ways the Japs could use to escape. Enduat deployed a group of fifteen men to go to the station and find suitable cover so they could fire on any of the unsuspecting soldiers trying to flee to the interior. The other main way out of town was the road to Kota Belud. It had not rained heavily for a few weeks so they knew that it would be firm and dry allowing vehicles to travel at some speed up the coast. If they could stop or at least slow down any attempts by the Japanese to leave Jesselton and regroup in the countryside then the Australian force would have a much easier task liberating the country. It would also save many lives by reducing any pockets of resistance. There was no need to worry about the airfield as they could see from the hill that it was completely destroyed with the runway pockmarked with craters and the buildings flattened. It couldn't possibly be used for many weeks. The same went for the wharf where they could see a variety of fishing boats and other craft at crazy angles in the water with many of them billowing out smoke and flames. No enemy soldiers would be leaving by sea or air.

To halt any movement along the Kota Belud road would not present any real problems. It was a narrow track barely wide enough for two vehicles to pass. At the Jesselton end for about five miles it was almost possible to call it a road as coral had been ground and flattened into the surface to make it firmer. This, however, resulted in many shredded tyres. For the remainder of its winding route it was a dirt track with a few log bridges taking it across small streams and rivers. Enduat considered blowing up a few of these bridges with hand grenades but decided that it would be too noisy and could draw unwelcome attention to them. In any case, if the Japanese saw a bridge down then they would be wary of an imminent attack and be more on their guard. He decided that the best plan was to conceal themselves in the deep storm drains on each side of the road and attack any passing vehicles with crossfire and, if necessary, the grenades. Rather than risk all his men in one place where they might be pinned down if the opposition proved too fierce they would split into three teams of five. Two of the teams would be on the roadside about two hundred yards apart with the third group staying back from the road ready to support the others if and when they needed it. That way, Enduat reasoned, it was unlikely that even a fairly large convoy would be able to break through without serious loss of life. He knew it was likely that some of the Japanese would make their way to Kota Belud despite his best efforts. But in order to help his father and Tom who would be coming in the opposite direction to join forces it was imperative that any opposition they might encounter should be as depleted as possible.

The landing by the 9th Division of the Australian Army was planned to take place just after dawn the next day giving Enduat plenty of time to prepare his traps. There was no point in remaining on the hill overlooking the town so he signalled to his men and they moved silently back into the trees and away from the stench of the burning. Once well clear they searched to find suitable a place to set their ambush on the road. Enduat had appointed an old boyhood friend called Dualis to lead the men going to the station. He knew he could trust him to do a good job and do all he could to prevent the Japanese using the railway as a means of escape. Dualis was to make his own decisions as how best to perform his allotted task when he had a clearer idea how well the station was defended. If it transpired that it was heavily fortified then they would have to go down the track and attack any trains from there. It would be much easier if he could prevent any of the small steam trains actually leaving the station. The railway was a vital link to the Japanese troops stationed in Papar and a larger contingent in Beaufort. To sever this vital artery would be of tremendous help to the whole operation. He kept his mind open as he moved his men, skirting the edge of the town, towards their goal.

By five o'clock the next morning, two hours before the landing, all was quiet on the Kota Belud road. The bombing had stopped the evening before and although the pall of smoke had gone they could still taste the burnt air. Enduat had placed two of the three groups of men along the road and was himself in charge of the third party ready to step in where needed. They had posted a sentry further down the road towards Jesselton to give them a sign if any army trucks or soldiers were sighted. All the men were ready and fully alert as they strained their eyes to see through the gloom.

Suddenly the silence was fractured by the incessant scream and thump of heavy shelling. This new bombardment was from the Australian Navy that was now positioned a few miles offshore. Its job was to accurately send a steady stream of fire over the heads of the men in the assorted landing craft to prevent the Japanese from making an attack as they reached the shore. This was an unexpected event that Enduat had not been told about. It was just as well he'd moved his men a couple of miles outside the town and not nearer to the devastation caused by the big naval guns that pounded the buildings near the shore relentlessly.

The railhead was the next prime target for the shelling. Dualis had only just got his men in position when the barrage started. They had observed the level of military security at the station and found it to be lighter than expected. The Japanese obviously didn't expect any immediate threat to their main exit from the area and had left it virtually deserted. Dualis watched the railway workers arrive and heard them going about their business firing up the locomotives for the day. They were civilians and he hoped to spare their lives if it was possible. His primary target was any Japanese soldiers who tried to use the train as a means of joining up with their colleagues down the line. He was determined that none of them would make it. But his plans came to nought as the heavy naval shells struck the station and the engine sheds. In a matter of a few minutes all the sheds were ablaze and the engines turned into twisted lumps of useless metal. He thought no Japanese or anybody else would be using the railway for the foreseeable future. Dualis decided to stay put for the moment as he guessed the soldiers in the town garrison would be unaware of the destruction and might still come towards the station hoping to escape. He gestured to his men to keep in position and be ready for action.

As the shells landed all around the edge of the town the first Australian soldiers landed and made their way carefully along the shore and towards what remained of the wharf. They dealt effectively with the little opposition they encountered and soon were established in various bomb craters and behind concrete blocks and assorted rubble. They were in a line behind the main street that ran parallel to the beach about a hundred yards inland. The battle for Jesselton now started. Many of the Japanese had hidden in shelters they had constructed months before and had strategically placed at road intersections in positions where machine gun fire could rake a wide arc of the town and prevent the Australians moving forward. The heavy bombing and the shelling hadn't managed to destroy all of these bunkers and they were in a strong position to repel any attack from the sea. Rifle and machine gun fire were exchanged for nearly an hour with Australian casualties mounting and no sign of the deadlock being broken. It looked as if it was going to be a long day with little useful ground gained. The liberation was not going to plan as the opposition was more organised and determined than the Australian command had envisaged. No Japanese troops were making any effort to leave the town so along the Kota Belud road Enduat waited impatiently with mounting frustration for some action.

At the station Dualis could hear the gunfire and realised the landing had taken place. The shelling from the ships had now stopped to prevent any casualties to their own troops. Like Enduat he waited for the Japanese soldiers to start moving towards him as they were pushed back by the 9th Division. There was no sign of them and he wondered if the invasion had failed. He decided to head cautiously back towards the town and see what was happening. As he moved his men in a fan formation towards the gunfire he took stock of the situation. So far they had not fired a shot. Enduat's group had the submachine gun on the road so Dualis knew his own firepower was relatively limited. He soon realised what was happening when he saw the first of the Japanese machine gun nests at the corner of a road leading to the main street that ran through the town. He could see it was pinning down a number of Australians by firing rapid bursts at regular intervals. It was also clear to him that the Japs were not watching their backs as he could see all the men clearly as they crouched behind the machine gun. He could see four of them and they were all totally focussed on watching the Australian troops in front of them. A smile played on his lips as he motioned to his men to move in towards him.

One of his men had proved to be a crack shot with a rifle

during their brief training with Tom so Enduat pointed to the machine gun and gave the man a thumbs-up sign. Raising his rifle slowly and holding his breath the man took aim and fired. They saw the soldier manning the machine gun crumple forward. The Japs didn't realise the bullet had come from behind them so he had time to pick off another one and then a third. The fourth man suddenly turned and looked straight at them but it was too late as Dualis had him in his sights already and he died immediately without being able to warn his comrades in other locations. It was too risky for Dualis to try to make contact with the Australians as they would probably have opened fire not knowing they had allies in the town. They knew the guerrillas would be active but had not expected to be given such direct support so soon in their campaign. Dualis moved round to the next objective; another machine gun nest in front of the old post office which, as it was built of stone, was virtually the only building still standing and relatively unscathed.

Again the occupants of the nest didn't think to cover their backs and soon they too had fallen to the accurate rifle fire of the Murut sniper. But another Japanese bunker, well hidden in the vegetation along the side of the road, had spotted what was happening and had seen Dualis and his men. As Dualis moved to find another target they opened fire and a withering storm of bullets tore into his men. They had no protection and soon only a few remained uninjured. Dualis died immediately as he was at the front of his party and the surviving men took cover where they could. One of them, angered by the sudden death of so many of his friends rushed from his hiding place and, before the Japanese could react, tossed a grenade into the bunker. It had the desired effect and the machine gun fell silent.

The Australian troops now realised they were not alone in the struggle to take the town and, with three of the Japanese positions eliminated from behind, were able to break out and destroy the others with very little loss of life to their own men. They met up with the, to them, strangely dressed warriors and with the universal language of signs and gestures thanked them for their help. Jesselton was now in the hands of the allies and it was time for them to secure the town and mop up any remaining enemy troops.

The few uninjured Muruts knew the importance of the railway to the enemy and took some of the Australian troops to the station. The locomotives there had been destroyed but they had no idea if there were any others still operational at various points down the track. The Japanese might still be able to use it to attack the Australian force as it led to all their main supply depots and a string of garrisons along its route to the interior. The nearest Japanese stronghold was at Papar about twenty miles down the line. It was situated close to the coast before the track reached the town of Beaufort that housed the main Japanese army camp and the new headquarters of the Kempetai. Their headquarters had been moved there as soon as the aerial bombardment of Jesselton had started.

The Australian command, thanks to Tom Field's earlier endeavours, had fairly accurate maps of the area. They decided that they would first of all try to take Papar as other allied troops had landed further down the coast and they were in communication with them. Those troops had encountered little resistance as they had landed in a very swampy area that was largely uninhabited. Progress had been slow because of the wet conditions but they were moving steadily northwards and Papar could now be attacked from two sides. They reckoned they could reach the objective in a matter of days so long as they didn't encounter any serious opposition to slow them down. Leaving behind sufficient men to hold Jesselton against any counterattack the majority of the 9th Division set out for Papar. The remnants of the Murut party decided that it would be better if they rejoined Enduat up the Kota Belud road. They would be able to tell him of their success tinged with the sadness of losing so many good men.

Chapter 22

Tom and Asampit, together with the crack Australian paratroopers, had reached Kota Belud at the same time as the landings in and around Jesselton took place. They were in contact with the Australian command but were unaware of how or if Enduat's men had been able to help. They knew nothing of how the landings had gone until they received a message that they had been a total success with much credit given to the Murut warriors behind the Japanese lines. Asampit was exultant until he was told of the high death toll. He had no idea if his son Enduat was alive or dead. All his thoughts were concentrated on the coming action as they prepared their assault on the Kota Belud garrison that had been strengthened with a few more experienced Japanese troops following the Kinabalu Guerrillas uprising. They needed to take the town using the advantage of surprise as a pitched battle was something that the Australians were keen to avoid as it would have meant a loss of men they couldn't sustain. Also they would have to attempt to prevent the Japanese trying to break out and fight man to man which they would do if they thought they had a numerical advantage. They knew the Japs were solely interested in victory and never considered the cost.

Tom guessed correctly that the bulk of the Japanese force in Kota Belud would be watching the coast and the road from Jesselton. He was sure they had heard of the landings in and around Jesselton and that their comrades had lost the town. It would, Tom reasoned, seem logical to the enemy that the Australians would advance up the road or stage another beach landing. They would, therefore, be totally focused on defending those two areas as they were hopefully unaware of the arrival of the joint Australian and Murut force at their rear. There was nothing to be gained from waiting any longer as any Japanese who had escaped the battle for Jesselton might be making their way to join their compatriots and strengthen the force at Kota Belud.

After a short discussion with Asampit and Lt. Harris the decision was made. Tom and Asampit would lead their men and try to force the defenders of the town towards the sea. At the same time Lt. Harris and his paratroopers would attack any troops defending the Jesselton road. The garrison itself would have to be left until later. They hoped that most of the enemy were deployed in the defence of the town and only a few would be left in the makeshift fort. Kota Belud had mainly escaped the bombing so there were still plenty of buildings standing to give them cover as they moved stealthily towards the town.

Before they reached the *padang* opposite the row of shop houses they split into their two groups and made their respective ways to positions behind the Japanese. The Muruts were not trained in formal battle tactics or techniques but their ferocity and courage more than made up for it. A difficulty that Tom thought he might encounter was that their enthusiasm could make them too vulnerable to a counter attack. They might overrun the enemy and end up being the ones with their backs to the sea. He hoped Asampit would help keep them together and not allow them to be dispersed over a wide area hunting down any escaping Japs.

Lt. Harris and his small army of paratroopers soon found where the enemy were holed up waiting for any movement up the road. As he expected they had set up a series of machine gun posts on each side of the road with more troops stationed behind them in the trees to move forward if required. He estimated that there were over fifty of them stretched out along about two hundred yards of the road. It was an extremely difficult situation for him to deal with as each nest was positioned to give covering fire to the next one. To attack through the trees would mean having to go through the back-up troops and lose any element of surprise. It was a big risk but they would have to try and work their way down the road and take out each post one after the other. In their favour was the fact that the nests had been set up facing Jesselton and not the direction from which the paratroopers would be advancing. Lt. Harris hoped that they would be able to move quickly and, using grenades and submachine gun fire, eliminate the enemy before they could turn round and the reinforcements waiting in the trees arrived. As with Tom's group, speed would be the key to success.

Although they had not planned it they both attacked at exactly the same time and the sleepy town was soon wide awake to the sound of explosions and bursts of gunfire. Local people took cover and parents clutched their crying children to them. The few Japanese soldiers in the garrison, most of whom were ill or injured, also kept their heads down as they had no idea who was doing the firing and assumed that it was their comrades pushing back the advancing Australian army. If they had realised they were in a position to attack both groups from behind then the outcome of the short battle could have been much different. They stayed put and out of the action as they saw no enemy troops coming towards them. They thought their forces were winning.

Tom and Asampit moved very quickly towards the beach and took the enemy completely unawares. They mowed them down before they could turn their guns to repel the advance. Dozens of them fell where they stood looking back in open-mouthed amazement at the sudden unexpected onslaught. A few managed to fire off shots from their rifles and a small number of the Murut men fell dead or injured. They had no time to turn the machine guns on the yelling warriors bearing down on them. The Muruts loved the hand grenades and took great pleasure in tossing them into any cover they thought might be hiding the enemy. Soon there were only a few stragglers left and these were swiftly despatched by bayonet and bullet. It went against Tom's better nature but he knew they couldn't take prisoners as there was nowhere to put them and no spare men to guard them. The Muruts never even considered taking prisoners an option and were delighted with the heads they had won. They flashed their red and black smiles at each other as they came together ready for their next orders.

Down at the road the battle was less one sided. Despite

the surprise element the paratroopers were soon embroiled in fierce fighting as they strove to wipe out all the machine guns. The Japanese fought frenziedly. Some of the reserve troops waiting in the jungle came towards the sounds of the conflict but misread the situation and swung round towards Jesselton with the intention of coming up the road behind the troops they thought had come from that direction. The result of their action was to achieve exactly the opposite and they found themselves head on to Lt. Harris's men making them easy targets. Those that survived the withering submachine gun fire melted back into the thick forest and tried to work their way round to support their comrades. But it was too late as the Australians had just completed the destruction of the last machine gun post and its occupants. When the Japanese troops saw that continuing to fight was futile they retreated further back into the jungle hoping to meet up with some of their other soldiers from different units and form some sort of useful fighting force again. Ever wary of an attack by the soldiers in the garrison Lt. Harris led his men and the walking wounded back to the town. He hoped he would be able to rescue the more seriously wounded men and retrieve the dead when the town had been fully secured. After a swift headcount he realised that only fourteen of his original twenty-four were still able to fight. Four had died and six were wounded. He hoped that there would be no further encounters until he had met up with the bulk of the liberating army when they broke out of Jesselton and made their move northwards. Now it was time to find out what had happened to Tom and his Murut companions.

Both parties made their way into the town and headed towards the garrison. Apart from the few very sick men it was deserted. The men there had realised that the joint actions had decimated their troops and some had run to take their chance in the jungle. It was a long way from Kota Belud to the main part of the Japanese army based in Beaufort and Tom reckoned it unlikely that any of them would reach there alive. As well as the group of experienced hunters that had been sent out by

Asampit to roam the jungle with their blowpipes seeking out any Japanese patrols or escaping stragglers there were also Muruts from other longhouses watching out for them. Prior to leaving his longhouse Asampit had sent messages to all his neighbours telling them of the Australian invasion and that there was now an opportunity to swell the contents of their head houses. He knew they wouldn't need a second invitation. Those Japanese leaving Kota Belud had set out on their own death march.

Tom, Asampit and Lt. Harris compared notes. They had suffered more casualties than they had envisaged but were now fully in control of Kota Belud and the land down from the town to the coast. Intelligence reports prior to the landings had told them that there were few Japanese north of the town apart from the small deployment in and around Kudat that Tom was well aware of. He hoped to renew his acquaintance with them sometime soon. They would be very unlikely to attempt to travel down the rough track towards Kota Belud and would almost certainly stay in Kudat vainly waiting for reinforcements.

Radio reports of the events in Jesselton were better than expected. Not only was the town fully under Australian control but the 9th Division had also taken Papar, the next station down the railway line. News also came that a hospital ship was now berthed at Jesselton making it possible to evacuate the wounded and have them professionally treated. Tom had not forgotten the men from the prison camp who were still in Asampit's longhouse. They would somehow have to find a way to get them to Jesselton as well as their own wounded. The news for Asampit was not so good and he learned that Dualis and nearly all the men with him had been wiped out. There was still no word about his son Enduat. He dearly hoped he was still alive and that they would meet up very soon.

It was going to be sooner than he realised as Enduat had become fed up with waiting. He knew from the survivors of Dualis's group about the action in Jesselton that few Japanese soldiers were now going to make their way up the road he had been guarding so he was making his way towards Kota Belud.

This time, on his way, he destroyed the few wooden bridges to make the road impassable to motor vehicles and thereby protect his rear from a surprise attack. This was an insurance against any possible patrols that might have been out of town when the landings started. They would almost certainly try to join up with other Japanese troops when they realised that Jesselton was now in allied hands and might head north to Kota Belud.

All seemed quite peaceful as the walked through the small villages lining the road. The people were going about their normal chores as if the war had never happened. Very few even bothered to look at Enduat's band of warriors as they passed. Occasionally Enduat had to ask for food for his men and this was always given resignedly and with blank expressions. Enduat knew they must have heard the bombardment of Jesselton and attempted to tell them that the end to the war was in sight but they showed little interest. He was sad to see how low in spirit they had been brought by the occupying troops. Even the children were subdued and only played lethargically at their games.

When Kota Belud was only a couple of miles away the men slowed their pace and became much more alert. They had no idea of the outcome of the joint action between the paratroopers and the Muruts. All they knew was that it was deathly quiet up ahead and that meant that no fighting was going on. But who had won? Enduat didn't want to risk running into an ambush along the road into the town so he took his men on a wide detour through the rainforest and up to the hill where the Rest House stood overlooking the town. The Rest House, now deserted, was a sort of small hotel found in most colonial towns. It was built for government officials and other travellers to stay in. Despite its strategically useful position the Japanese had preferred to stay in the town in the police station and jail. Enduat cautiously looked down and saw to his relief that the soldiers sitting outside the coffee shop were definitely not wearing the Imperial Japanese uniform. He motioned to the others and they swiftly made their way down the hill and into

Kota Belud.

The Australian paratroopers saw the motley band of dishevelled men charging into town and immediately grabbed their rifles, dived for cover and had Enduat covered when Asampit rushed forward and warmly embraced his son. As Enduat was obviously no threat the soldiers somewhat sheepishly returned to their tables.

'I'm so glad you're safe,' a relieved Asampit said. 'What happened to you in Jesselton? We heard nothing.'

'That's exactly it – nothing,' replied Enduat. 'We heard all the bombing, gunfire and shelling from our positions along the road but we waited and waited for ages and still there was no sign of the Japs. While we were waiting the surviving few of Dualis's men joined us and we learned a little more about the battle and the successful taking of the town. You probably know much more than us if you've been in contact with the Australian command. Are the Aussies still winning?'

Tom came forward and also gave Enduat a hug. 'Yes,' he said, 'and they have also taken Papar to the south. We have been told to stay put and hold Kota Belud in case there are any Jap patrols still out there who might try to retake the town. I think it's extremely unlikely as we managed to kill nearly all the enemy troops stationed here. In fact, the local people have only just finished burying the bodies. We intend to have a small ceremony honouring them and our own dead later today. I know they wouldn't do that for us but that's no reason to stoop to their level of ignorance and depravity.'

'Too right,' added Lt. Harris, 'they've shown themselves to be cruel and heartless. It's up to us to remain above all that and show our own men and the local people that there's another way of conducting a war. Bloody it may be but it doesn't have to be bestial.'

Now that the two groups were reunited they started to think about the third group out in the jungle with a roaming role to kill any of the enemy they could find. Although they were not in radio contact with them Asampit was confident that a couple of his warriors could soon make contact if they ventured into the jungle towards where their longhouse lay. Tom thought this a good idea as he thought they had probably completed their mission and that few, if any, of the escaping Japanese had made it to join their fellow soldiers on the other side of the mountain range. It would be a good time to consolidate their force to be ready for any task the Australian command allotted to them. Having a force of nearly a hundred men could prove useful if there was an emergency anywhere along the coast. He didn't tell the others but he still harboured designs on Kudat. Asampit sent out the men and, after discussion with Tom, agreed that if possible they would bring back with them the three very sick ex-prisoners so they could be taken to the hospital ship.

The next few days were rather boring and the men just waited for action. They kept in shape by regular physical exercise on the grassy *padang* and the occasional swim in the warm China Sea. An Australian versus Murut soccer match was arranged and ended in both sides collapsed in helpless laughter as the standard of play was so abysmal. The rules had been simplified to make it easier but the Muruts had the idea that if the person in goal could handle the ball then they should all be goalies when the occasion demanded it. In many ways it resembled an Aussie Rules game. Total chaos ensued and even with Tom as a neutral referee the game rapidly descended into farce. While they attempted to maintain their fitness Lt. Harris kept in constant communication with his superior officers on the ships and in Jesselton. The regular updates on the progress they were making gave rise to much satisfaction among his men and the Murut warriors he had grown to trust and respect. He hoped to be called into action again soon, preferably joining up with his compatriots in the push towards Beaufort, but was a good officer and would willingly undertake any mission given to him and his men. Another reason for wanting to go south to Jesselton was to take his wounded and the injured Muruts to the hospital ship. The conditions in Kota Belud were not ideal and now, after David Wong's execution, there was no trained medical help available. To prevent further infection setting in it was imperative to move them within the next few days. There was also the chance that Asampit's men would return with the three men being looked after in the longhouse. He decided to make his case to his superior officers the next time they were in radio contact.

That evening the contact was made and Lt. Harris explained the situation and how desperate it was becoming for the most badly injured men. He assured the officers in Jesselton that it was safe to use the Kota Belud road despite the bridges being down. He knew that the 9th Division would have brought with them the know-how and the materials to quickly replace a few wooden bridges. They informed him that a convoy of trucks and jeeps would set out the next morning and could be with them by evening. To be on the safe side they asked if a patrol could go part of the way down the road to meet them thus ensuring that the Kota Belud end was genuinely safe from ambush by any rogue enemy still on the loose. Lt. Harris naturally agreed and said the patrol would go out that evening so they could be almost halfway to Jesselton by daybreak. They could meet up at the small village of Tamparuli where the road forked and the main track led to Kota Belud with a smaller one going towards Ranau and Mount Kinabalu. This village also was the site of the largest bridge on the road and a few extra hands might prove useful in repairing Enduat's damage.

When he was told of the plan Enduat immediately offered his services as guide to the patrol. He knew the road and possible places that might spell danger. Lt. Harris was very grateful although Asampit, despite being proud his son had offered to help, was reluctant to let him out of his sight again. He wanted to go as well but Tom explained that his place as headman was with his warriors and it would serve little purpose having him away when the conflict might suddenly flare up again. In any case Enduat would be back the next day with the motorised group of pioneers and medics to take the wounded back to Jesselton.

The patrol and their guide set out as soon as they had kitted up and they made good progress down the familiar road out of town past the scene of their earlier engagement. It was as quiet as it can be when moving through a jungle at night when it seems that the living creatures of all sizes are competing to make the loudest croak, click or squawk. As the night progressed it quietened down somewhat and the men could listen for any unexpected sounds that were not part of the usual cacophony. They relied heavily on Enduat's knowledge of the jungle for any signs of danger and were pleased that he had offered to help them find their way through the unfamiliar countryside. At some points, especially where the track curved or the jungle encroached, he stayed ahead of them and they waited for a signal from the flashlight they had given him. When they received the all clear sign they moved forward to join him.

This process slowed them down but it was worth it as at one point the torch stayed off and they all dived for cover in case of enemy fire. It turned out that Enduat had stumbled across a couple of the Japanese who had escaped into the trees after the battle for the road and had decided to make their way south towards Jesselton rather than take their chances crossing the hills to join the others. They were camping out for the night but Enduat had smelt the remains of their fire and found them a few yards into the trees. He returned with the news to the sergeant in charge of the patrol. The sergeant and two of his men crept forward to the spot indicated by Enduat and before the two Japanese could even wake they shot them at point blank range. They left the bodies sprawled in the vegetation and continued towards the meeting place at Tamparuli.

The rest of the night proved uneventful and as dawn broke they were close to the small village. Rather than alarm the villagers they decided to stay hidden from sight until they heard the troops arriving. As they were coming in vehicles then that wouldn't be difficult. They could see the bridge that Enduat had demolished. It was now a tangle of splintered wooden spars and boards that hung at a crazy angle over the swift flowing river. They hoped the pioneers had brought all that was needed to either repair the bridge or put a new one across. It would have to be fairly substantial to take the weight of the trucks and jeeps. Lt. Harris wondered if there was anything they could do to help before the others arrived but decided that it was a job best left to the experts in the 2/2nd Pioneer Corps. They had vast practical experience in many areas of emergency construction and bridging rivers was an everyday task.

Just before midday they heard the noise of engines in low gear coming up the track. Still unsure as to whether it was friend or foe they stayed put and observed from their safe hiding place. As the first jeep came into sight they were relieved to see it was one of their own and they could go down and meet the convoy albeit from the other side of the river. A collection of trucks followed the heavily armed jeep and stopped just before the chasm. A number of men got out and shouted greetings to Lt. Harris and his men before quickly unloading a pile of perforated metal strips and a variety of other equipment. They made an A-frame and used it to swing some of the wooden spars across to the other side where they were gathered by Lt. Harris's men. Following the instructions shouted to them they made another A-frame so that ropes could be slung across the two and anchored to nearby trees to make a stable structure that would support the metal decking. It was a basic suspension bridge just wide enough for the trucks to edge carefully across. The whole operation had taken less than an hour and Enduat had watched in admiration as the bridge took shape. He reckoned he could use what he had learned that morning to improve some of the rough bridges they had built over rivers near their longhouse. These often fell down at inconvenient moments dumping unfortunate travellers into the water below.

Once the convoy was across they picked up Enduat and the patrol and headed for Kota Belud. There were no more bridges on this section of the track so they made good time and arrived there by late afternoon. Even so it was too late for them to make an immediate return so they set up tents on the *padang* and settled down for the night intending to make a return early the next morning. The medics with them assessed all the wounded including the three ex-prisoners of war who had arrived that day from the longhouse. All were pronounced fit to travel. The Captain in charge of the convoy told Lt. Harris that he was to accompany them on the return to Jesselton with most of his men to join the main force in the push towards Beaufort. He was, however, to leave one of his sergeants and half-a-dozen men to ensure that Kota Belud was held. Tom was wondering if there were any orders for him but it seemed that the clandestine nature of his activities had not filtered through to all the officers in Jesselton and he was now apparently supernumerary to requirements. He decided to head for Kudat by borrowing one of the jeeps but first he had to make a heart-wrenching visit.

Tom found out where David Wong had lived and with some trepidation went to see his widow Ah San. He approached the traditional house set on stilts to keep out any floods and knocked on the wooden post leading up the steps to the living area. A young man appeared and looked at Tom gravely. He spoke in English as he had been educated in the mission school and realised that Tom was unlikely to speak Mandarin or any of the Chinese dialects.

'How can I help you?' he asked politely.

'Is your mother there? I would like to speak to her.'

'Yes but she is resting at the moment. She finds life difficult after the death of our father. Do you know her?'

'No, but I knew your father. We met here once before the war and again when he was bravely organising his resistance movement. I'd heard of his murder by the Kempetai and wanted to see if there was any small thing I could do to help your mother.'

'Just coming to see her will be enough. We're all proud of his efforts to defeat the Japs and it'll lift her spirits if he's acknowledged by one of the liberating army. I'll go and tell her you're here.' He turned on his heel and went back through the door. A few minutes later he reappeared and beckoned Tom to come in. Tom removed his boots and went into the cool and tidy living room where Ah San sat in a rattan chair.

'We haven't met,' Tom said apologetically. 'Please forgive me for taking the liberty of calling on you unannounced. I met your husband before the war and then again a couple of years ago and just wanted to pay tribute to his courage.'

'Thank you,' replied Ah San in unaccented English. 'It has been a difficult time for our family. Fortunately the Japanese have left us alone since they executed David but life is still a struggle. My children are rapidly growing up and the oldest two are already working in menial jobs to help put food on the table. The younger ones have had to leave school as we can't afford the fees. I don't know what will happen to them in the future. Often it all seems too much.'

'That's why I'm here. When I first returned to Borneo to see David I was given some money to help bribe informers. None of it was ever spent and I left it safely with a good friend. I've brought it with me to give you as some small recompense for your tragic loss. Please accept it as a present from the Australian government in acknowledgement of your husband's brave efforts against the Japanese invaders.'

After he had given her the package Ah San leaned forward and took his hand in hers. 'Thank you again. This will make all the difference to our family's future. I hope we can meet again when this dreadful war is finally over and life returns to something like normal. Although for me it can never be the same again. I loved David with every bone in my body and each day I see him in our children and my heart feels it's breaking. I hope the end of the war brings you more happiness than I'll ever experience again. Will we meet again? I'd like you to see how my children grow up and make their way in the world.'

'I sincerely hope so,' said a subdued Tom. 'I might one day return with my wife and family to our old home in Kudat. I want to go there soon to see if it's still standing. If we set up home in North Borneo again I'll make sure we visit you. My wife would love to meet you and your children. Good luck.'

At that Tom left and with a great deal of emotion still visible on his face he made his way back to see if a jeep could be lent to him. He asked the Captain in charge of the convoy and explained what he wanted to do. It was a little unorthodox but the Captain could see the benefit of a small force going to Kudat to retake the town if there were any Japanese still in occupation. Tom had a radio so the reconnaissance would be useful to the 9th Division command and help them gain a fuller picture of the progress of the liberation away from the main towns. He contacted his headquarters and asked permission to hand over a jeep and some fuel. This was readily given and Tom was to start as soon the next day. He decided to ask Enduat to accompany him with three of the best Murut warriors. Hopefully they would meet little or no resistance until Kudat but it was better to be prepared. They would take a submachine gun with them as well as grenades and some high explosives with detonators. It would be a bit of a squeeze in the jeep but they didn't mind. Tom had never driven a jeep before so if would be a novelty to him and he wondered if one would be useful for getting around the plantation after the war. He knew Mary would probably prefer a smaller vehicle to the large truck she had fought with so valiantly in the early days.

Chapter 23

In Jesselton the senior officers of the 9th Division were contemplating their next move. They had received news that the 24th Brigade of the 9th were to land at the tiny town of Weston which was on the other side of Beaufort to the south. They were coming from the now secure island of Labuan that was only a short sea crossing from the mainland. With them attacking Beaufort from the south and the main force from Papar in the north they felt the Japanese threat would soon be extinguished. It was now late July and the war in the pacific was almost won with American troops close to Japan itself. They surmised that the war would soon be over and wanted to limit the loss of further lives as best they could. They were unaware of the resistance that the enemy would put up making them fight for every inch of soil. So far the invasion had gone to plan and relatively few lives had been lost. But now the Japanese had their backs firmly against the wall and would fight to the last man standing.

In high spirits they sent their men down the railway to Papar. An inventive mechanic had measured the gauge of the railway and found it to be almost identical to the axle size of their jeeps. A few modifications to the wheels and they had an efficient means of transporting goods and men down to the front line. Unfortunately the brakes were useless on the steel rails and there were a few collisions with water buffalo and other livestock. This problem was partially solved by slamming the jeep into reverse. Not too good for the gearbox or the passengers who were thrown forward with some velocity.

On approaching Beaufort all seemed calm and peaceful. There was no sign of the enemy. The Australians sensed a trap and were correct. As soon as they reached the first houses there was a series of almighty explosions that sent men and vehicles high into the air. The Japanese had booby-trapped the houses and detonated the explosives just as the allies were outside them.

A hurried retreat followed and the soldiers regrouped ready for further orders. They realised now that it was not going to be easy. It was decided to try a less straightforward approach on a number of different fronts. The 24th Brigade were in position on the other side of the town so they moved forward in three groups to try and give each other cover if they came under fire. They had flame throwers to set ablaze all the wooden buildings and force out any Japanese hiding in them. It was obvious that the local population had long since deserted the town so it was just the two opposing military forces in occupation.

It was a bit of a stand off with a few shots exchanged but no face to face action. Both sides seemed reluctant to take the initiative. The Japanese because they knew that to force the Australians back required far greater manpower than they had at their disposal, and the Australians because they were unwilling to incur a high death toll when the war was almost over. The situation remained unresolved for two days with neither side making a decisive move. Food was becoming scarce for the Japanese troops and they had no way of finding any more. They would starve to death if they didn't find a way to break through the enemy lines that held them in such a tight grip. Rather than have minor skirmishes they decided they would try one final assault using all the men still able to hold a gun. It happened just before dawn and the Australians were suddenly confronted by a wave of soldiers pouring out of every building and crater. The noise they made as they charged towards the enemy positions would haunt many of the Australians for years. It was a high pitched screaming that went on relentlessly as if it gave the onrushing men a cloak of invincibility. As they reached the machine guns many of them were cut to pieces and the ground was stained red and littered with body parts. A few got through and used their bayonets to try and stop the guns firing on the troops following behind. The Australian soldiers had no time to retreat and just stood their ground as best they could until reinforcements came up from the rear and the Japanese attack was finally repelled. As the surviving Japanese retreated back to their own positions they were under constant fire and many more were slaughtered. The air stank of blood and gun smoke.

The Australian officers had a meeting and decided they didn't want to experience a repeat of the Japanese attack so they would have to take the initiative and move forward themselves. They wouldn't make a full frontal frenzied assault as the enemy had but a systematic taking out of each group in a controlled manner. Lt. Harris and his paratroopers were ordered to try and take a particularly difficult set of three machine gun nests positioned on the edge of the town in a thickly wooded area behind the Rest House. It was of particular strategic importance to the Japanese as if those particular guns were silenced then the way was open for the allies to cut their force in half and the battle would soon be lost.

The direct approach to the nests gave little cover and any man venturing out into the open would be immediately taken out. Lt. Harris selected four of his men and, moving quickly from one small piece of cover to another, they made their way to the edge of the woodland out of sight of the gunners. It would now be possible to sneak up on the Japanese, hopefully unobserved. As the Lieutenant moved out from the shelter of a large baobab tree a single shot rang out and he fell with a bullet hole neatly in the centre of his forehead. There was a sniper who had them in his sights and the remaining men had only a vague idea where he was hiding. The sergeant took off an empty ammunition pouch and, using a broken branch, moved it out to the side of the tree's trunk. Immediately another shot rang out and this time they could pinpoint the position of the sniper. He was in the town's Rest House on the first floor which gave him a wide scope to ply his deadly trade as there were windows overlooking most of the town and all he had to do was move from room to room looking for new targets. The sergeant knew it would be impossible for them to continue until the man had been neutralised so he sent one of his men back to the command post to ask for assistance.

It came swiftly. As soon as the commanding officers heard

about the death of Lt. Harris and news of the sniper, who was a danger to all the troops, they put the Rest House under a bombardment of fire ranging from machine guns to rifles. Under cover of this fire a squad of men with flame throwers torched the building and as it was wooden it was soon ablaze. They saw the man run out screaming with his hair and shirt on fire and mowed him down. It was a merciful death. The only sounds now were the crackling of the flames punctuated by the occasional crash as another beam gave way. The Rest House was soon completely destroyed.

The way was now open for the sergeant and his men to tackle the concealed machine guns. They moved towards the first position and took out hand grenades to throw. As the sergeant half rose to throw his grenade he was struck down by a burst of fire that virtually cut him in two. His grenade then exploded in his hand and ripped apart the rest of his torso flinging gory bits of flesh, bone and internal organs over the men cowering beside him. With an unearthly scream one of the privates suddenly charged the nest and tossed his grenade accurately so that the Japanese were consigned to oblivion. Instead of stopping there he continued his run to the next position and destroyed that firing his Bren gun from the hip. The third one was dealt with in the same manner and then the soldier fell prone onto the ground. His two comrades thought he was dead or badly injured so they inched forward to rescue him. To their astonishment he was still alive and had suffered no more than a few scratches from the undergrowth he had forced his way through. He was, however, suffering from extreme shock as the adrenaline rush left his body and had to be half carried back to the command headquarters. There he was given a hot sweet mug of tea and gradually he returned to normal.

'That was either the bravest or the most stupid act I've ever seen,' his commanding officer opined. 'Whichever it was I'll certainly be mentioning you in despatches as a candidate for a medal. I won't be surprised if you receive the highest honour a soldier can get. What's your name?'

'Private Peter Strachan, Sir. Sorry for being a little hasty and acting without direct orders but both my Lieutenant and Sergeant had been killed. I sort of saw red and thought I'd try and sort out the Japs myself.'

'I'm glad you did even though the risk you took was tremendous. Your action almost certainly saved many lives and our task is now far easier. We should have complete control of the area within the week.'

After liberating Beaufort they intended to work their way down the rest of the railway line through Tenom to the end at Menlalap. Before reaching the busy little town of Tenom, which is on the other side of the Crocker Mountain Range, the line follows the River Padas as it goes through the Padas Gorge. This is a frightening ride at the best of times and an ideal spot for an ambush by the retreating Japanese. The track starts on the plain and winds its way staying close to the river until it starts the climb towards the gorge. Here the line clings precariously to the rocky side of the gorge and is in constant danger of rock and tree falls. The sound of the river is deafening and it is so close to the line it splashes the train as it passes. From here it climbs higher up the gorge until the sunlight is blotted out by the steep walls and the vegetation covering virtually every inch of rock. It would be a challenge to follow the track without putting many men in danger of attack. Using the jeeps to pull carriages along the line was not a viable option as the gradient was too steep and anyway a train would be very vulnerable. The Australian command debated for a long time about how best to overcome this obstacle and eventually came up with quite a novel solution.

The railway line had been constructed through the Padas Gorge as it was the only route that was passable for the locomotives they possessed. Other routes were surveyed but were too hilly and would have needed either tunnels or major earthworks to reduce the gradient of the track to one that was acceptable. Using one of Tom Field's accurate maps the officers found a track running south of the gorge but in the same direction. This would take the troops over the Crocker Range to a point south of Tenom in the Pegalan river valley. From here it was relatively flat all the way up the valley to where the remaining Japanese soldiers were based. Once they were dealt with them the campaign would be over.

They transported the troops along the railway in shuttles by jeep until they arrived at the rapids tumbling out of the Padas Gorge. Here they waited until they had assembled all the men and equipment needed for the thrust. They moved off along the faint track that would lead them over the mountains with scouts going ahead and reporting back to avoid any surprise encounters with the enemy. It was fairly tough going but the men were fit and well trained so they made good time and soon found themselves crossing the top point of the pass and having the satisfaction of looking back down to where they had come from. Spread out in front of them was the wide valley floor and along this to the left they could just see the town of Tenom and the railway snaking along to its end. They could see no signs of any Japanese forces so they made their descent over the slippery rocks and jumbled roots to the lower ground.

There was little cover on the plain so they fanned out in a 'V' formation with the point at the front. This way they could give each other some supporting fire if they were attacked. They came under some sniper fire as they moved forward and lost a few men. There were a couple of minor skirmishes with Jap patrols but they met no serious opposition until they reached the town. Here it was obvious that the enemy had dug in and were waiting for them. They had withdrawn their troops from the gorge when they realised the Australians were not going to come that way and now had all their men waiting to defend the town, their final foothold in Borneo. The battle was bloody but the 9th Division prevailed and the Japanese were overrun. The few survivors fled the town and headed up the valley towards Ranau and Mount Kinabalu.

Even when they were informed that Japan had surrendered unconditionally on August 15th after the dropping of two atomic bombs the enemy refused to give in. They retreated further and further into the jungle and many were killed by the Muruts who also didn't know the war was over or, if they did, chose to ignore the fact. When the fighting eventually ended the 9th Division were in control of a large area which encompassed the entire coast of North Borneo up to Kota Belud and inland over the Crocker Mountain Range and up towards Mount Kinabalu.

Chapter 24

The convoy carrying the wounded and its accompanying paratroopers set off south for Jesselton as Tom and his companions boarded the borrowed jeep and went north towards Kudat. From Kota Belud the optimistically named Kudat Road soon became a very rough track that was heavily rutted where the rains had washed away the soil exposing the glutinous orangey clay underneath. This was extremely slippery in any parts where it was wet and caused the jeep to slither and slide in every possible direction as Tom tried to keep it steady and on course. The men in the back were looking rather sick with the rolling motion and clung on to the jeep and each other in order to stay aboard. After about fifteen miles of being thrown around they were all ready for a break and Tom stopped by a small stream so they could have a drink and recover their land legs again. It was good to be able to dangle their feet in the cool water although they still remained on guard with one of the group standing and watching the road for any sign of the enemy. They knew that for the next twenty or thirty miles they would be very unlikely to meet any Japanese as the road left the coast as it headed towards Sikuati. It would be after passing through Sikuati and going on to Kudat that they would once again be in what they thought might still be enemy controlled territory. With no clear idea as to the strength of the opposing force they would have to take it very carefully.

They jumped aboard the jeep feeling much refreshed and jolted their way past small hamlets and isolated plantations until they had to stop where the road crossed a shallow river. There had never been a proper bridge at this point but boulders had been strategically placed in the river bed and a liana stretched out across the river to give support to anyone crossing on foot. Tom was unsure if the jeep had sufficient ground clearance to be able to cross without getting stuck on the larger rocks so he cut a stick and measured the clearance before wading into the river to measure the depth at the critical points. It was important to know the depth to keep the exhaust pipe and air inlets out of the water thereby preventing the engine from stalling and leaving them marooned. After going backwards and forwards across the river three or four times Tom was still undecided. Without the jeep they would have a long trek to Kudat and be unable to carry all their weapons and ammunition. But just staying where they were would achieve nothing so it was a risk he would have to take. He levered himself into the driver's seat, started the engine, engaged low gear and slowly let out the clutch. The jeep edged forward into the river and Tom endeavoured to follow the line he had identified that would keep him away from the bigger boulders and the deepest pools. All went well until he was just over half way across when one of the rear wheels suddenly slid on one of the slimy rocks and the jeep veered sharply to the left. With a lurch it stopped. Tom, who rarely swore, cursed loudly. 'Bugger, bugger, bugger! Now what?'

There was no answer so he waded out into the water and back to the bank. The jeep sat forlornly at a strange angle with the river washing its wheels. Tom looked round for Enduat but he was missing. The other three men sat on a fallen log and seemed unconcerned at the plight of the jeep. They probably were pleased that it wasn't going to torture their digestive systems anymore. But what had happened to Enduat? Tom was becoming concerned at his absence. Then there came a crashing through the undergrowth behind them and the sound of voices accompanied by swishing and smacking noises. The source of this commotion soon became clear as Enduat emerged from the trees with a small party of Kadazan villagers in tow. They were carrying ropes and leading a reluctant pair of water buffalo towards the scene of Tom's misfortune.

'I thought we might need a little more power,' laughed Enduat. 'When I saw you measuring the depth I decided to go and do some exploring. I know that villages are usually to be found near where rivers and roads meet and I wasn't wrong.

These villagers live just around the corner and I persuaded them to come and help rescue you if anything went wrong. Again, I was right.'

'Yes you were. Will those beasts be able to pull us out?'

'I'll have them taken to the other side and then we can tie the ropes to the jeep and haul it from the river. All you have to do is steer it generally in the right direction.'

The amused villagers cajoled the buffalo into the water and over past the jeep to the far bank. Enduat attached the ropes to the front axle and Tom climbed into the driver's seat and waited to be rescued. The buffalo took the strain and heaved. Slowly the jeep righted itself and it was soon safely on the road again. Tom now had to dry out the electrics and check that no water had gone into the carburettor. He knew the wheel bearings should really be repacked with grease but they weren't going far and that chore could wait. Eventually it spluttered back to life and they were able to resume their journey but not before Tom had made the villagers a present of a rifle and some ammunition that they could use for hunting. They were more than pleased with the gift and swore allegiance to the strange white man and his fearsome Murut friends.

As they drove off Enduat told Tom he had also asked the villagers about the Japanese and had been informed that they hadn't seen any for months. It appeared that the Japs had retreated back to their bases in the towns and no longer ventured out into the countryside. That suited Tom's plans exactly. It was now time to push on towards Sikuati and then Kudat.

The road was much easier to drive along now as it was on the sandy soil of the Kudat peninsular and nearer the coast. They made good time and Sikuati soon came into view. It looked no different to the time when Tom and Mary had gone there to buy some goods at the market before their picnic at Bak Bak all those years before. Tom looked fondly at the row of wooden shop houses with the raised walkway in the front. But this was not the time for reminiscences and they had to move on to Kudat before nightfall. Enduat took in his new surroundings. The buildings were very similar to those in Kota Belud and the few children playing in the trees gave the place an air of normality. This worried Enduat as nothing had been even vaguely normal for a long time and he knew his life had changed for ever. He wondered if the others felt the same. Nursing the submachine gun in his lap he forced himself to focus on the road ahead and be ready for action. They approached Kudat via Bak Bak where Tom had landed from the submarine and eventually been captured. Without stopping they continued on to the edge of the town and Tom turned sharp right and up a coral track that led to St. James's Primary School and Church. It was situated on the top of a small rise and Tom knew that from there they could have a clear view of the town right up to the wharf. He stopped and they all clambered out, stretching their legs and arms. Using a pair of field glasses Tom looked towards the town. It wasn't there.

The only buildings still standing were the Chinese temple and the police station. The remainder of the town had been completely flattened and it was difficult to work out even where the main street had been. The wharf had also disappeared and Tom could see a few hulks of sunken boats jutting out of the sea. He could recognise the *padang* as it was the only green open space in the town but the club on its edge had gone. There were a few sandy coloured dogs mooching about in the rubbish that had once been the neat and pretty town that Mary had so loved but no sign of human life. He focused his binoculars on the police station and thought he could see some movement through one of the glassless windows. It was impossible to tell if the shadowy figure was one of the Japanese so they would have to move nearer to find out. He handed the glasses to Enduat who also scanned what remained of the town and shook his head sadly.

'There isn't much life down there,' he said. 'If those are Japanese in the police station then I don't think they'll put up much of a fight.'

'They'll fight for their lives,' replied Tom. 'If I've learned only one thing about the Japanese army it is that they never, ever give up. We might still have a battle on our hands. Let's get it over with.'

They left the jeep at the bottom of the school drive and went on foot past the debris of the club towards the police station. When they were about two hundred yards away and hidden by a few still standing casuarinas Tom lifted his rifle and fired a shot. There was an immediate response. A barrage of rifle and small arms fire came in their direction and they hurriedly hit the ground. Raising the binoculars Tom could make out one figure behind one of the gateposts and another at an upstairs window. He then realised something was not quite as it should be. There were no vehicles parked anywhere near the building. That was very odd as the Japanese always kept transport on hand. He crawled closer and called out in Malay. The reply came, also in Malay, and he then knew then that they were not the occupying force but local men who had somehow taken control of the police station. Both parties exchanged a few more words to be sure that they weren't in a trap and then the men emerged and came towards them. Tom didn't recognise any of them but it was obvious they weren't the enemy. They warily exchanged greetings and Tom found out that the Japanese had left Kudat a few weeks earlier when the bombing was at its worst. They had left by truck and had headed down the road Tom had just come up. Where they had ended up no one knew or cared so long as they were well out of the way. Tom and Enduat certainly hadn't encountered any on their trek up the road. Since then all had been quiet and they had taken charge of the police station. They were fishermen who normally operated from the nearby islands but had been forced to live in Kudat by the Japanese who, with some justification, didn't trust them. Now all they wanted to do was to salvage what they could of their boats and return to their families still living off the coast. Now that Tom and his men had arrived they felt that their job was over. They parted amicably and Tom and Enduat wandered over to the police station and went in. It was a painful reminder to Tom

225

of his previous visit and he told Enduat a little more about what had happened there than he had related to Asampit previously. The Japanese had obviously left in a hurry as some of their paperwork was still in the drawer of one of the desks. Tom idly wondered if he featured in any of it.

There was no point in going any further into the desolate wreck of the town but there was one place Tom still needed to see. Leaving Enduat in charge he made his way back to the jeep and drove off towards mile 5. The road was still as familiar as it had been but it was with his stomach in a knot that he turned off to his old house. It looked a bit run down and the garden was overgrown but otherwise little had changed. He slowly got down from the jeep and stood silently, taking in the scene. His eyes misted over. Suddenly there was an almighty yell and before he could move a figure charged out of the house and threw itself at him. He was almost flattened by the force of the clumsy embrace. He pushed the man off roughly and held him at arm's length. It was his houseboy Kim Bong.

'Welcome home *tuan* Tom.'

Author's Notes

This book is a work of fiction woven around some of the events that actually happened in North Borneo (now Sabah, Malaysia) before and during the Second World War. Other events described in the story are completely from my own imagination. I have not attempted to either glorify or sanitise the war as I believe evil deeds should be remembered just as clearly as heroic ones. I changed the names of all of the people who were actively involved.

The Vyner Brooke incident with the nurses is true as were the death marches from the Sandakan Prisoner of War camp. The real commandant of the camp, Captain Susumi Hoshijima, was tried and executed after the war for his part in those horrific events. Colonel Suga, who was the commander of all the Japanese troops in Borneo, committed suicide by cutting his throat with a table knife.

There was an exceptionally brave Australian who single-handedly took out three machine gun nests in the battle for Beaufort, killing seven men. Private Leslie Thomas Starcevich was awarded the Victoria Cross for his conspicuous gallantry under heavy fire. It was the last Victoria Cross of the war to be awarded. Afterwards Leslie Starcevich returned to Australia where he died in 1989. A memorial with a plaque celebrating his bravery can still be seen in Beaufort.

The Australian Service Reconnaissance Department (SRD) was originally called the Inter Services Department (ISD) and was formed to organise local resistance, establish lines of communication, disseminate anti-Japanese propaganda and be involved in acts of sabotage and subversion. It was restructured and named the SRD in 1943 with a new HQ in South Yarra. The training took place at Camp Tabragalba (known as Camp X) near Beaudesert which is south of Brisbane. The surrounding countryside was ideal for training as it is very similar to Borneo with rainforests, rivers and mountains. It is true that few of the

227

operatives sent to Borneo survived.

Many of the British and other characters in Kudat are composites of people I met there in the early 1960s. Sadly none of them are still alive. I was working for Voluntary Service Overseas at the time and fell in love with the wonderful people of various ethnic origins that I was fortunate to meet. The beach at Bak Bak still holds for me many fond memories of lazy days spent swimming, drinking Anchor beer and eating the ubiquitous curries. It was an interesting time as the British were handing over power to the State of Malaysia and I found I was living in a war zone as Indonesian President Sukarno's army were attacking the borders of Sabah claiming it belonged to them.

I was also very lucky to stay for a while in a Murut longhouse and join them in their everyday activities and celebrations. The *tapai* was as foul as could be but the alcoholic content took the edge off it. The villagers were wonderful people who willingly shared their food and friendship. At that time they and I didn't know that their simple and dignified lives were soon to be shattered by the logging industry destroying their ancestral hunting grounds.

A great many myths have built up over the years about what actually happened during the occupation. The Kinabalu Guerrillas, led by a very brave man named Albert Kwok, actually did exist and were the only civilian group to successfully rebel against Japanese oppression in any country during the course of the war. Unfortunately their fate was much as I described it. Stories still circulate about the longhouse feast and the massacre of the Japanese officers but I have found no conclusive proof it really occurred. The Japanese continued to fight to the very last man and the fighting continued in Borneo until October, two months after the war had officially ended.

Apologies for any factual or military errors – I take full responsibility for them.

Acknowledgements

To Brian MacArthur for his excellent book 'Surviving the Sword' which gave me an insight into the horrific treatment of the Australian POWs in Sandakan and the death march to Ranau as well as some excellent descriptions of life in a Murut Longhouse.

Also Ronald J. Brooks for his most entertaining book 'Under Five Flags' which was invaluable for the information regarding the Kinabalu Guerrillas and the general treatment of the civilian population in North Borneo.

Credit must also be given to the Internet which enabled me to research the armaments and transport used at that time; the history, work and training of the Australian SRD; various accounts of the sinking of the Vyner Brooke and the VC awarded to Private Starcevich.

To Ben, an Australian teacher I met travelling in India, who critically read the first few chapters and whose encouragement and sound advice persuaded me to complete the book.

To my friends in the King Bill pub in Histon, Cambridge. Dick Lane who kindly read and helped correct the manuscript and Keith McAllister for his beautiful artwork for the book cover.